Grab A F...

You get *Black File 10* free with this book (see Table of Contents for details).

Die Forever

Angel of Darkness Book 10

Steve N. Lee

Copyright

Published by Blue Zoo, Yorkshire, England.

Die Forever

Chapter 01

DRENCHED IN THE darkness of the derelict store's doorway, Teddy slunk as far back as possible into the blackness as male voices drifted through the cold night air – he couldn't risk a witness being able to testify that they'd spotted him lurking here.

Two guys meandered along the sidewalk arguing over whether or not a foul had been a good call in some basketball game. From the sanctuary of the shadows, Teddy watched them amble by, completely unaware of his presence.

The threat passed, Teddy smirked. This was way too easy.

He shuffled forward again so he had a better view of the street in each direction. He peeked out.

So, what was it going to be tonight – blonde, brunette, or redhead? Man, it was such a tough call when he could have literally – literally – any woman in New York City.

A tough call?

Hell, tough wasn't the word for it. At times, he almost wished he was a sex-starved geek again, invisible to every woman under fifty who wasn't a blood relative.

He'd always imagined being spoiled for choice would be heaven, but it could be absolute torture. Picking a super hot babe, just one, not knowing if an even hotter one would happen along just seconds later... torture. Yep, it was a tough life when he had to 'settle' for perfection. Especially if his idea of perfection didn't meet with the approval it deserved.

Johnny's whiny voice came over his phone's earpiece. "Oh, this one, Teddy. Get this one. She's goddamn gorgeous."

Shrouded in the shadows, Teddy stole a glance. A young woman sashayed down the sidewalk in the direction of his hiding place, wearing a tiny black leather skirt and a white top. She shivered. He stared at her breasts. It was such a chilly spring night her nipples had to be like screw heads.

As he watched the woman approach, a bead of sweat ran down the side of his face. Not from the stress of their covert activities, but because of the sweltering warmth of the two puffer jackets he was wearing. He wiped it away.

The woman in the leather skirt wiggled by the store. Yes, she oozed sex, all right, but they'd had so many like that now. The whole point of this wasn't to get the first babe that happened along, but to get something extraordinary – the kind of smoking-hot ass that wouldn't even look at a guy unless he'd been on the cover of *People* magazine or owned a penthouse overlooking Central Park.

Teddy's voice was as low as it was steady. "We're not having another goddamn co-ed that's barely got pubes. I want a woman. A real woman."

Over his phone, voices spoke in the background.

Adam said, "Hey, Niko, your mom free tonight?" As usual, he snickered at his own joke.

"I hope to God yours ain't," replied Niko. "I wouldn't touch that blimp's cooch if I was shipwrecked, blind, and had only an hour to live."

"You sure?" said Johnny, "You'd be onto a safe bet because I hear she's got a thing for men with small dicks."

"Well, you'd be the expert there," said Niko.

They all laughed.

Teddy heaved a sigh. "Guys, if recess is over, d'you think we can get back to the plan now?"

Still in the background, Niko said, "Johnny, tell him we want something born this century. His last one was hot, but she must have gone to school with my grandma."

"Yeah, maybe we should set an age limit," said Johnny.

Teddy had to stamp this out. This was his turn, so he'd pick who the hell he wanted. "Your grandma, Niko? Really? She was twenty-five if she was a day. Twenty-five. Jesus, have you always been such a math savant? And what would you like me to choose, Johnny? Another fat-ass black chick who'll give us all crabs again?"

"Whoa, bitch fight," said Adam.

A deeper, gruffer voice broke in. "Will you all just shut the hell up and pick something, for Christ's sake?" said Larry. "My ass is going to sleep sitting in the back of here."

It was then that Teddy saw her. "Shhh." He pulled back into the shadows.

A woman strolled toward his hiding place. Long, long legs that looked toned even through jeans. Tits so

9

firm even her zipped leather jacket couldn't squash them down. And the kind of angelic face a guy just couldn't look at without picturing his dick in her mouth.

But it wasn't just her looks. Man, how she moved. So fluid. So graceful. She had to be a Broadway dancer or something.

He grinned, then whispered, "Hold the front page, boys, we got us a winner."

Johnny said, "Oh man, not that one. I watched her walk by. She must be pushing thirty, for God's sake."

Teddy squashed himself back into the darkest corner of the doorway as the woman passed, swinging a small brown grocery bag in one hand. Hidden in the gloom, he ogled her. He couldn't help but mouth 'wow' to himself. And couldn't help but notice the aching sensation growing in his crotch.

Such a tight little ass. God, how he was going to pound that.

"Come on, Teddy," said Johnny, "let's wait for something else."

"You had your turn on Wednesday," Teddy whispered. "Did I tell you what to pick? Now quit your whining – it's radio silence till the cat's in the bag."

Checking under his jacket's hood, Teddy ensured his mask was positioned on top of his head so he could slip it down in a second, then he stepped into the orangey glow of the streetlamps. He nodded to the white cargo van parked up the street, facing in the direction the woman was walking.

Near the van, a couple meandered along arm in arm, but they were too far away and moving too slowly to be a problem. Likewise, there was nothing close enough up ahead that would pose a realistic threat.

Everything looked good to go.

He slunk up the sidewalk after the woman. Even though he was wearing the softest-soled sneakers he could find, he still tried to tread lightly as he gained on her with each stride.

An old man walking a dog neared them. Teddy turned his face toward the road as the old boy shuffled past.

The intersection lay less than thirty yards away. That would be where they'd hit her. About seventy yards beyond that, dark shapes moved this way, but they wouldn't make it to the intersection before the woman did. And then it would be too late.

Teddy smirked again. Yep, they were good to go. He glanced over his shoulder. The van prowled slowly down the street.

His mouth dry, he swallowed hard. He was breathing so heavily it was as if he'd been running. It was always the same. Weird. He would have thought he'd have gotten used to it by now. But man, talk about the thrill of the chase. This made him feel so good. So alive. Like he was a great hunter stalking a man-eating tiger.

He eyed that tight little ass just twenty-five feet ahead of him. God, he was going to pound that so hard. So damn hard.

He checked back along the sidewalk. As he'd figured, that couple was walking way too slowly to catch up and were far too engrossed in each other anyway. Besides, his two puffer jackets were so bulky they'd hide anyone immediately in front of him from anyone behind him.

The van crawled along, Adam driving. The guy was so small in such a big vehicle, he looked like a kid at the wheel.

Teddy wiped the sweat off his palms on his jeans, then stuffed his hands in his jacket pockets. In the right one, the stun gun felt hard and cold.

The intersection loomed before him. And that little ass just kept wiggling its way toward it. If only she knew what was waiting for her. Hell, she might even get a kick out of it. After all, who was to say she hadn't fantasized about something like this? Some chicks did. It was a well-known fact.

He quickened his pace. It was this spot or not at all – the next intersection had a street cam, so they couldn't go anywhere near there. And boy, he did not want to miss this one.

Ten feet from the intersection, he looked left and right down both the smaller side streets. No one was near enough to matter.

Game time.

Without turning, he stuck his arm out and gave the thumbs-up to the van.

Almost on her, Teddy pulled his Dracula mask down from under his hood and hid his face.

The woman stopped at the intersection and looked for traffic.

Adam eased the van around the corner just as Teddy came up behind her. Muffled rock music came from the van's radio.

As the vehicle pulled even with her, the woman took a step back from the curb, as if wary of it.

Too little, too late.

Larry ripped the side door open, a Frankenstein's Monster mask hiding his face. Rock music blared into the night.

At that precise moment, Teddy lunged forward. He grabbed the woman around the neck and rammed the stun gun into her lower back.

He clicked the switch.

Though it was almost lost amidst the raucous guitar and pounding drums, the gun made its unmistakable *ratatatatat* noise as it shot electricity through her.

The woman's back arched and her whole body went rigid as her muscles involuntarily contracted. Teddy thought she cried out, but the music drowned that out too, as it always did.

In a werewolf and a mummy mask, Johnny and Niko yanked her into the van through the side door, knocking her grocery bag from her grasp as they did so. A cabbage and some carrots rolled into the gutter. The two guys slung her onto the van floor and Johnny immediately dropped onto her left arm to hold her down.

Teddy scrambled in and leapt on her, straddling her stomach to pin her down with his weight. Niko then clamped her other arm to the floor, laughing with excitement.

With Teddy safely inside, Larry slammed the door shut and Adam hit the gas. The van took off down the street.

Teddy fished out a little black wallet from his inside pocket – she wouldn't be incapacitated for long, so they had to move fast.

Holding the woman's arm, Niko grinned. "Oh, she's nice, this one. I tell you what, if you don't want your go, Johnny, I'll do her twice and you can have my turn next time."

"Hey, *I* didn't say I didn't want a go. You were the one complaining." Johnny groped her left breast with one hand, holding her arm with the other. "And quit with the names, asshole."

"Like she's gonna remember anything," Niko said.

Teddy removed a prefilled syringe from his wallet.

"I don't care," said Johnny. "Quit it." Snickering, he reached around Teddy and felt her crotch over her jeans.

Though groggy, the woman broke free of Johnny's one-handed hold and lashed out. A feeble punch glanced off Teddy's face. It wasn't hard enough to hurt him, but it knocked his mask sideways to reveal part of his face.

He recoiled, hiding behind his hands.

Johnny jerked back and grabbed her hand to pin her again.

"Watch her, for fuck's sake." Teddy realigned his mask as quickly as possible.

"Sorry, man," said Johnny. "She got away from me for a second."

Teddy punched him on the arm.

The guy sucked through his teeth. "Jesus, I said 'sorry.'"

"Screw up again and you're off the team. Understand?"

"I was just—"

"Just fucking around. Yeah, I know. Now, stick to the goddamn plan. We get sloppy, we get caught. Okay?"

"Okay. Okay." Johnny mouthed something else, but he was only trying to save face. If he hadn't been, he'd have said it out loud. Then Teddy would have kicked his ass. Or at least have had Larry do it for him later.

Turning back to the woman, Teddy slapped her across the face. "And you, bitch, you'll pay for that."

"Give her an extra dose," Niko said, "I don't want her biting or scratching the crap out of me."

"An extra dose might kill her," said Teddy.

"Yeah, right."

"I'm sorry, but did you do two years of pre-med? Oh no, that's right, you were too busy serving fries so you had time to write that novel that was going to change the world. How did that work out for you, Niko?"

From the driver's seat, Adam shouted over the pounding music, "So give her an extra half."

An extra half dose would probably be safe. Well, fairly safe. Okay, there was a slim chance it might leave her in a coma, but Niko had a point – Teddy didn't want her biting a chunk out of his face while he was banging her.

He planted a hand on her forehead to immobilize her head, then took a second to stare at her tits. Oh, yeah, she was going to pay in all sorts of ways. He stuck the needle into her neck.

Chapter 02

"HELLO?" SAID A male voice. "Hello...? Can you hear me? Are you okay?"

The woman's eyes flickered half-open. A frail man with gray hair peered right into her face.

"Oh, you had me so worried." Nicotine-stained teeth smiled at her. "Now, don't worry, I've called 911 and an ambulance is on its way."

Why should she worry? And who was the ambulance for?

The woman slowly turned her head to see where she was. But the effort of turning was like trying to push the world around.

Green.

Everywhere was green. A blurry green.

And brown. A blurry brown.

She looked up. Squinting at the brightness.

Was she outside?

She blinked and shook her head to clear it. But instead of clearing her head, the shaking shot pain through her skull as if someone was tightening it in a vise.

"Oww…" Wincing, she felt her forehead. Something hard and rough was caked to it and her hair seemed to be matted into it too. Had she been bleeding?

Her vision came into focus. Kind of.

Yes, she was outside. Those green things were trees. But where outside?

She peered down and then around behind her. Why was she slumped on a small patch of grass against some big gnarled oak tree?

"Do you know what happened?" the old man asked.

She just stared at him. What happened when? She looked down at herself. Her clothes were ripped and disheveled, and damp with dew.

"You're lucky we found you." The man gestured to his small white poodle. "We don't usually come this way, do we, Percival?"

The woman pushed to get up, but groaned. Hell, had she been on the bender to end all benders last night?

"Can I help?" The man reached out, but he looked like he'd snap if he took her weight.

The woman studied the man's face. He seemed genuine. Grabbing his wrinkled hand to steady herself, the woman clambered to her feet. She swayed. Felt herself falling, so she grabbed the tree for support.

Where the devil was she?

Standing beside the oak, she scanned the area to try to figure out the answer. Trees and shrubs left vapor trails as her gaze passed over them.

Was it a park?

It kind of looked like one.

But which one?

"I don't know what the world's coming to, I don't," said the man. "I tell you, most days Percival and I don't set foot outside the door after seven."

The woman pushed away from the tree and took a couple of teetering steps.

"You really should wait for the ambulance, you know."

Without looking, the woman waved her hand at the man to decline. She staggered forward, then stopped and half-turned. "Th—" Her mouth was so dry she could barely speak. And she had an awful bitter taste at the back of her throat.

She tried again, her voice croaking. "Thank you."

The man said, "Are you sure you won't wait for the ambulance?"

The woman didn't reply, but staggered on. Again, her legs wobbled under her. She lurched to grab the backrest of a wooden bench, to keep herself from falling.

She missed.

Crashed to the ground.

Blackness swallowed her.

Chapter 03

THE WOMAN'S EYES flickered open.

Blurry shapes greeted her again. But not greens and browns. These were whites and grays. Where the hell was she now?

She turned her head to check her surroundings.

Everything was on its side.

Either that or she was. Was she lying down? In a bed?

"Oh, hello there," said a chirpy female voice. "Doctor, she's conscious."

From her left, a chunky woman in a pale blue uniform loomed over her. "Don't worry, you're safe now."

"Wh—" Christ, her mouth was so dry. And that goddamn bitterness. What the hell was that? She swallowed and licked her lips. "Wh—where am I?"

She pushed to sit up, but was so weak, she barely managed to lift her head off the pillow.

On the other side of her, a balding black man in a white cotton coat appeared. "I'm Dr. Phillips. Now hold still and don't try to get up, please."

He flashed a light from one of her eyes to the other, then said, "Do you know your name?"

What kind of a dumbass question was that? Of course she knew her name. And this guy called himself a doctor.

"Where..." She tasted her mouth again. "Where am I?"

"Pupils are responsive," Dr. Phillips said, "That's good."

Wincing with the effort, the woman moved her arms to get better leverage to sit up.

"Now, we'll have none of that, young lady." The doctor rested a hand on her shoulder, making it clear he wanted her to stay put. "You've suffered quite a trauma, so you're going to be with us for a while yet."

He took her pulse. "Do you know what day it is?"

Why did he want to know what day it was? "I... um... Sunday?"

Wasn't it? Okay, maybe Monday. One of the two. Her brain felt like congealed stew. What was wrong with her that she didn't know what day it was?

"And what's your name?"

That dumbass question again. Why all the stupid questions when what she wanted was answers? What the hell was going on?

"Do you know your name?"

She thought for a moment, then said, "Tess. Tess Williams."

"Good. And do you know where you are, Tess? What happened to you?"

She gasped, reliving the moment she'd felt an electric jolt hit her in the back just the way it had in Shanghai when Sergei had shown her what it was like to

20

be attacked with a stun gun. Pictures and sounds flashed through her mind.

Blaring music.

'If you don't want your go, Johnny, I'll do her twice.'

Dracula. And cabbages and carrots.

A punch in the face. Her face.

'... bitch, you'll pay for that.'

What had happened? With so many weird, disjointed memories floating around in her mind, she struggled to piece together the events. Then something clicked.

Tess's eyes popped wide open.

Oh God, no. *That* hadn't happened.

No. Not *that*.

Not to her.

Not again.

It couldn't have. It had to be a nightmare she'd had. A drug-induced nightmare.

But that would explain why someone had pumped her full of drugs.

Oh God...

Adrenaline surged through her body as anger surged through her mind. The hospital room came into focus – all sharp whites and sanitary grays.

She heaved herself up, which yanked on the intravenous drip that ran into her hand from a bag of fluid dangling over her. The steel IV stand rattled.

The doctor grabbed the stand to steady it, then again eased down on her shoulder. "Please, Miss Williams, we're flushing as yet unidentified drugs out of your system, plus you're seriously dehydrated and have mild hypothermia. Believe me, the best thing for you is to stay exactly where you are now."

Tess knocked his hand aside, then ripped the intravenous needle out. Blood spurted across the back of her hand.

The nurse gasped and backed away. "Shall I call security, Doctor?"

Tess heaved up and around to dangle her legs over the bed. She panted as if she'd just done a hundred pushups.

Blocking her way, the doctor held his open hands up. "Please, Miss Williams, you've suffered considerable trauma, both physically and mentally, if—"

Tess glowered at him, the adrenal rush coursing fresh energy through her wracked body. "While I appreciate what you've done, if you don't get out of my way, you'll suffer physical and mental trauma, too."

Backing away, the doctor pointed at the nurse. "Get security up here."

The nurse scurried out.

Tess looked about the room. Objects blurred as her gaze skimmed over them, like a hand smudging pencil marks on paper.

Jesus, what the hell had they pumped into her?

She struggled up and finally stood. Swayed, but caught herself.

Someone had stuck her in a white hospital gown. The crap in which they dressed invalids and the dying.

"Where are my clothes?"

"Miss Williams, I must insist—"

She grabbed the doctor by the collar and yanked him down so she could stare him in the face. "I won't ask again."

22

"They're in the Dispatch Office, level one, waiting to go to the forensics lab, with the DFSA kit."

Her mouth fell open.

As her grip relaxed, the doctor pulled away from her.

A DFSA kit? A Drug-Facilitated Sexual Assault kit?

Oh God, no.

It wasn't a drug-induced nightmare.

The hospital had taken semen samples.

Semen from *inside* her.

Tess clenched her fists.

No, not again. This was not happening. Not again.

With a guttural scream, she lashed out sideways at the bedside table. A jug of water crashed against the wall.

The doctor adopted what he must have believed was his most soothing tone of voice. "Anger is a perfectly natural response to—"

She heaved off the bed and lurched toward him and the open door. "You examined me without my permission?" She panted, but from fury, not exertion.

"Miss Williams, please," said the doctor, backing away, his voice now wavering. "You've been unconscious for over twenty-six hours. The SANE thought it wise to collect any evidence while it might still be viable."

Tess didn't care that a SANE, a sexual assault nurse examiner, had taken samples of God only knew what. No, what she cared about was what that nurse had done with them.

Tripping over her own feet, Tess clattered into the door. She clung to it to steady herself.

She needed her body to function. She'd never get out of here and do what needed doing if her goddamn body wouldn't work.

Tess pounded her fist into the door, beating it against the white-painted wood to force her adrenaline to fight the disabling drugs overwhelming her system.

In the hallway, a pudgy orderly pushing an empty gurney stopped. "Is everything okay, miss?"

The doctor took her arm. "Please, Miss Williams, let me help you."

She shoved him away.

As the orderly darted toward her, he shouted over his shoulder to the nurses' station. "Get security. Now!" A redheaded nurse picked up a white phone.

The orderly shuffled toward Tess, his arms out wide to corral her back into the room. "Please, Miss, back in your room."

She couldn't risk being sedated. Couldn't risk having to talk to the police. Couldn't risk the trail going cold.

And most importantly, she couldn't risk the police getting to those bastards first.

If the authorities tested the DNA from the sperm and got a match on CODIS, the national database, they could have the 'suspects' in custody before she could even walk straight. How the hell would she get to them then?

No, she had to get out of here. Now.

When the orderly got within reach, Tess flicked her hand out toward his crotch. As he threw his hands down to protect himself, she shot her hand up and lashed her fingers across his eyes. The strike wasn't hard enough to blind, but would ensure his eyes stung and watered so much he'd never be able to stop her, even if he tried.

To be sure he wouldn't hamper her, she kicked his feet out from under him, and he smashed into the mottled blue-and-gray floor.

Tess tottered down the corridor, holding a hand out wide to push off the pale green wall to keep her steady. The harsh tube lighting made her squint.

Patients and staff hugged the far wall to stay as far away from her as possible.

Painted in navy, a one-foot-tall number 2 was on the wall beside the stairwell door. So, if her stuff was on level one, that was just the next floor down. Thank God. She didn't know how many flights of stairs she could handle in this state.

Tess flung the door open. The curved metal handle banged into the wall.

Gripping the banister rail, Tess half-fell, half-ran down the steps. At the next floor, she burst out of the doorway into a corridor almost exactly the same as the one she'd just left. Slumped against the wall, she stared up at a large blue sign with white lettering that faced the stairwell, arrows pointing this way and that.

The sign's letters and numbers danced in the air, as if they were individually suspended on elastic. Tess rubbed her eyes and drew a long, steadying breath. The letters stabilized.

She scanned the departments listed but didn't see Dispatch Office. Not surprising – the signage was for patients and visitors. Members of staff would know where they were going.

An Asian doctor trudged past, head buried in a chart.

Tess called out. "Dispatch Office, please?"

He didn't even look up, just gestured over his shoulder the way he'd come.

Tess pushed away from the wall and staggered down the corridor, swaying from side to side as if she'd downed a bottle of tequila.

Now she'd have her belongings. Then she'd have the monsters who'd done this to her.

Chapter 04

PEOPLE STARED AS Tess lurched along, but no one tried to stop her until a Latino nurse spotted her. She gently grasped her arm.

"Here," said the nurse, "let me help you back to your room."

Tess shoved her away. "Touch me and you'll bleed."

The nurse scuttled away.

At the end of the corridor, Tess checked left. Nothing. But away to her far right, high up on a wall, a sign read: Dispatch Office.

She darted toward it.

Her goal in sight, she flew down the hallway, steadier and stronger with each step.

As she burst through the opaque glass door, a weedy guy with thick glasses jerked up from looking at his computer, his eyebrows raised with surprise.

Her breathing heavy, she panted as she spoke and rested a hand on the blue counter that separated them. "You've got my clothes and a rape kit."

"I'm sorry, what?"

She hammered her fist down onto the counter. "Tess Williams. Clothes and semen sample. Where are they?"

"Miss, I'm going to have to ask you to step back and calm down," said Thick Glasses.

If the hospital needed to secure items that might be used as evidence, where would it store them while they awaited collection?

Tess scanned the office. She dragged her hand over her brow, gasping for air.

A row of cubbyholes ran down either side wall. In the middle sat a table with a number of neatly piled boxes, while at the back stood a row of metal lockers.

A secure area? Obvious.

She flung the counter's flap up and over. It banged down onto the countertop with an almighty crash.

Thick Glasses held his hands up to bar her entry. "Miss, this is for hospital employees only."

She lurched through the gap in the counter and into the staff area, fixated on the lockers.

"You have to leave or I'll be forced to—"

Grabbing one of his hands, she twisted to clamp him in an armlock, and then slammed him facefirst into the countertop. Tess grabbed a box cutter that the guy probably used to open packages and held it to his throat.

Leaning right into his ear, she said with an even tone, "I don't want to hurt you. All I want is what's mine. Understand?"

He nodded, panting with fear, eyes wide.

"Tess Williams. Clothes. Rape kit. Where?"

His free arm trembling, he pointed back at the lockers.

"Which one?"

28

"F—f—fifteen."

"Keys."

He fumbled with a bunch of keys hanging from his belt. They jangled as he struggled to unclip them.

She tweaked her armlock just a fraction tighter to hurry him along.

He jumped and snatched a breath, then fumbled with greater urgency, the keys jangling all the more.

She needed to get her things before security arrived. Getting caught, getting sedated, getting interrogated... no, she couldn't risk that. She needed to get out of here. Needed to find those bastards. Needed—

He slammed the keys down on the counter.

Thank God. Now to get her things and get the hell—

"Freeze!"

Nooo!

Two security guards in blue uniforms stood in the double doorway. Guns drawn. Aiming at her head in the classic feet-apart-two-hands-on-the-gun stance.

On the left, a black guard with a shaven head stared at her, his gaze as steady as his aim.

The other guard's gaze constantly flicked from her to his colleague and then back to her. That was all she needed – a potentially trigger-happy new recruit. Worse still, from the acne on his porcelain white chin and forehead, it looked like he was barely into his twenties, so wouldn't have any life experience to draw upon.

The black guard's voice was calm but assertive. "Put the knife down and release Mr. Talbot."

Yep, that was experience talking – remaining composed and humanizing the victim by naming them. Not that it would get him anywhere.

Tess dragged Talbot up off the desk, retaining both her armlock and the blade. Using him as a human shield, she shuffled backward toward the lockers at the far end of the room. She was getting out. One way or the other.

"I said drop the knife." The black guard cocked his revolver.

The rookie's pimply chin quivered. He was obviously in way over his head. That could be a problem – he wouldn't have to squeeze the trigger deliberately because any sudden sound could make him jump and the place would become a bloodbath.

Tess couldn't see his face, but Talbot whimpered as if he was crying.

He was just an innocent bystander in all this. Just some schmo doing some crappy job who happened to be in her way. But she needed that stuff. Needed it to get the bastards who'd... Jesus, how had this happened to her?

She shuffled back another step.

The black guard glared at her. "The knife. Now."

Time all but froze, and there was no sound. Not even her own heartbeat. Tess locked eyes with the black guard. Could she call his bluff, get her stuff, and then fight her way out? Or would he and his trigger-happy partner blast her apart?

She stared into his eyes, trying to judge the future from his resolve.

Oh, God. He was just like her – not the type to back down.

Trapped.

No way forward. No way back.

Tess gulped, her gaze swinging all around her. What to do? What to do?

She stared. Her thoughts blurred.

She usually had such clarity. Could usually make life-or-death decisions in an instant. Could usually... think! What the devil had they pumped into her?

She fixed on the black muzzles aimed at her face. How the hell was she going to get out of this?

Chapter 05

A VOICE SHATTERED the deadly silence of the Dispatch Room. A different voice. A calm voice. A male voice that Tess knew.

"Easy, everybody. Let's all take a moment here. Everyone's going home healthy and happy today."

A dark-haired guy dressed in ordinary street clothes stood between the two guards. To resolve the situation, he didn't hold a gun, but a badge. A detective's badge.

Square-jawed and muscular, he looked every inch the hero. Any woman would be crazy not to feel a flood of relief sweeping over her if he ran to her rescue. Yet he was the last man on the planet Tess wanted to see.

He said, "Detective Josh Hardy. You've done a great job, guys, but I can take it from here, thanks."

The guards lowered their guns a fraction, but then Tess tightened her grip on Talbot and he squealed. She couldn't help it. Seeing Josh. And him seeing her. He was the last person who should know what had happened to her.

The instant Talbot squealed, the guards' guns jerked back up to aim at her.

Her fingers clawed into Talbot and he squealed again.

She stared at Josh.

Her stomach clenched as if those monsters were taking her right that moment.

Not Josh. Please. Not now. Not here like this. She could handle anything else. Anything but seeing him. Now.

She shook her head at him. Her voice wavered. "Please, go."

Josh stepped in front of the guards, easing their guns down without looking.

"Tess, I know what's happened," Josh said. "Let me help. We can fix this."

"You know this psycho?" the rookie asked.

Josh tutted, then said quietly, "That's not helping."

He stepped through the gap in the counter, his arms wide, unthreatening, welcoming. A part of her ached to run into them, to be swept up and carried away from this nightmare.

"We can fix this," Josh said. "Let me help."

With her adrenaline drained from the effects of the drugs still clawing at her and now Josh appearing out of nowhere... Tess's legs buckled. She crumpled to the floor.

Talbot scrambled away from her.

Josh shoved him aside and dashed to Tess. He cradled her in his lap.

"I'm so sorry, Tess," he said.

"I..." What? What could she possibly say?

"Shhh. It's going to be alright. I promise."

The black guard said, "Tell me you aren't going to let her walk just because you know her."

33

Josh looked back at him, squinting as if vaguely remembering something. "Johnson, right? From the Eighteenth?"

The black guard shrugged. "So I do a little moonlighting here. So what?"

"Still married to...?" Josh grimaced, obviously searching for a vital piece of information that had slipped his mind.

"Gracie. But don't pretend we're friends, so everything is cool. That psycho needs booking."

"Okay. But tell me, Johnson, when you go home tonight and Gracie asks how your day went, what do you think she'll say when you tell her you busted a young woman who lost it after being shot full of drugs and gang-raped?"

"What...?" He rubbed a hand over his face. "Hey, man, no one said anything about that." He holstered his revolver. "Jeez, we were only told a crazy had gotten loose."

"So now you know."

The guard looked at Tess, his voice soft and calm. "I'm truly sorry, ma'am. I hope they catch the bastards."

Catch the bastards?

No. No. Nooo! She wanted them. She deserved them.

Tears ran down her cheeks as emotion finally swallowed her. She buried her face against Josh's chest.

Why him? Why Josh? Now? Of all people, why did he have to know?

The guard turned to leave and then frowned at the rookie, who still had his gun drawn.

"Good God, Henry," said the black guard, "the woman's hurting, for Christ's sake. Do I have to do all the thinking for the both of us? Put your goddamn gun away."

Josh held Tess. Tight. He didn't say a word. Just held her. It was exactly what she needed to hear.

After a few moments, she turned her head a fraction so she could speak. "How did you know I was here?"

"You know how fast word spreads. And you've got more friends in the department than you think. Now, what do you need me to do? Anything. Just say it and it's done."

35

Chapter 06

JOSH PUSHED TESS'S apartment door open and then stepped aside for her to enter, handing her the keys as she did.

Tess cocked an eyebrow at him. "I'm not sick, you know."

"I know. Now shut the hell up and let me look good."

She strolled in.

Home.

Finally.

Relief flooded her body as if cocooning her in a warm goose down comforter.

She moseyed over to a small round table beside her sofa on which swam a red Japanese fighting fish in a little tank. The feeblest of smiles wavered across her lips.

"Hey, Fish," said Tess.

Groaning, she crouched down to him. The gang hadn't just sexually assaulted her, but given her a beating as well, so she had aches and pains everywhere.

Tipping food into his bowl, she said, "Did you think I'd run away and abandoned you, buddy? I'm sorry."

"He okay?"

Tess's smile widened as Fish gulped the food drifting down through the water, then she turned to Josh. He was still standing near the door, as if unsure whether or not he was welcome to come further into the room. Not surprising, as he'd never been allowed across her threshold in the past, even while they were sleeping together.

He surveyed her apartment – a brown sofa, brown rug on bare brown floorboards, a brown table for Fish, a small brown bookshelf. No paintings, no ornaments, no photographs.

Beside the door, two rucksacks leaned against the wall, each packed so full it looked about to burst.

He gestured to the bags. "Taking a trip?"

Tess's smile faded. Her gaze flicked from Fish to the mantelpiece, where a plane ticket to China was sitting – the ticket she was supposed to have used eleven and a half hours ago to start her new life across the other side of the world.

She forced another smile. "No. It's for Goodwill. I've been doing some spring cleaning."

"And none too soon. I've never seen a place so cluttered." Fidgeting, he remained standing next to the door.

"Are you going to sit down or what?"

"Sorry, I didn't know it was allowed. I must've missed that memo." He shot her that roguish smile of his. Hell, she'd missed that more than she'd dared let herself believe.

She'd never invited him in before because she'd firmly believed there was no place for him in her life. How could there be? A cop and a killer? Like that was

37

the proverbial match made in heaven. But things had changed. She'd changed. He was a great guy. Good God, he hadn't just rescued her at the hospital, but on the way over there to offer his support, he'd bought these clothes for her to go home in, knowing that hers would have been taken as evidence. That said more than words ever could.

He meandered inside. "I see you have another little playmate. Who's he?"

"What?"

He nodded to the corner of the room, where a cage was pushed up against the wall.

"Oh, crap!" Tess bolted for the kitchen. She filled a shallow bowl with water and ripped open the refrigerator. It was completely bare except for a milk carton, a carrot, and half a lettuce. Tess grabbed the vegetables and darted over to the cage. She stroked the white-and-brown rabbit inside. "Sorry, little one." She put the food and drink inside.

The rabbit immediately started chomping on the carrot. She stroked him again. "You're okay, aren't you, boy?"

He was the reason she'd been out that evening – last-minute supplies before she handed him over to the little girl whose heart she'd broken by saying she was leaving the country.

Josh ambled over to the sofa and nodded to her brand-new widescreen television. "I see you finally got a TV."

"A gift from a friend."

"Ah."

"A friend friend, not *that* kind of friend."

38

"Hey, it's none of my business." He rubbed a hand over his mouth, his body language suggesting that was far from the case and that there was more he wanted to say.

Tess preempted any follow-up comment. She remembered how awkward she'd felt the last time she'd knocked on his door, only for it not to be he who answered.

She said, "So, how's *your* little friend?"

"Who? Oh, uh, Christine? Good, thanks."

He rubbed his hand over his mouth again.

Tess nodded, just looking at him.

"Listen, you disappeared for six months," said Josh. "Six months. What was I supposed to do?"

He wandered over to her bookcase with two bare shelves and a handful of books slung onto the other: Joyce, Faulkner, Wilde, Twain, Hemingway... Her book collection was mainly digital, but nothing could beat occasionally curling up with real paper and ink.

"So, is it serious?" Tess asked.

He dragged a hand over his face and heaved a sigh. "Tess, do you really want to get into this right now?"

"Get into what? I'm just catching up with an old friend."

"An old friend, huh?"

He picked up her copy of *Wuthering Heights* and turned it over to the blurb on the back.

Tess had read that book to Fish, who'd seemed to enjoy it, but she couldn't see Josh being enthralled by a dark tale of love, betrayal, and sacrifice.

After a few seconds, he shook the novel at her. "Do you know how long I looked for you? Hell, I even filed a missing person's report."

A missing person's report? Maybe Heathcliff's tormented yearning for Cathy wouldn't be lost on him after all.

"I'm sorry. But…"

Her gaze drifted about the room as she struggled for words. But what? She'd been recuperating from an almost-fatal stabbing she'd suffered while taking out a local crime boss with her bare hands. That wasn't an excuse for an ordinary boyfriend, let alone a by-the-book homicide detective.

Josh hung his head for a moment, then slotted the book back in place.

"Hey, no, it's me who's sorry," he said. "Obviously, I have questions, but there's only one that really matters."

Great. What was he going to hit her with now?

He locked her gaze. "Right this second, what can I do to help?"

Hold her.

Hold her so tight it was like he'd never let her go.

Then catch the gang and torture them to death.

Like any of that was going to happen. His love for 'Christine' and for the letter of law would make damn sure of that. That left only one thing he could do to help her.

Tess said, "Ice cream."

"Ice cream?"

"It's a frozen dessert made from dairy products."

"Is that so?"

"You can get it almost anywhere. I'm surprised you haven't come across it."

"Well," said Josh, "I'll have to see if my buddy in Vice can hook me up sometime."

40

Tess sighed. That was all she had, joke-wise. She needed him to believe that she was as okay as she could be, and humor was the easiest way of achieving that.

He gestured with open hands. "So, rocky road, cookie dough, rum raisin...?"

"Lemon."

"Lemon. Just lemon?"

"Uh-huh. You can get it at the convenience store three blocks down, next to the Irish pub."

He nodded. "I know the one. And that's all you need? No food, drink, toiletries" – he gestured to the rabbit – "carrots?"

"Na-huh."

"Okay, so just lemon ice cream it is." He made for the door, then turned back as he opened it. "When I come back, it's going to be time for your meds." He pointed at her. "I want to see you take them – actually see – to be sure you have. Okay?"

Dr. Phillips had called it post-exposure prophylaxis – a course of treatment to prevent her from developing any sexually transmitted infection to which she might have been exposed, such as gonorrhea, chlamydia, even HIV. It was a serious issue, so she'd be taking her self-medication equally seriously. But it was sweet of Josh to be so concerned.

She arched an eyebrow at him again. "What am I? A kid?"

"Considering what you've been through, I'm amazed you're even on your feet right now. So, to make sure there are no nasty surprises down the road, I'm going to make damn sure we do exactly as the doc said. We clear?"

With a stern expression, she saluted him.

41

"Give me strength." Shaking his head, he pulled the door open and stepped out into her hall. As he was closing it, she called out.

"Josh?"

He poked his head back in, eyebrows raised. "Hmm?"

"Thank you."

He smiled. Then disappeared.

Tess stared at the closed door. What they could have had if only her life had turned out differently. Maybe there was still time. She hung her head and heaved an almighty breath.

Time? There was time for only one thing.

She checked to make sure Fish's automatic feeding machine was still on and then topped it up so he had the full seven days' worth. Then she grabbed her spare leather jacket and her black backpack. Finally, she removed the rabbit's water, picked the cage up, and headed for the door.

Josh had wanted to do something for her, and he'd done it – he'd left. Now she had to do something for herself.

Chapter 07

TESS PUSHED OPEN the door to Gamma apartment and strode into a living room even more sparsely furnished than the one at Alpha, her main apartment, where she'd gotten rid of Josh. Bare it might be, but it had everything she needed in a safe house.

The air smelled damp, so thick she could almost take bites out of it. And it felt cold. Colder than outside. That was only to be expected, as she hadn't visited for six months to do so much as crack a window, let alone fend off the vicious winter the city had suffered.

In the taxi over here, pangs of guilt had clawed at her over how she'd run out on Josh when he was trying to be so supportive. But she couldn't be with him now. Not like this. Not when she'd pictured being with him again so differently. No, she needed to be alone. Plus, the fewer distractions she had, the quicker she'd be able to work through this and do what needed doing.

She put the cage on the floor beside the fireplace with a white wood mantel and put fresh water in it. The rabbit seemed content enough as it chomped on its food, but she'd have to get something else for it later.

She grabbed a bottle of water from the refrigerator and then pulled open the doors to the two main kitchen cupboards. Stacked high like in a prepper's glory hole, cans of soup, meat, beans, fruit, and vegetables stood alongside powdered whey, milk, and eggs. At the far end, packs of rice, oatmeal, and pasta squared off in neat lines. If she had to, she could hole up here for three months without needing to set a foot outside.

Trudging to the mottled green sofa, she sipped her water, then slumped down and took the medication Phillips had given her. She lay down and stared at the ceiling.

Apart from the two showers she'd had at the hospital while Josh had waited in her room, it was the first moment she'd been alone since waking from her nightmare. It felt odd.

She pushed up. Speaking of showering.

She ambled to the bathroom, wincing as she rolled her shoulders – she had aches and pains all over her body. However, at the bathroom door, she stopped.

Pounding her fist into wall, she grimaced. "Goddamn it."

She was clean. She knew she was clean. She'd scrubbed herself so hard for so long, the patches of red raw flesh all over her body proved she was clean. Another shower would do nothing but prolong her pain by pandering to a nonsensical craving.

She wandered back into the living room and collapsed onto the sofa, but immediately bounced back up.

God, she wanted that shower. Wanted it so badly. Would just one more hurt?

"Fuck off!" She hurled the bottle across the room. It hit the wall, splattering water across it.

Pacing behind the sofa, she hung her head, deep in thought.

So, what was she going to do?

She had to do something. Hiding away here feeling sorry for herself would drive her nuts.

But unfortunately, it wasn't a case of what she *would* do, but of what *could* she do.

The forensic examination of her clothing and the rape kit could take forever. Quite literally. It was a scandalous fact that the system was backed up with rape kits waiting to be tested. Kits often sat for months. Longer. But when there were around 100,000 forcible rapes reported across the country every year and most police department budgets were stretched to the limit, why would anyone be surprised there was a backlog?

But even if Josh called in every favor he could, and then some, and managed to get it tested, there was no guarantee it would lead anywhere. CODIS only maintained DNA records of people who'd been busted, so if none of the gang had a jacket, there was no way to trace them that way.

At least if she'd managed to secure the kit, she could have paid for a private analysis to know one way or the other and not be left in limbo like this. But she hadn't been able to get it. She had nothing.

In the good old days, she'd just have phoned Bomb. His computer wizardry could often trace someone within a matter of hours. But the good old days were long gone. Firstly, Bomb was out of the game. Secondly, even if he wasn't, she had nothing to give him to go on – no description, no evidence, no witnesses. Nothing.

She slumped against the wall and then slowly slid down it to sprawl on the floor. Nothing.

Oh... no, that wasn't true. She remembered a white van. And a name – John. But like that would be a help in a city of eight million people.

Even if Bomb was still with her, he couldn't work miracles.

But he wasn't with her.

She was alone.

Totally alone.

What was she supposed to do?

She couldn't be with the man she wanted to be with. She couldn't have the new life she'd spent months creating. She couldn't trace the gang who'd attacked her and ruined that life. What the hell could she do?

And as if that wasn't bad enough, she could still feel them on her. Their stink. Their filth. It was there. All over her. Festering. Crawling. Spreading.

She had to get it off.

Had to.

She leapt up. Ran for the only thing that could ease her pain.

Chapter 08

SO MUCH STEAM filled Tess's bathroom that it was like a fall morning on the docks as the fog rolled in from the Atlantic.

The water from the showerhead beat down relentlessly, but no matter how much poured out, it washed away nothing and merely flowed straight down the drain as clean as when it jetted forth.

Tess hadn't made it into the shower. She'd undressed, turned it on, put her foot in, but then frozen.

What would happen if she got into the shower? Again?

How long would it be before she craved another one?

How many more times would she need to bathe before she felt clean, before she had washed their stink off her, their filth off her?

Now, huddled in a ball between the toilet pedestal and the closed shower door, she sobbed. Naked. Shaking. Lost.

If only she could see a way out, a means to drag things back to how they used to be.

But things could never be the same. Not after what they'd done. They'd used her. Used her as a thing. Not a person. A thing. A thing they could fuck and then toss away like garbage.

And she'd let them. Let them!

Why hadn't she fought back? For God's sake, she'd spent nearly a decade in the Far East training to kill with her bare hands, so what had happened to all her moves?

And since coming home, she'd tracked down more killers than a whole precinct of New York's finest, so how the hell had she let someone snatch her so easily? How?

Jesus, everything about it was just so dumb. Right from the way they'd grabbed her. Why hadn't she seen the van? Sensed the threat? There was a time she'd have taken a step away from the curb on seeing a van slowly approaching. Most people would have called that paranoia, which was why those people were targets and she never had been. Why hadn't she stepped back? Given herself an extra second? Time to think. Time to act. Had she been out of the game so long? Or had she been so distracted by her new life in China? A new life that was now as dead as every other dream she'd ever had.

Images of that lush river valley in China flashed through her mind. Such stunning scenery. Scenery that was supposed to have become her backyard.

She smashed her fist into the blue tiled floor.

But it wasn't just distraction, no.

Even once they'd snatched her, it had all gone to hell.

Yes, they'd stunned her. Drugged her. Beaten her. But so what? She should have fought, for Christ's sake. She should have goddamn fought.

"Shit!" She hammered the floor. Again and again and again. "Shit. Shit. Shit. Shit."

She was trapped in a nightmare, and the reason she couldn't see a way out was because there *was* no way out. She couldn't wake up and escape when she was already awake.

She pounded the floor again.

She was trapped. Trapped. Helpless. Alone.

And still the water beat down in the shower. Tormenting her. Trying to tempt her in. Coaxing her to cleanse herself. Over and over and over. Forever a victim. A junkie craving another fix.

She sobbed. She felt like she was dying. Like she was going to die every single day for the rest of her life. Die forever.

What could she do to make it end?

Chapter 09

RAIN BEAT DOWN. But it did as much to wash the filth off Tess as the shower had done.

The reflections of streetlights smeared across the drenched black asphalt as traffic crawled along the city street with a shushhh, not a grrr.

Tess trudged past an old man scurrying along the sidewalk in the opposite direction. She bowed her head and turned away. Her puffy red eyes were a dead giveaway that she'd been crying. Not just crying, sobbing. She hated that anyone seeing her would instantly judge her as weak.

A dark-colored van approached.

Tess whipped around and peered into it. It was the wrong color, but a van was a van. Who said they had only one?

Through the rain and darkness, she only caught a blurry, shadowy glimpse of the driver. It could have been an aging Chinese guy as easily as a Caucasian cheerleader. Not that she'd recognize any of those bastards if she saw them. But that wasn't the plan – she was hoping they'd give themselves away with their reaction to seeing her.

That said, some hazy image kept rearing from the back of her mind – a blond-haired twenty-something Dracula. What the hell was all that about?

The attack was still one huge blur of weird images and odd sounds, the drugs and stun gun having warped her memories into the strangest jigsaw puzzle ever created. It felt like she was never going to get the pieces to fit together.

Tess tramped down the street. Her shoes squelched. Her clothes clung to her like a sodden burial shroud. Yet still she lumbered on.

With each step, the knot in her stomach tightened as if she was about to vomit, and only sheer force of will was keeping everything down. She'd wanted to puke her guts up since leaving the hospital and realizing how futile a search would be.

But she had to go on.

She would not be just another weak victim.

She would not relive that hell day after day.

She would not allow her own mind to torture her over something she couldn't change.

Shower?

Fuck showering.

She was never going to goddamn shower ever again.

A sound behind her made her jump. She spun around, fists up.

Nothing there. Again. There wasn't another person within fifty feet.

Christ, she could barely walk ten steps without checking behind her to see if anyone was following.

Her hair matted to her head and droplets hanging off her eyelashes, she peered up at a street sign. West 68th Street. That was the one she wanted.

She turned the corner and lurched down a street dominated by brownstones. Drenched in shadows, the buildings looked even darker drenched in rain too. She eyed them warily.

She'd been walking around in circles for hours. Her thinking was so clouded, the only plan she had been able to come up with was to search for the van and the guy who'd stunned her by spiraling outward, street by street, from the point at which she'd been snatched. It was a decent plan.

But it wasn't working.

Vans had passed. So had guys. But none had been the ones she was hunting.

For the first couple of hours, having a plan had buoyed her spirits. She'd had a goal, a purpose, maybe even a means to resolve the nightmare she was living. But after dragging herself around the streets for so long, with not a damn thing to show for it, she didn't just feel tired, she felt exhausted, as if the very next step would see her fall flat on her face.

And in the back of her mind, a little voice kept screaming that she needed another shower to wash that filth off.

Gasping for air, she slumped against the black iron railings guarding the stoop of one of the brownstones. She rested for a moment and then pushed off to continue her search, but fell back against the railings, her energy completely spent.

She had the strength to walk all night if she needed to. She knew that. Physically, the gang hadn't hurt her so much. No, the problem was all in her head. But she just couldn't heave herself away and take another step. What was the point? She wouldn't find them, no matter how far she trudged, how long she searched, so what was the point of wasting her life on taking even just one more step?

But she had to go on. She had to find them. It was what she did. What she was. She wrought justice when all hope was lost. No one ever escaped her. No one. It defined her. So she had no choice but to hunt them down. To be vengeance itself.

Didn't she?

No, she didn't. Because she couldn't.

All she could do was accept that it was beyond her. Become the victim she'd always been. Accept that was her life. Victim. Victim. Victim!

She slumped back. Slid down the rails. Sat on the soaked paving stones.

And the rain beat down. Washing away nothing but her hope.

If only she had someone to turn to, someone to talk to, someone who'd understand and know what to do.

The rain ran down her forehead and drip, drip, dripped off her nose.

Maybe there *was* someone.

He'd always been there for her in the past; maybe he could be there for her now. Maybe. If she could just clamber to her feet and make it to him.

Chapter 10

TESS STOOD IN the middle of the room. Dripping. Shivering. And smiling.

She'd been roaming the rain-soaked streets for so long and gotten so wet, water pooled beneath her on the bare floorboards as if she'd peed herself. But she didn't care.

She gazed at him. Smiling. He was always there for her. No matter what problems she faced or created. It was so stupid that she hadn't turned to him to start with. How lucky she was to have a friend like him in her life.

But now she was standing here – face-to-face – what should she say? How could she tell him what had happened? Happened to *her* of all people? What would he think of her?

Her breath breaking as she drew a huge gulp of air, she braced herself, then sat on the floor before him.

"Fish... I'm in trouble." Her chin quivered. Clenching her teeth, she struggled to control her emotions. Still a tear rolled down her cheek.

Her voice rose in pitch. "I don't know what to do."

Fish looked at her, his mouth opening and closing as he gulped water.

"I can't think straight. Nothing I try works. It's like I'm not in control anymore. Like they didn't just" – she drew another faltering breath and looked away from him – "didn't just take me, they took my life."

Smearing her palms over her cheeks, she wiped her tears away.

Fish still looked at her. Listening. But not judging.

She shook her head. "I don't know what to do. I just don't know what to do."

Cupping her hands to her face, she stared at him. Searching for answers. He'd always helped her in the past. Helped in ways that other people would have thought impossible – he was only a fish. Yet if anyone could help her, it would be him.

"What should I do?" She leaned closer to his little tank. "Please, Fish, I need help. What should I do?"

She stared at him.

And waited and waited and waited for an answer.

But Fish just floated in the middle of the tank looking back at her, opening and closing his mouth to take in water.

Tess leaned her head against his bowl. And sobbed.

There would be no answer. How could there be? Fish was just a fish. She loved him, but this was probably one of the stupidest things she'd ever done. Like a fish could ever help her resolve such a nightmarish situation.

After a few moments, she pushed up off the floor and half rose to leave, but she stopped. A frown wrinkled her brow.

She sat back down.

Stared at Fish.

He stared back. His mouth opening and closing. Opening and closing. Opening and closing.

He… he was talking to her.

Tess studied him. She shook her head. "I can't, Fish."

Opening and closing. Opening and closing.

"I can't. It's not fair to ask that."

Opening and closing. Opening and closing.

"Fish, no."

Opening and closing. Opening and closing.

"Fish…" Tess buried her face in her hands. She couldn't do that. She *wouldn't* do that.

Drawing her hands down her face, she looked at him again, hoping he'd changed his mind. He hadn't.

"Fish, you don't understand. That's too much to ask."

But Fish was adamant.

Tess snapped at him, raising her voice. "Okay. Okay. I will. Just shut the hell up about it."

She took out her phone and placed a call. As it rang, she looked at Fish.

Fish still opened and closed his mouth, opened and closed his mouth, saying one word over and over again, "Bomb. Bomb. Bomb."

"I'm calling, okay?"

56

Chapter 11

"YO, TESS. ARE you forgetting the time difference, girl? It's still the middle of the night over here."

"Bomb…"

He yawned. "How was the flight?"

"Bomb, I'" – her voice wavered – "Bomb, I'm in trouble."

"Yeah, yeah. Very funny, Tess." He snickered. "You've been there like, what, an hour and you're already bored and looking for something to do. Didn't I tell you this was going to happen. China, for God's sake. Jeez, what were you thinking?"

"I'm–I'm still in Manhattan."

"What?"

"I–I—" She sniffled.

"Tess? What the hell's going on?"

"I'm sorry. I know we did our last job, but" – her voice rose in pitch again – "I need help."

Instantly, she heard him clicking away on a keyboard. "Give me everything. Whatever you need, you got it."

57

Over the next twenty-three minutes, she recounted the entire sordid tale, all of which Bomb documented. The simple act of going through the story in detail and hearing Bomb typing gave her hope. They'd never yet worked a job they hadn't cracked, never hunted a monster they hadn't nailed.

Tess rested a hand on the glass of Fish's tank. She smiled at him. How would she ever manage without him?

"You're sure you don't remember anything else about the van except it was white with a sliding side door?" Bomb asked.

"Such as?"

"Did it have windows in the rear section? Was there panelling in the interior and if so, with what? Did it smell of oil, flowers, baked goods – anything that could tell us what it's usually used for?"

"I don't know. I'm sorry."

"That's okay."

"No, it isn't. It's a fucking disaster, you know it is. If we got so little from a client, we'd want to walk away because it would be an impossible job. You know that."

"Tess, no one is walking away from nothing. You'll be surprised, but there's more here than you think."

Really? Or was he just shooting her a line to try and cheer her up? "Like what? A white van, someone called fucking John, of all things, and maybe, just maybe, Dracula is a blond? Come on, Bomb, we both know the odds of cracking this."

She leaned her forehead against the edge of Fish's table. Despite having Bomb with her now, she had to be realistic if she wasn't going to end up hurting even more when everything came crashing down again later.

"Since when have we let the odds factor into a job?" said Bomb.

Tess hated to be defeatist, but… "There are eight million people in the city. Twenty million in the tristate area. How the hell are we going to find just five guys in twenty million?"

"Okay, cut out all the women, that's down to ten million."

Tess snickered. "Yeah, that's so much better."

Bomb ignored her. "Let's be generous and say ten percent of those are blond – that's a million. Around seven percent of the population is eighteen to twenty-five, so that takes that mil down to seventy thousand. Again, let's be generous and say one in fifty know how to handle a needle – that's just fourteen hundred people."

"Why filter by handling a needle?"

"If your average Joe has a needle, where's he going to stick it? In your neck, or in your arm or leg? I tell you, most guys are way too squeamish to go for a neck shot. That says our boy knows something about drug absorbency, and you don't learn crap like that from *ER* reruns."

With everything that was going through her mind, she hadn't thought of that. Bomb was right – fourteen hundred certainly sounded a hell of a lot better than twenty million.

"But where do we start?" asked Tess. "It's not like we've got photos of those fourteen hundred, is it?"

"No, exactly. And that fourteen hundred figure is going to climb anyway because, realistically, we need to factor in med students, trainee paramedics, military medics, and groups like that. Maybe even people who got first aid training with the Red Cross, who knows? Plus, some of these groups I'm not going to filter for blonds in case this guy's is out of a bottle."

"So we're back to tens of thousands."

"Hey, if it was easy, they'd all be off their heads on K2 in the yard at Sing Sing already. But that's not what we need to focus on. Here's what's going to happen – after I've set my bots loose on social media, the first job is to hack the student records databases of all the med schools within a hundred miles and get you mug shots of all their male students. This blond guy sounds too young to be a doctor, but he has basic skills and access to restricted drugs, so who's to say he won't be the first picture you look at?"

Tess wasn't stupid enough to imagine his face would pop up in the very first picture she saw, but this was starting to sound like they actually had a real chance.

She pushed up to her feet and meandered around to the back of her sofa, where she usually did her best pacing to mull things over. "So, we might seriously have a chance of catching these bastards?"

"I tell you, Tess, whether it takes a day or a year, we're gonna burn these motherfuckers."

She picked her backpack up from where she'd slung it. Water dripped from it onto the floor. She'd be needing it after all, so she ambled into her bedroom for her hair dryer.

"You really think social media might give us a lead?" Tess asked.

"Twitter, Facebook, Instagram – the bots will do all the work, so it's not like it will be pulling me from something potentially more productive."

Tess came back from the bedroom and placed her hair dryer next to Fish so she wouldn't forget to dry her backpack with it.

"Yeah," said Tess, "but after they executed the snatch with such military precision, are they really going to be so brainless that they give themselves away in some dumbass tweet?"

"Remember the Kim job and the video of the dog?"

Fair point. The video that the killer had posted online had helped Tess identify him and get a lead on his accomplices. People could be surprisingly dumb when it came to making themselves look big online.

"But that's an interesting point – military precision," Bomb said. "It could give us an extra lead."

"You think?"

"Damn straight. The snatch was so clean it tells us two things. A: to have devised such a plan and have had the discipline to pull it off, one of the gang could have been to a military academy. B: for everything to have gone so smoothly, it's unlikely that you're the first victim."

Tess gasped. She sank onto her sofa as the realization dawned.

She'd never thought of that. She'd been so consumed by her own pain and humiliation that it had never crossed her mind that she might not have been the first woman the gang had attacked.

"Oh, Jesus. There could be dozens of victims."

"Exactly. So that could be our best lead. Except something like less than twenty percent of sexual assaults ever get reported. But of course that leads to another question."

Tess waited, but Bomb said nothing.

In the end, she said, "What question?"

He huffed as if he didn't want to say anything. Most unlike him.

"Bomb, what's the question?"

"Isn't it obvious?"

"Would I be asking if it was?"

"Well..." He huffed again. "Josh."

Tess jumped up off the sofa and started pacing again. "Oh, no. We're not going there."

"Tess, I can probably hack the case files, but you know as well as I do the files are only half the story."

They were. Files only included the facts. They did not include hunches, opinions, rumors – all the elements that often led to a breakthrough in a case. No, for those, you needed to discuss a case with someone who knew it intimately, who'd analyzed all the ins and outs, not just glanced over the Cliff Notes.

Bomb said, "After you and Josh were so close, what harm would there be in feeling him out on this?"

"Bomb, are you fucking kidding me? If Josh gets so much as a hint of what we've done in past, or what we're doing now, he'll slap the cuffs on us both himself. No hesitation." Detective Josh by-the-book Hardy was a great guy, but sadly, he was also a great cop.

"And what if no matter what we try, all we get is squat?"

"Then, we'll just have to—"

A vague memory stopped her dead. A snippet of gossip she kind of remembered, which, at the time, she'd completely ignored. Was she remembering it correctly?

62

She stood motionless. Wading through the muddy memories in the far reaches of her mind for the tiniest flicker of light.

"Tess?"

"Hold on."

"What is it?"

"I think I might know where we can get the inside track on these bastards."

Chapter 12

ON A WOODEN bench overlooking the Hudson River in Lower Manhattan, Tess slumped forward, her elbows on her knees. She sighed.

Before her, the river slithered by, dark and cold like a gigantic snake that would devour anyone whole if they came too close.

She looked back at the city towering over her. At some point, she'd have to make a move. If she could ever figure out just what that move involved.

A slab of gray hunkered down over Manhattan's skyscrapers, as if it was trying to crush them into the ground. The odd shaft of light struggled through, making the huge concrete and glass monoliths gleam, but then was quickly strangled by the cloud, leaving gloom to once more hang over everyone and everything.

Tess clasped her hands behind her head and screwed her eyes closed. She just couldn't think straight. Everything was a complete jumble. Normally, she'd breeze into a situation like this, get what she wanted, then breeze back out. But today?

How was she going to handle this guy today? He'd given her information in the past, but each time, she'd had to pay a price. Paying it hadn't been a problem. Then. Now? This time it would be too high. Way too high.

She'd already suffered one traumatic encounter today when she'd dropped the rabbit off at Mary Jo's, believing the little girl would be at school, so there'd be no emotional upheaval. But Mary Jo was at home with a head cold.

Other than Bomb, the little girl was the closest thing to a true friend Tess had, and Mary Jo looked on Tess as a replacement for the big sister she'd lost. The poor little thing had been devastated when Tess had said she was leaving New York City. Tess had wanted to get her a dog, but that would've been way too much work for the family, so a house rabbit had seemed a great second choice – something unbelievably cute that demanded little and yet was there for Mary Jo to cuddle whenever she felt down. What could be better? And for a few brief seconds, Mary Jo had smiled that cheeky smile that had so endeared her to Tess. And then came the tears when Tess tried to say goodbye.

More emotional trauma was the last thing Tess wanted. But if she didn't face her demons, how many other women would be forced to suffer the nightmare she'd endured?

"Oh, God…" She placed her hands on the wooden seat on either side of her, preparing to stand and face what she must. If she didn't at least try, she might as well run home and curl up in a cringing ball of pain and self-loathing and just stay there forever.

With the groan of an arthritic old man getting up from a low chair, she heaved up off the bench and trudged toward the nearest street, her feet feeling like blocks of concrete.

Eight minutes later, a skinny guy in a bloodstained blue apron looked up from poking inside the torso of a wrinkly old woman on a stainless-steel autopsy table.

"Tess? Oh, my God."

She smiled meekly. "Hi, Myron."

He ripped off his bloody gloves and apron and scampered over to her, arms wide.

Stepping back, Tess held her hands up. "Please. It's not a good time right now."

Every single time she'd gone near this guy, she'd had to bang him to get the information she needed. She couldn't face that today. If he so much as looked at her below chin-level, she was out of here.

"Tess, I heard." He beckoned her. "Come here." He moved closer as if to hug her.

She cringed. "I can't, Myron. Not today."

He put his arms around her and gently hugged her.

"Hey, what kind of unfeeling monster do you think I am?" he said. "You should know me better than that by now."

Instead of being repulsed, Tess felt strangely warmed. Always having pictured him as the ugly runt of the litter, she had a soft spot for Myron, but though she'd banged the guy on and off for years, it was surprising to learn he had this level of empathy.

For a few moments, she basked in the sensitivity of another person, like old friends who'd received mutually distressing news.

"How did you know?" Tess asked, breaking the hug.

"Joe Corrigan." He gestured to the body he was slicing apart. "This is his case."

66

Joe was a homicide detective on the Upper West Side. He was one of her favorite cops – he didn't just work the streets, he cared about what happened on them.

"Does everyone and their dog know?" Tess asked.

"For a big city, it's a surprisingly small town."

Tess meandered further into the autopsy suite but didn't get too close to the body. The discoloration and bloating from internal gasses hadn't yet set in and that lovely aroma of decomposition was yet to truly take hold, but rotting meat was rotting meat. That stench clung to the nostrils like nothing else.

Beside each of the three stainless-steel autopsy tables stood a chrome stand from which hung a large pan used to weigh organs. The pan beside the body had what looked like lungs inside it.

Tess ambled over to the pan beside the middle table. She pushed it down and then let it elegantly bounce back up. How could she get what she needed if she didn't want to bang him and didn't want to discuss what had happened to her?

She pushed the pan again, and again it slowly ascended to a state of equilibrium.

Despite having rehearsed what to say beside the river, she had no idea how to now say it in a way that wouldn't implicate her later if five rapists turned up dead.

Finally, Myron broke the silence. "I know you're probably hoping for good news, but according to my sources, the department has zilch, so I'm sorry, but there's not going to be an arrest anytime soon. If ever. I really can't tell you how sorry I am. I wish I had something more positive to share."

She didn't look at him. Just focused on depressing the pan and letting it return to a balanced state. It was stupid to think he wouldn't know why she was here. All she ever used him for was information.

He shrugged. "If there was anything I could do, you know I would, but…"

"When I saw you about the new Butcher, you mentioned a gang of rapists, didn't you?"

"That I did."

"It's them, isn't it?"

"There's no question it fits their MO – a white van, monster masks, no street camera coverage… While I like to deal in cold hard facts" – he gestured to the dead body on the slab – "so few details about these cases have been made public that I think it's safe to assume there's little chance we're dealing with a gang of copycats."

"So what can you tell me?"

"I can tell you to leave things to the authorities and to try to get on with your life."

Finally, she looked at him. "Myron, I need this."

He crossed his arms, one hand rubbing his chin while he stared at her, obviously hoping to weigh her up as easily as he weighed body parts.

He snorted out a breath, then said, "They" – he made air quotes – "'think' it's a gang of at least five men. Caucasian. Twenty to twenty-five years of age. Other than that, like I said – zilch."

"That's it?"

"They wear masks, fingerprints are a bust, and there're no hits on CODIS for DNA, so…" He shrugged.

"Seriously? That's all the authorities have?"

"I'm sorry."

"You're sorry? Well, that's alright, then." It wasn't Myron's fault, and he was doing what he could, but she just couldn't help lashing out.

He turned his back on her and strode away to his computer without another word. Instead of sitting on the black swivel chair, he leaned down to it and started clicking away.

Great. He'd been her best shot at a decent lead. But that was gone. She had nothing. It was going to be impossible to find them. They'd gotten away with it.

She heaved a breath. "I'm sorry, Myron. I appreciate you trying to help. It's just…" She buried her face in her hands and heaved another sigh.

He didn't even turn around to face her when he spoke. "As good law-abiding citizens, all we can do is hope is that, one way or another, someone puts those animals away for good."

He was her one hope. She needed something. Anything. "Myron, please, isn't there—"

Without turning from fiddling on his computer, he reached back and held up an index finger meaning for her to be quiet.

"In this instance," he said, "the $64,000 question is who can possibly catch them when the police have nothing. Of course, anyone can hire a PI, but, well, some of them are so unscrupulous they're little more than criminals themselves and break all kinds of laws to get the job done – for the right money, of course. God only knows what would happen if one of those miscreants got hold of the wrong information."

He glanced back at her for a moment. "I'm sure you've come across that kind of lowlife scum when you've been researching your crime articles."

He clicked the mouse once more, then his desktop laser printer hummed into action.

"I just need to pop out for a second." He pointed at his printer. "Please don't touch that. I don't want to have to print another copy if anything happens to that one."

Without another word, he sauntered out.

Tess darted to the printer as it spewed page after page. When it finally stopped, she stuffed the collection of sheets into her backpack and shot for the door. Myron was leaning against the blue wall of the hallway outside. Without even looking at her, he waltzed back into his autopsy room.

All around outside, pedestrians rushed about as if avoiding the pouring rain was a matter of life and death. The gray world felt unforgiving, vindictive, heartless. Yet Tess no longer saw a world mired in gloom. Hers had the tiniest speck of light glimmering in the far, far distance. If she could nurture it…

She marched for the nearest subway station, paying little heed to anything happening around her.

She ached to read the file, but she couldn't risk it getting soggy and falling apart. Question upon question screamed in her mind, but only one mattered: what secrets hid in these papers to help her catch this gang?

As the steps down to the subway came into sight, her phone rang.

"Yo, Tess."

"Bomb. I've got something."

"Me too. It's uploaded and waiting for you. I suggest a big screen."

She'd thought she had questions before, but now she had even more. Between them, surely they would have enough to find those bastards. And bury them.

70

Chapter 13

TESS HAD HER tablet in her backpack, but Bomb was right – the bigger the screen the better for this type of task. She strode along the avenue of trees in Bryant Park as quickly as she could without running, aching to explore what he'd uncovered. Overhead, buds were forming on the massive London plane trees to herald the spring, but the wintery rain and the onset of dusk meant few of the green metal chairs along the path were in use on the South Promenade.

The bad weather had packed pedestrians onto the subway train, so Tess hadn't looked at the file Myron had provided. Being jostled and losing something vital was too much of a risk. Now, curiosity gnawed at her like a maggot at a juicy apple.

Having rounded the corner onto Fifth Avenue, Tess glanced at Patience and Fortitude, the lions captured in white marble on either side of the stone steps up into the public library.

This had been her favorite place in the entire city when she was a kid. Even nowadays, she still felt a chill of excitement at seeing the lions, knowing their magnificence was only a precursor to the wonders she would find within the library's books.

But today?

Today, it was just a building of cold stone in which was something she needed.

Inside, taking two steps at a time, she dashed up toward the Catalogue Room on the third floor. Normally, she'd have sauntered up while basking in the architectural glory of sumptuous French walnut and pink marble, décor befitting a European palace, but today, she raced straight on by it all as if it didn't exist.

Finally, sitting at a computer, she entered her password to access Bomb's darknet, a website buried so deep on the Dark Web that normal search engines could never find it. And even if someone happened to stumble upon Bomb's site by accident, the NSA and FBI combined would never crack its AES-Twofish-Serpent cascaded three-cipher encryption.

She froze with the site open, completely torn. Should she study Myron's file first or Bomb's?

Well, there was only one real choice. She opened the folder in the darknet, inside which were three subfolders: 'Tri-State Graduates,' 'Tri-State Undergrads,' and 'Tri-State Pre-med.' Myron's file could give her leads, but Bomb's could give her an actual target.

The graduates subfolder had the fewest megabytes, suggesting it had the fewest images. It seemed logical to start with that one and get it out of the way first.

Would Bomb be right and the first image she saw would be of that blond Dracula who'd pumped her full of drugs? She'd only caught a blurry glimpse of part of his face when his mask had slipped, but because of what he'd done, she'd never forget it.

She opened the first image. A fair-skinned guy with red hair stared out of the screen at her. Okay, so maybe the next would be the one. She clicked the forward arrow. A big-nosed young man looked at her through half-closed eyes.

Okay, so she hadn't really expected to hit the jackpot right off the mark, but maybe she'd be lucky and he'd be somewhere in this first batch. Looking at the number of images in the subfolder, Tess rubbed her brow and her shoulders slumped.

"Oh, you're shitting me."

Someone coughed nearby. Tess glanced up.

The bespectacled librarian who'd given her access to the computer stared at her. The woman shook her head and put her finger to her lips. Tess mouthed 'sorry.'

Sighing, Tess looked at the number of images again: 1374.

And that was the smallest subfolder? She didn't even want to look at the two bigger ones. Man, had she been stupid getting all excited thinking the first image to pop up might be one of the guys she was looking for.

Altering the layout of the image viewer, Tess looked at two portraits at once. But on that scale, it would still be nearly 700 screens she'd have to study. And she meant study – she'd only glimpsed Dracula's face for a split second, so she couldn't risk only glancing at the photographs and accidentally skipping over the very person she was hunting.

Giving each picture a full second or two to properly digest it would mean she'd be here for hours. So, maybe she should download the file to her phone and study them on the go while she pursued whatever leads Myron's file provided.

No. Again, that could lead to mistakes.

She had no option but to give this her complete attention. The gang could be hiding in this file, so she couldn't risk not spotting them. Thank God she'd decided to study the photographs on a large screen here and not on her tablet at home. She slapped her forehead. She didn't only have a tablet at home, but that lovely big TV that Bomb had bought her. Why the devil hadn't she gone home and used that?

Okay, she wasn't used to there being a TV in her life, but that didn't alter the fact that her head obviously wasn't completely in the game yet. All the more reason to stay here, where over the years, she'd done some of her most comprehensive research, and not go home, with all the distractions it held.

Ensuring she wasn't slouching to avoid backache, she sat as comfortably as she could and paged through to the next two images. Then the next. And the next.

Eighty-one minutes later, she clicked the forward arrow, then immediately clicked the back arrow – her mind had drifted yet again, so she hadn't properly looked at those last two. Unfortunately, neither was the face she was looking for, so she hit forward once more.

No, not him either.

Forward again.

Nope.

Forward.

Nothing happened.

She'd reached the end of the first subfolder.

She slumped over the wooden desk on her elbows and buried her face in her hands. He wasn't there. The other two folders were so big she'd literally be here all night if she tried to study those now.

Rubbing her face, she heaved a breath.

It was no good; she needed a break. Her mind was so messed up that she couldn't concentrate for longer than a few minutes at a time before she drifted off and thought of anything but analyzing the photographs in front of her. She needed a rest so she could come back to the photos with a renewed vigor and give them the scrutiny the task demanded.

She took Myron's file from her backpack and flicked through the pages to get a rough idea of whether she was going to be equally disappointed with the potential leads he'd provided.

"Oh, God." Only five other women had come forward claiming to have been assaulted by a gang of up to five men in a van.

Five. Though it meant they'd all have had to suffer horrendous abuse, Tess had hoped for three or four times that to be sure of getting something solid to go on.

Yet in another way, five was a horrifically large number, because if Bomb's statistics on the percentage of rapes actually reported was correct, it meant that there could really be thirty to forty victims. Victims she could never find to help her. Victims she could never help by nailing these monsters.

Struggling not to be defeatist, she leaned back in her chair and started combing through the police reports Myron had provided. The first two she read gave her nothing she didn't already know. When she picked up another one, something caught her eye, but she didn't immediately know why.

The complaint had been filed by Sammie Hogarth, a blonde fifteen-year-old who'd been grabbed on her way home from her gymnastics class. The report was dated less than two weeks ago.

Tess paused and gazed away into space as she filtered through her memories.

Two weeks?

That was around the time she'd gone to Myron for information on the new Butcher who was terrorizing the city by hacking up kids. That was what she'd half-remembered – a snippet of gossip Myron had dropped into the conversation about a gang of serial rapists.

Oh Christ, if Tess had listened to Myron that day, if she'd acted on the information then, maybe she could have stopped the gang back then. Stopped them and saved Sammie. And saved herself. Oh, dear Lord.

It hadn't clicked earlier, but now it was clear – if she hadn't been so selfish, so consumed with leaving this life behind and running away to China to establish a sanctuary for animals, she could have stopped this nightmare before it had ever happened. She'd have changed the very future there and then.

Tess stared blankly at nothing.

She'd done this to herself.

She'd had the power to prevent it, but her own selfishness had brought this torture upon her. Upon her and God only knew how many other women too traumatized to come forward and report it.

Her vision blurred as tears filled her eyes.

She'd done this to herself. Running away had been so goddamn important that she hadn't seen what needed doing, and that only she could do it.

Worse still, she could have saved other women from suffering such hell, but hadn't, because she'd put her own selfish dreams first.

Tears streamed down her cheeks.

She deserved what had happened to her.

Deserved it.

Something prodded Tess's shoulder. She jumped.

The librarian said, "Are you okay? Have you had some distressing news?"

Oh God, yes. The most distressing she could ever remember.

"I'm sorry, I—" Without another word, Tess logged out of the darknet, scooped all her belongings into her backpack, and leapt up out of her seat. Once out in the hall, she ran through the building and out into the street, where the rain poured down.

She had to get away. Far away. But to where?

Where could she go to hide from herself?

Nowhere.

That was the problem with guilt. With shame. With responsibility.

No matter how far she ran, no matter where she hid, it would always follow her. A malignant shadow.

Tears streaking her face, she barged through the pedestrians on Fifth Avenue. She didn't see where she was going. Didn't see where she'd been. Only that there were people all around her. People whose lives she'd put in jeopardy because she didn't care enough.

She had to get away.

Had to.

But to where?

Where?

She couldn't be the only person in the world to suffer a crisis. What did everyone else do in such a nightmarish situation?

Well, there was one thing…

77

Chapter 14

THIRTY-SEVEN MINUTES LATER.

On a barstool in the Rolled Dice, Tess nodded to the barman with a glass eye as he placed her drinks before her – a third bottle of imported cider on her right and a first shot of tequila on her left. Not wanting to talk to anyone and believing her nod had sufficed, she slid a twenty across the bar top. Drinking worked for many folks in the face of an overwhelming crisis, and though it was doing squat for her so far, she hoped another few rounds might rectify that.

Cradling her cider, she watched a droplet of condensation trickle painstakingly slowly down the side of the brown glass bottle.

Rock music played in the background, glasses chinked, and pool balls clacked, while gossip floated on the air from all directions. She usually gravitated toward rock music bars: their clientele was generally easy-going. In Manhattan's trendy nightspots, too many weak-willed pussies worried whether the emoji they'd just texted was cool or being scoffed at in tweets with the ironic hashtag LOL. Tess couldn't do those people even on a good day.

Normally she'd have felt quite at home in the Rolled Dice and enjoyed the refreshing taste of her cider as it sparkled on her tongue. But not tonight. Tonight, Tess heard nothing and saw nothing. Nothing except the droplet fighting its way to freedom.

Raped.

Her.

How could that have possibly happened?

To her?

What had she done wrong?

She always tried to be so aware of her surroundings. Aware of the objects in it, the people meandering through it, the natural and unnatural phenomena dictating its environmental condition. How could someone creep up and catch her so unaware? Had her mind already been in China even though her body was still here? That had to be it.

This would never have happened a year ago, when she was at her peak on the streets. Had she lost so much edge due to her injury and the resulting recuperation period?

Tess threw the tequila down in one and then slammed the glass down on the counter. As she did, she spotted a chubby guy at the far end of the bar where it curved around. He was just a guy swigging on a bottle of domestic beer. About 200 pounds. Brown hair. No discernible distinguishing features. Yet he was a guy she thought she'd seen before. But where? When? And why did it feel important? She stared, trying to place the stranger.

"Hey," someone said beside her.

A dark-haired guy in a faded black T-shirt with a list of concert dates on the back looked at her. He'd been sitting a few stools down with his buddy, but now he leaned on the bar, grinning at her.

The guy said, "Cheer up, sweet cheeks, it might never happen."

Tess didn't react. Didn't speak. Didn't look. Didn't flinch.

"Whoa, all your bad days come at once, huh? I tell you what always works for me: vodka. Here, let me get you one."

He waved to get the barman's attention, then said, "Two vodkas."

It wasn't this guy's fault she was suffering like this, so there was no reason to spoil his day.

Tess said, "Thanks, but no."

"Believe me, it works wonders," he said. "Listen, we'll have a drink, have a dance, and I bet by the third shot you can't even remember what you're all bent out of shape over."

Sipping on a bottle of beer, he eyed her up and down.

The barman placed two vodkas on the counter. The guy paid for them, then slid one over to Tess.

"Get it down you, sweet cheeks. We'll have you up and partying in no time."

Vodka Guy threw his shot down.

Tess pushed hers back toward him.

"Hey, loosen you up." He slid it back to her. "We're both here looking for a good time, aren't we?"

Tess didn't look at him. "No."

"No?" He chuckled. "Hey, I'm going to have my work cut out making you smile, aren't I?"

80

Leaning on the bar, he stroked her hand. "Come on, have a drink. I'm a real nice guy, when you get to know me."

She turned to him. Stared coldly. Jet-black bangs hung down over a lined face that looked like the lines were more from smiling than aging, as if laughter came easily to this guy.

"What do you say?" Vodka Guy asked.

"No."

"What? Hey, you'll have the time of your life, I promise you, or my name ain't Earl."

Tess spoke slowly, purposefully. "No means no."

"But it could so easily mean yes." He winked.

The barman leaned over. "Is there a problem here, folks?"

Without taking her eyes off Vodka Guy, Tess said, "I got this."

Vodka Guy frowned. "Oh, you got this, huh? What's with the goddamn attitude when I'm being so nice? Shit, I tell you, the only problem you got is the size of the goddamn stick up your ass."

Tess continued staring at him without a flicker of expression on her face. "Walk away. Don't speak. Don't look back. Just walk."

He stabbed a finger at her. "Who the hell do you think you're talking to?"

Again, the barman leaned over. "Please, guys, let's keep things peaceful, okay?" Looking at Vodka Guy, he said, "The lady didn't ask for company, so why not just let her drink alone, huh?"

"I said I've got this." Tess pushed her drink away and stood. "Shirley here was just leaving."

She shoved Vodka Guy in the chest and knocked him back into his buddy, a guy with a bushy beard and a hairstyle that must have been the height of fashion during the Neolithic Period.

Neolithic Man pushed Vodka Guy away and then clambered to his feet.

He glared at Tess. "What's your fucking problem?"

Now she had two guys totally pissed at her. Right at that instant, she couldn't think of anything she wanted more.

Vodka Guy stalked back and leaned into her face. Spittle hit her as he spoke. "Who the fuck do you think you are?"

"A woman who said no."

She shoved him again. "Now, run along like a good little girl." She nodded to Neolithic Man. "And take your boyfriend with you – he looks like he'll burst if he doesn't get a good fisting soon."

Sneering, Vodka Guy leaned closer. "Don't think I won't hit a woman, bitch."

Tess said, "And don't think I won't." She headbutted him.

He staggered back, clutching his face.

Before Neolithic Man could react, Tess hammered a kick into his groin and then slammed a punch into his throat. He slumped over the bar, gasping for air, bottles and bowls of nuts skidding everywhere.

Vodka Guy flew at her, blood gushing from his nose. In typical bar brawling style, he swung his right fist back and then fired a haymaker at her head.

Tess sidestepped and ducked under it. In rapid succession, she crashed her knee into his gut, powered her fist into his kidney, then stamped into the back of his knee.

He crumpled to the tacky floor.

Scooping her arms around his neck, she tightened a reverse choke hold and levered back, forcing him to arch backwards and stare up at the ceiling.

Vodka Guy spluttered for breath.

Tess squeezed harder.

"Pl—please." His face twisted and flushed with blood.

She held him tight.

Vodka Guy raked her forearms, his breathing making horrible gargling sounds.

Onlookers gawked. They'd probably never seen a woman fight with such skill, such savagery.

Tess stared down into his wide terrified eyes. If she tightened her grip, she could kill him in a matter of seconds.

She relaxed her hold. He splattered to the floor, red-faced and gasping for air.

Tess scanned the dumbfounded faces. "Anyone else not understand the word 'no'?"

She snatched her cider from the bar, took a last swig and then stormed out.

The cold night air made her cheeks prickle. She checked behind her as she walked down the sidewalk. Just let her see a curb-crawling van or a guy tailing her now.

The bright lights of another bar burst out onto the sidewalk ahead, and when the main door opened, the faint sound of some crooning boy band drifted toward her. Should she risk another beer? Risk more hassle? Another confrontation?

Or should she go home?

She looked at her hand. The one Vodka Guy had stroked. She brushed it on her jacket. Rubbed it with the cuff of her other sleeve. Dragged it across her black jeans. But still she could feel him on her.

Beer? No, she had to get him off her. Had to. Now!

Chapter 15

TESS'S EYES FLICKERED open and she immediately frowned.

Where the hell was she this time?

Turning her head, she groaned and grabbed her neck. Instead of feeling joy at the dawning of another day bristling with opportunities, she cringed as pain shot through her neck and shoulders.

On Alpha's bathroom floor, she'd wedged herself in between the shower and the washbasin, too terrified to step under the still-jetting water for fear that if she succumbed to this pathological need, she'd never again be able to function like a normal human being.

She'd managed not to feed that craving, but that was where her victories had ended. Every time she'd left the bathroom, she'd sweated, fidgeted, and shaken, desperate for clean water to wash away her pain by washing away the filth. But she knew it couldn't. It never would. No amount of water could wash away something that was all in her mind.

Massaging her neck, she eased herself out of the tight space and grabbed the washbasin to pull herself to her feet.

The hot shower having run all night, the air was wet, like that in a Thai jungle during the rainy season.

She turned off the shower, then wiped condensation off the mirror and stared at herself. This couldn't go on. Something was going to give, and she knew what. Unless things changed, she was going to end up in a psych ward, in prison, or in the morgue. Whichever it was, it didn't end happily ever after.

Locked on her own gaze, she studied herself.

The average Joe probably thought a fighter's most deadly weapon was a devastating hook, or a lightning-fast jab, or a kick that could shatter bones. Tess had trained to maim or kill with her hands, feet, elbows, knees – just about every part of her body – but none of those were her deadliest weapon. That title went to her mind.

If her hand was broken, she wouldn't be able to form a fist to punch. But she'd still be able to punch with her other hand, or kick with her feet, bite, headbutt, strangle, stomp... The loss of one hand would be problematic, but not a game ender. However, she only had one mind, so if that was broken, she wouldn't be able to think, to react, to function. A messed-up mind meant only one thing – game over.

She intended to hunt down a gang of five men. Whether they were trained fighters or not didn't matter. What mattered was that there were five of them. And that this was real life, not a Hollywood movie. Five guys was way too many to take on because punches and kicks could come from any angle. They'd be impossible to avoid. And when one connected and put her on the ground, that would be the end. Period. No one would withstand five grown men stomping on their head and body, no matter what training they'd had.

No, she needed her mind not just to fight, but to plan. So, if her primary weapon was broken, the obvious solution was to fix it. Fortunately, she had an idea how she might attempt that.

***

Mallard ducks quacked away in the distance as Tess strode through the park, but the commotion barely registered. She ambled along, head down, gazing at the asphalt path instead of at the plants reawakening after a long winter.

Why was there so much evil in the world? How could people do the appalling things they did and live with themselves?

Tess had struggled with this conundrum for years, ever since that night in her grandpa's store, but never – never – discovered an answer that truly satisfied her.

Rhododendron bushes lined the path down into the heart of the park. Every time Tess saw them, she was instantly transported to the time so many years ago when she'd strolled in the Himalayan foothills.

The sun had beaten down, yet the air had been so cool and fresh, Tess could still taste it. Indira had led them over a hilltop Tess had never explored before and down a winding dirt path through rhododendron bushes bursting with pinky-red flowers, the air thick with their sweet scent. This was the furthest away from civilization and Indira's ashram that Tess had been. This was India at its wildest. Or so it at first appeared.

Before visiting the place, whenever Tess had thought of the Himalayas, she'd always pictured Mount Everest, snowcapped peaks, and life-or-death struggles over jagged rock faces, but the Himalayas were so vast, the landscape so varied, it constantly surprised her with its devastating beauty.

Clearing the rhododendrons, they meandered further down the path through a hillside field. A field carefully tended to yield a bountiful crop. Cannabis plants towered over Tess, six, eight, ten feet tall. Starlike leaves basked in the sun, rebellious and proud.

Ambling along, Indira, who normally couldn't say enough, was strangely quiet. Her long black hair streaked with gray swept out behind her like a cape in the light breeze.

"Shouldn't we tell someone about this?" Tess asked.

Without looking back, Indira said, "I'm sure they know."

"So we could burn it."

"Why?"

"Why...? Well, okay, it's not heroin, but it will still get people hooked and waste their lives. And God only knows what the drug money will be used for."

Indira glanced over her shoulder. "You're so sure it will end up in schoolyards and not pharmacies? Killing, not healing?"

"So it's medicinal cannabis?"

Indira shrugged.

"So we should tell someone."

Indira stopped. She reached up, plucked a leaf from one of the plants, then stuck out her index finger and balanced the leaf across it.

"This plant walks a tightrope," said Indira. "A tightrope between light and dark. One moment it's helping people cope with chronic pain, the next it's dragging the misguided into crime and self-destruction."

She held her finger higher. The leaf seesawed in the breeze but remained balanced.

Indira said, "Do we have the right to push it one way or the other, and seal its fate forever, or should we believe the balance of the universe will allow it to choose its own path?"

With her other hand, Indira gave the leaf a gentle nudge and it seesawed more vigorously, but still remained on her finger.

Tess frowned. "It's a plant. How is it going to choose anything?"

A wry smile spread across Indira's face. With her free hand, she knocked the leaf off her finger and it spiraled down into the dirt. She stamped on it and ground it into the dirt.

"Is the world a better place now?"

How could it be? "Yeah, I bet there're drug lords all over the world shitting themselves over making their mortgage." Tess nodded to the acres of cannabis plants.

"So is the world better with regard to this one plant?" She stroked the bushy eight-foot tall plant from which she'd taken the leaf.

Losing a single leaf would make no difference to the plant or the drug trade at all. "With one less joint in the world, I suppose a musician somewhere might make it out of bed before lunchtime," said Tess.

Indira pointed to the leaf at her feet. "So, is it better for the leaf?"

"The dead leaf?"

89

"Exactly. The world is not better in any way whatsoever." Indira turned and set off down the track again.

So what just happened there? Was Tess supposed to have learned something from all this hippie-dippie bull, or had Indira been discreetly chewing the leaves all morning?

Tess picked up the leaf. "I don't get it."

Indira stopped and wandered back to her. "There is darkness in the world and there is light. For a time, each of us must balance on the tightrope between the two before choosing in which world we want to live. However, for a lucky few, there is a third path – to walk that tightrope, forever journeying through a gray world of shadows."

Indira took Tess's hands in hers. "You are one of these lucky ones who walks this tightrope. You experience the wonder of both the darkness and the light. However, remaining balanced, remaining on that tightrope will be a constant struggle."

"And what if I don't want to be on a tightrope? Don't I get a say in this?"

"For there to be light, there *must* be darkness, just as for there to be love, there must be selfishness. We cannot eradicate one without diluting the power of the other. So when we meet a personal crisis, we shouldn't ask, 'why me?' as if we believe we are being unfairly punished. No, we should consider ourselves lucky that we have the chance to walk that tightrope and to experience both the world of light and the world of dark, and from it gain the strength to be a survivor, to have the chance to do what few people ever get to do."

"So, I'm supposed to be grateful when bad shit happens?"

"Today, you are physically and mentally stronger than you would be if you hadn't suffered the life you have. You've experienced more cultures and seen more places in the last eight years than most people would in eighty. And now, purely through the strength of your own will, you have the skills, quite literally, to change the world."

Indira took the leaf from Tess, then opened Tess's hand out so her index finger pointed. She balanced the leaf on it. "Like this plant, your greatest challenge will be balancing darkness with light. Ultimately, only you can decide on which side of the tightrope you'll spend the most time – helping people, or harming them." She knocked the leaf off Tess's finger. It spiraled to the ground.

Thinking of Indira's words from all those years ago, Tess fought to find solace in them as she slunk through the park to her special place beside the lake. She'd spent years clawing her way out of the darkness, then more years fighting it so others wouldn't have to, harnessing the darkness in herself to bring more light to the world. Now, after all her sacrifice, she'd had an opportunity to make a new life for herself. A completely fresh start. Why had it been denied her?

On a small grassy knoll jetting out into the lake, an elderly woman and a tiny girl threw scraps of bread to waiting ducks. The mallards quacked appreciatively.

After studying with Indira in India and Chen Choa-An in China, Tess had come to appreciate that bad things happened to good people for absolutely no other reason than they simply did. Unfortunately, she was one of those

91

people. When she was only eleven years old, she'd had her life ripped apart, and yet, purely through her own strength of will, she'd managed to build a new life, a life that had true purpose. After battling the odds like that and struggling for so long to make the world a better place – after endlessly sacrificing for the greater good – didn't she deserve a second chance?

Everything had been in place. Paid for. Organized. Finalized. Everything. All she'd had to do was be on that plane.

Yet instead, she'd been unconscious in a hospital bed, dragged down into the darkness once more.

She'd been determined to leave the life that brought so much death and destruction into the world for one that brought only joy and life.

But it wasn't to be.

She'd never believed it, but maybe there was a God. Or karma. Or maybe existence was nothing but some cruel virtual reality game played by some twisted cosmic behemoth. Whatever it was, maybe this life was all she deserved.

Tess marched over to her willow tree on the bank of the lake. With only tiny brown blobs where soon there would be showers of lush green leaves, the willow's branches swayed to and fro in a light breeze. Tess lowered herself to the grass to sit leaning against the trunk.

Just like balancing on a tightrope, life was a struggle. But it was only through knowing this struggle that people could know love and sharing and joy. Tess understood that. Understood it completely. However, sometimes there was a need for wisdom; other times, there was only a need for blood.

If someone was dragging her into the darkness once more, man, had they better be prepared for just how dark she was going to be.

A male mallard quacked as it swam after a female just feet from Tess, the iridescent green plumage on its head glistening in the sharp sunshine. Spring was a time for rebirth, for rejuvenation, for resurrection.

Tess closed her eyes to meditate, to still her mind enough to conjure a plan from the chaos. When next she opened her eyes, she too would be renewed. And then there would be no darkness so dark it could hide those bastards from her.

Chapter 16

WITH RENEWED VIGOR, Tess marched up the brick path from the sidewalk. On either side, the yard didn't have a lawn, like most of the little houses on the street, but unkempt grass fighting for space with weeds. She climbed the four steps to a porch littered with dead leaves, presumably from the previous fall.

A sign hung on the doorjamb with red letters on a white background: No Cold Callers. Below that, the doorbell's name plate had a piece of black tape obscuring the homeowner's name. Very welcoming.

Tess rang the doorbell.

A green blind covered the glass panel in the door, shrouding the interior, so Tess couldn't see in. The blind was faded down one side, as if it had once hung somewhere else and had recently been moved to here.

A few seconds passed, then a finger curled around one side of the blind and eased it an inch to one side. A beady brown eye peered out through lank, straggly brown hair.

A wavering woman's voice said, "Yes?"

"Jill Masterson?" Tess asked.

"Who wants to know?"

"My name is Tess Williams. I'd like to speak to you about a personal matter."

"Read the sign." The finger let go of the blind.

Great. It looked like this lead was going to be just as successful as all the others she'd tried over the last few hours.

Tess knocked on the door and called out, "I'm not selling anything."

She waited. Stared at the spot where the finger had appeared. It didn't appear again.

Banging on the door, Tess said, "Miss Masterson, I need to speak to you. It's vitally important."

Again, she waited. And again, she got no answer.

Tess hammered her fist on the door, which rattled in its frame. "Miss Masterson, I'm not leaving until you speak to me."

The finger didn't appear, but through the closed door, the voice said, "I've called the police. You better go."

"Miss Masterson, I need your help."

"I've got a gun."

Tess drew a long, slow breath. She didn't want to have to say what she was going to say because saying it would make it real. It *was* real. She knew it was. But saying it only acknowledged it and made it ten times more real. But she had no choice.

"Miss Masterson, I... I was raped. I think it was by the same men that attacked you."

She waited. Stared at the blind.

It didn't move.

Tess continued staring. Willing it to move. Under her breath, she said to herself, "Come on, come on. Look at me and open the door. Why would anyone lie about a thing like that, for God's sake?"

Finally, the voice said, "Who are you?"

"Tess Williams."

"Why do you want to speak to me?"

"Because I think I can catch the gang who did it."

The finger curled around the blind again and the eye stared at her once more.

Tess simply stared back. This wasn't a time when a big beaming smile would work in her favor. On the contrary, morose would probably work far better. To hedge her bets, Tess remained impassive.

The eye pulled away and the blind fell back into place.

Tess waited for the door to open. It didn't.

"Goddamnit." Rubbing her brow, she heaved a sigh and stared at the porch floor.

This strategy had appeared to be the answer she'd been searching for. Her lakeside meditation had done the trick and given her the modicum of clarity she needed to see how she might undertake this job. The moment she'd thought of it, she couldn't help but feel how stupid she'd been not to have come to that conclusion earlier.

Five women had reported being attacked by the gang. Tess had been looking at them as five other victims. She couldn't have been more wrong. They weren't five victims with cases to be studied, but five eyewitnesses with information to share.

Tess had caught a fleeting glimpse of one of the gang, had heard rock music, had realized she was in a white van, and had heard a couple of things the attackers had said. By themselves, that wasn't enough to catch them.

However, if she thought of those as jigsaw pieces, all she needed was more seemingly meaningless pieces that, when fitted together, wouldn't be meaningless at all, but would reveal vital clues to the identity of the attackers.

It couldn't be simpler.

Of course the police would have tried to do this. But she had hoped that a victim talking to another victim – a mini support group – might unveil far more than any detective in a sterile interview room could, no matter how sympathetic he tried to be.

But... it wasn't working.

Tess had organized the list of victims based on the ease of getting from one to the next. Helen Miles, the first on her list, had moved to Kansas.

The second, Gloria Jackson, had refused to come to the door, and when Tess had declared why she was there, Gloria's two-hundred-pound boyfriend had threatened her with a baseball bat.

Victim three, fifteen-year-old Sammie Hogarth, who Tess could see being home-schooled from the doorway, told her mom she'd like to talk, but her father stepped in and stopped her.

Jill Masterson was the fourth on the list. Tess had gotten closer to talking to her than any of the others, but it too had ultimately been a disaster. That left only one more lead – Antonnia Wosniak. If she was a dead end, that was it and Tess was right back to square one. Bomb was trying his best, but so far, he had less than she did.

Tess stared at the door. At the blind. Praying it would move. Okay, she couldn't stay here all day so she'd give it just thirty more seconds.

She counted to thirty. Slowly.

And continued on to forty.

Then sixty.

Her shoulders slumped. That was it. Another potential lead lost.

Tess trudged down the three steps from the porch. What the hell was she going to do?

She kicked a pebble off the red brick path. It skipped along and into the gutter along the road.

"Goddamnit." She'd been sure this was the answer. So goddamn sure.

"Why do you think you can catch them?"

Tess gasped, freezing in midstride. She spun back to the house.

The front door ajar, a drawn face stared out through a nine-inch gap. The woman's lank brown hair looked like it hadn't been washed for a month.

"Because I have friends who specialize in this kind of thing."

The woman's eyes narrowed. She stared at Tess, as if judging whether or not she could trust what she was saying.

Tess took a step toward the porch. And the door closed four inches.

Tess stepped back.

The door opened again, but not as wide as it had been.

"I can't do it alone," said Tess, "but with your help, I'm sure I can make them pay."

The woman continued staring, continued judging. Her narrowed gaze drilled into Tess.

"I just need five minutes," Tess said. "Five minutes to make them pay."

Tess waited. Frightened to say more. Frightened to move. As if she'd seen a rare butterfly and the slightest sound or movement would spook it and this once-in-a-lifetime opportunity would be gone forever.

Tess stared at the door. Please let her be the one. Please.

Finally, the aching silence was broken by the door hinges squealing. The door didn't open. But neither did it close. A gap appeared just wide enough for someone to squeeze through.

Tess dashed back to the house and in through the narrow gap.

The woman slammed the door shut, bolted it top and bottom, then placed a carving knife on the stand beside it.

"Thank you." Tess dared a half a smile. Finally, she was in. Together with another victim, surely they could piece together some sort of lead for her to nail the gang.

Chapter 17

FINALLY FACE-TO-FACE WITH another victim, Tess needed to establish a rapport as quickly as possible. The easiest way was to humanize herself.

"Tess Williams." She stuck out her hand.

The woman shook hands. "Jill Masterson." She pushed ropes of greasy long brown hair back behind her left ear and only held eye contact for the briefest of moments. "Sorry, I wasn't expecting guests."

The place would make the locker room in an old-style boxing gym smell positively fragrant. Tess guessed that Jill hadn't been receiving guests for quite some time.

Jill ushered Tess toward a blue sofa. Magazines and dirty clothes engulfed it, as they did much of the room, leaving just one place clear in which to sit. A pile of empty fast food cartons lay on the floor next to that spot on the sofa as if Jill ate there every day and then simply tossed the containers aside. Most were emblazoned with a green-and-white logo for an Italian fast food restaurant.

Jill scooped up an armful of clothes and magazines from the sofa. "Sorry, I don't entertain much, these days."

"You don't have family in the city?"

"Michigan."

A reddy-brown splodge stained the chest of Jill's gray sweats, probably pasta sauce.

"Can I offer you a drink?" asked Jill. "I think I've got cream for coffee. Or I have juice."

Dirty cups, balled tissues, and overflowing ashtrays littered the coffee table in front of the sofa. It looked like Jill had been so traumatized by the assault, she was now little more than a shut-in, having food delivered when she needed it and rarely stepping out the door herself. Maybe why she'd let her personal hygiene slip. Or maybe she felt safer being dirty, believing no one would ever attack her in that state.

"Thanks, but I'm fine," Tess said.

"So, what makes you think you can catch this gang when the police can't?"

"I'm a freelance journalist, so I've made a fair few contacts over the years. Some of them... how shall I put it? Let's just say they're not exactly what you'd call 'law-abiding citizens,' so where the police have to deal with Miranda rights, chain of custody, and client/attorney privilege, these guys don't."

Jill nodded.

"I'm not proud of knowing people like that," Tess said, "but at a time like this, it would be stupid not to ask them for help, don't you think?" She purposely phrased it as a question to engage Jill in the hope it might encourage her to see a real chance for justice... or revenge.

Jill nodded again. "And you really think they can help?"

"I'm sure they can. There isn't much they can't do when they really want to."

After staring at her coffee table for a few seconds, Jill said, "So, can they tell me why it happened? Why me?"

The gray sweats couldn't hide that Jill was tall and slender, with the kind of full breasts some women paid thousands of dollars to possess. On top of that, washing off the grease and grime would reveal high cheekbones, pouting lips, and hair that, whenever she flicked her head, probably swung like in a shampoo commercial.

Jill stared at Tess as if seriously believing she had an answer. "Why? Why me?"

"I think..." Tess had asked herself that same question. "I think just because they could. A bunch of guys concoct a crazy plan that lets them have any woman they like and, guess what, they get away with it. So, all raging hormones and hard dicks, why wouldn't they keep doing it when they believe they can't get caught?"

"But it's just... just evil."

"Yeah, you're right. But my guess is they see it more like a game than a crime."

Jill's chin quivered. "A game? They think ruining people's lives is a fucking game?"

The woman was obviously way too fragile for a frank analysis. Tess needed to get any information she could before the woman fell apart.

"But let's try and be positive," said Tess. "Do you remember anything that might help us catch them? Something about the van, maybe? Or something that was said? Or maybe you even managed to see one of their faces?"

"So they just get to use women and walk away laughing about it?"

"No, that's why I'm here."

Jill stared at the cluttered coffee table. "Use them, as if they're jerking off into a goddamn Kleenex they can throw away?"

"If you can remember any—"

Jill looked back at Tess. "How can they do that to another person?"

"They'll pay for what they've done. One way or the other." Tess placed her hand on Jill's thigh. "Believe me, they'll pay."

Jill lunged at Tess and flung her arms around her. She clung on, digging her fingers into Tess's skin as she sobbed.

Tess had never been one for revealing her feelings. Especially toward a stranger. However, sharing such a life-changing trauma made them far from strangers. Tess had done all her sobbing, but she hugged Jill. Squeezed her tight.

As Tess had discovered earlier when Myron had hugged her, it felt surprisingly good to share. Despite the pain, despite the shame, a flicker of warmth glowed in her belly and gradually emanated outward. It didn't kill the hurt, but it lifted Tess a fraction closer to some form of equilibrium. She hugged Jill tighter.

"It's okay, Jill. Everything's going to be okay. I promise."

Her words breaking as she blubbered, the woman said, "How–how could they d–do that?"

There was no real answer to such a question, so Tess didn't try to give one. She just did what needed doing – she held Jill. Let her know that there was still goodness and caring in the world. That she wasn't the only person who was hurting. That she wasn't alone.

Ninety-four minutes later, Tess pushed aside one of the ashtrays and squeezed her third cup of chamomile tea into a spot on the cluttered coffee table.

Jill hadn't said a word for twelve minutes now. All she'd done was stare at the television screen, even though the set was switched off. Her breathing still juddered and she occasionally sniffled, but the sobbing had stopped. Not a surprise – from how soaked Tess's shirt was, she'd be shocked if Jill wasn't on the verge of suffering extreme dehydration.

Tess didn't want to ask another question because every time she did, it set Jill off again. That meant there was little point in lingering here.

"Listen, Jill, I'm going to get off now."

Jill gawked at her, her eyes like those of a puppy watching its owner leave the house for the first time.

"What? Already?" She grabbed Tess's forearm. "Are you sure? Stay and have something to eat first. It's the least I can do." She grabbed her phone from the table. "I'll have something delivered. What do you like?"

"I'm sorry, I can't. I have an appointment soon."

"Oh." Her face drained of life. "Okay. I understand."

"But I can come by again," said Tess.

"When?"

"I, er—"

"Tomorrow?"

"Maybe, but I can't promise." Tess fished something out of her pocket. "Look, here's my card. If you think of anything that could help us catch those bastards, phone me. Anytime. Okay?"

Jill studied the card. "Yes, of course." She looked up. "And if you need to talk or anything, come around anytime. I'm always here."

Tess left, glancing back halfway down the path. The beady eye peeked out from beside the blinds. And a solitary finger waved goodbye.

Guilt ate at Tess for leaving when her visit had obviously helped the woman so much, but she had her own pain to ease. And there was only one way she was ever going to be able to do that.

After a short walk to the subway, she hopped on a train to Downtown. This was going to be her last shot.

Chapter 18

AT 4:53, A twenty-something woman escorted her to Hauser, Horst, and Liebermann's conference room. The woman's clothes looked so immaculate it was hard to believe they hadn't come straight out of the store just seconds earlier.

As Tess approached the conference room's glass-paneled wall, a woman gazed out at the city from the twenty-fourth-floor windows. Streaks of red smudged across a darkening sky as the sun sank behind the skyscrapers.

Tess's heart hammered and her mouth dried. This was her last chance. Her last great hope for a lead. This had to pay off. Had to. If it didn't, the gang would escape justice forever. She couldn't live with that. After she'd brought a bloody justice down upon so many criminals over so many years, it would be a cruel God that denied her now.

She'd already been a victim for nearly two decades, but finally, she'd thought she'd left that life of pain behind and replaced it with a life of hope, where she could be happy and have a new purpose. That could never happen now. Yet she couldn't go back to her old life either – continuing to spend her life as a victim would destroy her. She needed closure. And that could only come in one form – blood.

In the conference room, the woman turned from the windows when her colleague showed Tess in for her five o'clock appointment with Hauser, Horst, and Liebermann's youngest junior partner.

The woman marched over, holding her hand out, but showing not the tiniest hint of emotion. "Antonnia Wosniak."

"Tess Williams."

"Please." Antonnia gestured for Tess to sit at the rosewood table that dominated the room. The air smelled of polish. Not surprising considering the glass-like sheen on the wood. Twenty-four chairs sat around the table, but a pitcher of water and two glasses had been placed in between a particular two, so Tess chose one of those.

Antonnia picked up the pitcher. "I can have tea or coffee brought in, if you'd prefer."

"I'm fine, thanks."

Chunks of ice clinked and a slice of lemon sloshed around as Antonnia poured herself a glass of water. She had the kind of figure that probably meant her male colleagues wouldn't merely see her sitting at this table, but picture her writhing on it. Probably some of her female colleagues, too.

Leaning back in her chair, Antonnia picked up a digital recorder and, without asking Tess if she minded or not, clicked the Record button.

"Now, Miss Williams, how do you believe I can help you?"

Tess studied Antonnia. She was austere. Disciplined. Impassive. A polar opposite to Jill Masterson.

"As I said on the phone, I was attacked by the same men who attacked you. I'm hoping you can provide information to help catch them."

"I've given a statement to the police," said Antonnia.

"It's not uncommon for victims to remember details weeks, sometimes even months after the event. Anything can spark a memory – a dream, a smell, a comment. I was hoping you might have remembered something new. Something the police aren't aware of."

Antonnia nodded, took a sip of water and then locked her stare onto Tess. "So wouldn't I just give that fresh information to the authorities? Why do you come into the equation?"

This wasn't going anywhere near as well as Tess had envisioned. Not least because Antonnia seemed needlessly aggressive. But then, she was a lawyer, someone whose job was to uncover all the facts about a case and then, whenever possible, use them selectively to her advantage.

Maybe appealing to her humanity would be Tess's best option.

Tess leaned forward. "Listen, those monsters don't only need punishing for what they did to you *and* me, they need stopping so no other woman has to suffer what we did. As it turns out, I have contacts in law enforcement and in other areas, so I—"

"Other areas? Do you mean in the criminal community?"

"I'm a freelance journalist, so I have a number of sources who aren't quite what you'd call law-abiding citizens, yes."

Antonnia put her glass down and leaned forward, too. "And you feel that these people can help you catch a gang of rapists?"

"Yes."

Nodding, Antonnia leaned back in her chair again. "So these people, who you freely admit are not law-abiding citizens, would of course follow the letter of the law to apprehend the individuals responsible to ensure that when brought to trial, there would be no possibility of any of them being released on any sort of technicality?"

Tess rarely had cause to deal with lawyers. She was starting to be very thankful of that.

She stared at Antonnia. The woman was obviously very intelligent, so why didn't she appreciate Tess was trying to help her?

Tess poured herself a glass of water. Maybe a more brutal approach was called for. "You don't seem particularly fazed that five assholes fucked you in a van like a cheap hooker."

Antonnia's expression didn't alter. She'd make a wonderful poker player – probably why she was such a hot property in the legal fraternity. "What do you want? Puffy eyes? Uncontrollable sobbing? An aversion to stepping outside?"

Swishing an ice cube around in her glass, Tess let it chink off the sides. "People handle things in different ways."

"So your way is to mount a personal crusade for retribution?"

"And yours is to deny it ever happened?"

Antonnia smirked. "What happened, happened. No amount of bawling my eyes out is going to change that. How that event impacts my future, however, is entirely under my control, and I choose to not let it."

She stared coldly at Tess. So coldly anyone would believe what she'd said was true. Maybe even Antonnia believed it. Consciously, that is.

Subconsciously?

A tiny twitch in the corner of Antonnia's right eye said differently. So, maybe not so hot at poker, after all.

"Is that what your shrink says to do?" asked Tess.

Antonnia pushed her glass away, suggesting she'd finished with it and, thereby, with this meeting. "Tell me, Miss Williams, if your toilet was to spring a leak, would you simply bawl your eyes out while drowning in your own excrement, or would you call a plumber, someone who specializes in cleaning up other people's shit?"

Tess shrugged. "Well, if psychoanalysis is what works for you."

"It is, so unless there's anything else..."

Tess slipped her card across the table. "Not all the other victims have such a well-adjusted attitude, probably because they can't all afford $500-an-hour shrinks" – or weren't such unfeeling fucking machines – "so for their sakes, if you think of anything that might help, please call me."

Antonnia glanced at the card but did not pick it up. "Goodbye, Miss Williams."

"Thank you for your time." Tess slouched out.

That was it. The last victim and the last chance for a lead.

Those bastards had gotten away with it. All she could pray for now was that they'd snatch another woman, and that they'd make a mistake in doing so.

Tess rubbed her head. Was she really praying for another woman to be snatched? How sick was that? Christ, what was wrong with her? But as she stepped into the brushed-steel elevator, she surfed the Internet looking for a news bulletin to that effect. It was her only hope. If it was there, she had to grab it.

None of the main media sites were reveling in a story of another gang rape. Though she hated to admit the shame of it to herself, the disappointment hit Tess like a baseball bat in the gut.

She couldn't face trying to do anything else, not that she could think of anything else to do, so trudged to the subway and slouched back to her apartment. She felt empty. Not just drained of energy, but totally empty. As if all the life had been sucked out of her. Despite the suffering she'd known, this had to be the lowest point of her entire life.

No sooner had she sat down on her sofa than her phone rang.

"Hey, Bomb."

"Yo, Tess. It might be a dumb question, but how you doing, girl?"

He'd already expressed enough sympathy and concern earlier. No way would he phone her just to chitchat. This wasn't good.

Chapter 19

THE HAIRS STOOD up on the back of her neck and she gripped her phone tighter. "What's wrong, Bomb? Have you found something?"

"Oh, boy." He noisily blew out a breath. "Tess, there's, er…"

"What?"

"I, er…"

"What, Bomb? Just spit it out."

"Yeah, I, er, I found something…" He trailed off again.

"And? Am I supposed to play twenty questions, here? I take it it's not good news."

"No, it is. Kinda. Well, I mean, if we look at it objectively. Like as a means to an end."

Anything that involved a 'means to an end' was rarely good. She swallowed hard and then drew a long, calming breath. "Bomb. Please. Just tell me."

"There's no easy way to say this."

"So just say it, then. What's the worst that can happen?" The moment she said that phrase, she cringed. Talk about tempting fate.

"I found a video."

112

"That's it? You found a video?" That's what all this fuss was about? A goddamn video. Why would a video be bad news? And not just bad news, but news Bomb was barely able to tell her about?

A nasty niggle slowly clawed its way from the back of her mind.

A video? A video of what?

Or more importantly, of who?

She felt a strange cold burning sensation as the blood drained from her face. Her legs weak, she slumped down on her couch. It was obvious what the video was. Obvious what it showed. Obvious who played the leading role.

The lowest point of her life had suddenly dropped a hell of a lot lower.

"It's, er..." She closed her eyes tightly, praying she was wrong. Her hand trembled as she rubbed her brow. "It's not..." She couldn't even say the word.

"It's you. I'm so sorry, Tess."

No, that couldn't be real. No way. It had to be some sick joke. Or a nightmare. But no one was laughing. And she was awake. Around the globe, perverts were jerking off while watching her getting raped. What kind of sick world was it?

Dumb question – she'd seen firsthand just how sick it was.

Her stomach churned. She swallowed hard, struggling not to throw up.

After a moment, she drew a wavering breath. "Can you—" Her voice cracked, so she cleared her throat. "Can you delete it?"

"No."

She snickered. "Yeah. Because that would be just too easy, wouldn't it?"

"I'm so, so sorry."

"Can we, uh, can we just back up a sec?" She rubbed her face with her hand. "You said… uh…" What was it he'd said? Something about good news, qualifying it with some tired old cliché? She couldn't think, her thoughts like mud being forced through a strainer. She wanted to slap herself. Snap herself out of this daze.

She tried again. "Why, um, why exactly is this good news 'kinda'? I'm sorry, but I'm just not seeing it."

"It's for sale all over the Deep Web."

"Oh, Jesus."

"It's one of the *Monster Bang* series."

Her mouth agape, Tess shook her head, staring blankly into space. She'd thought being gang-raped was the worst thing that could ever happen to her. It wasn't. Being gang-raped and then knowing perverts everywhere were reveling in her suffering…

She covered her eyes. She just wanted to crawl into bed, pull up the covers, and die. Not metaphorically. Literally. Die.

Bomb continued talking, but she didn't hear any of it.

Her hand dropped down over her mouth, then she screwed her eyes shut. She curled forward into a ball, so her head was on her knees. She squeezed her eyes closed tighter and tighter, trying to block out the whole world.

But the world wouldn't go away.

Finally, she said, "Bomb, I'm sorry, but… I, uh, I drifted off. Can we, um, can we maybe back up again. Sorry, but I'm still struggling to see how this is good news. Please tell me the video shows someone's face and you've got an ID."

"Sorry."

She rubbed a trembling hand over her brow.

Bomb said, "Couldn't even ID the type of van because they'd hung black plastic sheeting everywhere."

This couldn't be happening. Really. It just couldn't.

"But…" said Bomb.

Tess's eyes popped open at the tiniest hint of hope. Maybe he'd analyzed the video's metadata and retrieved the New York location from where it had been uploaded to the Web. Under her breath, she said, "Please let there be GPS data. Please let there be—"

"I do have a location—"

Yes!

"—for the distributor."

"Shit!"

"Hey, this means we're a step closer to finding those assholes."

"You couldn't get anything from the metadata?"

"I checked – it got scrubbed when the video was reprocessed. But this ain't nothing."

Tess hung her head. "I suppose." Yes, it was something, but just nowhere near as much as she'd hoped for. "So, what have you got?"

"Well, it's not much yet—"

Tess closed her eyes again.

"—because the only info I've been able to dig up leads to a shell company called WestLine."

"Can't you… I don't know… use some of that Bomb 'magic'?"

"That's how I've gotten this far. I had to pull a phishing scam with some of the footage from our last job. Luckily, they replied and—"

Tess's head snapped up. "Whoa, whoa, whoa. What? What do you mean 'from our last job'?"

"From our last job – from Thea Dworkin's cloud storage."

Her jaw dropped. "What? You're telling me we're using kiddie porn as bait? What the hell, Bomb! We don't pull shit like that."

When she'd scammed Thea Dworkin at the Chelsea art gallery, Bomb was supposed to have destroyed everything he hadn't left for the authorities to find.

"Tess, we didn't make it. And it's not like we're raking in bucks off it. So what's wrong with using it for a good thing?"

"A good thing? Seriously? Kiddie porn?"

"Is it any different from you collecting semen, or hair, or fingernails to leave as fake evidence?"

"Yeah, it's real fucking different. These are innocent kids, Bomb, for Christ's sake. Innocent kids. We don't pull shit like this."

"Okay, so here's the thing, we—"

"There's no 'thing.' Forget the 'thing.' We're *not* doing it."

"Too bad, because it's already done. And it worked. Now, do you wanna bust my balls like a crusading college freshman, or do you wanna know what I've got?"

Tess buried her head in her hands. Just when she thought things couldn't get any worse, the world kicked her in the gut to prove how wrong she was. "Promise me you'll delete the files you've got."

"Okay."

"Promise me."

"Okay, I promise. Now shut the hell up and listen. I analyzed the distributor's email header and got their IP address. The problem is, the only info I've tracked from that leads to this shell company, so I have no idea who it is we're actually dealing with – it could be a kid in his mom's basement just as easily as it could be a cartel of Uzi-toting psychos."

"So, just give me a location and I'll scout it out."

"Yeah, about that." He gave a little nervous laugh. "Remember how I always say you can deal this kind of shit from anywhere in the world? Well, it was always gonna be a million-to-one shot that the distributor was in our backyard."

"Yeah, I appreciate that. So what are you telling me?"

"I ain't gonna sugarcoat it – again, we've got good news and bad news. The good is I've got a street address. The bad is it ain't in the US."

"So where's the problem? Just get me on a plane."

"Tess… hmmm… I…" He heaved a breath as if exasperated. Why was he being like this? Bomb was usually the only person in the world she could rely on to give it to her straight. She'd trust him with her life. And frequently did.

"Bomb, am I missing something here? If you can't get what we need, I will."

"I could call in a few favors and get—"

"No!" She trusted Bomb. Only Bomb. Period. "No way. *We* deal with this. Alone. Just tell me what you need and I'll get it. Simple."

"But it isn't, is it?"

"Isn't what?"

"Simple."

"Why not?"

"Look, you know I love you, girl, and I'd do anything for you, so I'm just gonna lay this out there. Okay?"

"Lay what out there? Bomb, what the hell's wrong with you?"

"Wrong with me? It's you, Tess. You."

Her mouth dropped open.

"You ain't fit for this, Tess. Once you're outta the country, I ain't gonna be able to have your back like normal. There's only gonna be so much I can do. And with your head so seriously fucked up, who knows how things are gonna play out? You could get nailed by the first goon that comes along and not even see him coming. So, no, I can't let you go. I just can't."

She was just fine. Her head was just fine. She was going to end these bastards. End of story. "While I appreciate the pep talk, get me on a goddamn plane, Bomb."

"Listen to me. We're not talking about visiting a beachfront condo in the Bahamas. We're talking dangerous shit here."

With her voice hushed, her words fought to get out through her clenched teeth. "So help me God, Bomb, if you don't get me on a goddamn plane this goddamn second…"

"Tess, let's just take a breath, yeah? Please. I can get everything we need. Honest. Just me. No one else involved. Okay? It'll just take a little time. But it ain't like those fuckers are going anywhere, because they don't know we're hunting them."

She shouted. "Get me on a plane, Bomb. *Now!*"

"Okay, okay, okay." She heard him hitting keys. "I'm doing it. Okay?" Over the clicking of keys, he muttered under his breath. "Goddamn crazy bitch better not come whining to me when she gets herself goddamn killed."

"I can hear you, you know."

"Good!"

"So where am I going?"

Chapter 20

THE SETTING SUN bathed Table Mountain in an orange glow. The guidebook Tess had bought at JFK said to try to get a window seat on the left when heading into the city from the airport, and boy, it was not wrong.

She ran her gaze along the rim of the monstrous beast. It was like a mountain had had its top sliced clean off to leave an enormous plateau swathed in cloud. Amazing. What kind of geological event could have created such a wonder? For a few moments, the sheer awe of the sight stole her away from the nightmare she'd been living for the past few days.

Her gaze drifted down the mountainside. In the sun's glow, the craggy rock face looked like a giant dying ember.

But as she'd learned on her travels around the globe, for her to know beauty, she also had to recognize ugliness.

The plains around the mountain and Cape Town weren't just home to natural wonders, but to man-made horrors. Her bus sped by a shanty town. Thousands of gray one-story buildings huddled together, some constructed of brick, some of corrugated metal sheeting, some of bits of wood. While her guidebook described the mountain as a must-see, it said this slum was a no-go, unemployment, squalid conditions, and drug abuse having given gangs not just a foothold but almost free rein in some townships. Gun violence was frequent and bloody. Luckily, this was as close as Tess was ever going to have to get to the place.

As the bus pulled into the city center, Tess studied the street map in her guide book. She alighted, got her bearings, and then set off for the tourist area on foot. On her way, she gazed up at the glistening skyscrapers of the business district. It was hard to believe these towering edifices, crammed with satellite communication and cutting-edge technology, were only a few miles from thousands of people who had no running water. She shook her head. It was the same every single place she went – people just couldn't resist screwing each other over for a buck.

Tess reached Long Street. With most of the skyscrapers behind her, the architecture here was very different, as if from a bygone age, like Bourbon Street in New Orleans, where the windows, balconies, and roofs brimmed with ornate decoration. The buildings were smaller than those in the business district, most being just three or four stories, and instead of gray concrete, they were vibrant blues and reds and yellows.

Ambling down the sidewalk, Tess entered a covered walkway where one of the buildings extended right out to the curbside, metal columns supporting a balcony with decorative wrought-iron railings.

Tess waited for the one-way traffic to crawl by, then crossed the road to a small aluminum-framed glass door between a bookstore and a place selling African art. A small sign above the door read: The Hostel Upstairs.

She pushed the door. Locked.

Set into the wall was a keypad and intercom. A laminated sign above it read: 'After entering the code and opening the door, please close it securely behind you. Thank you, The Management.'

She pressed the intercom's buzzer.

"Hello?" said a woman with a South African accent.

"Hi. My name's Meuller. You should have a room for me."

"Hi, come on up." A buzzer sounded and the door clicked unlocked. Tess pushed it and entered. When she closed the door, she shoved it hard until she heard it latch and lock, then she headed up the steps to the next floor.

A chubby black woman checked Tess in, smiling constantly as she did so. Tess paid in cash and then received a short tour of the facilities – a pool room with vending machines for soft drinks and snacks; a large kitchen with doorless cupboards in which masses of mismatched dishes were stacked; and a communal space with a TV, three brown sofas with sagging cushions, and a rack overflowing with brochures from local tour companies. Ideal.

A few minutes later, Tess opened the door to her room. She slung her small rucksack and her black backpack onto the floral comforter covering the double bed and then turned sideways to squeeze between the bed and the walnut-effect armoire to reach the window. She peeked out. With night closing in, lights shone from bars and late-night stores up and down Long Street, while people moseyed about in all directions.

She opened the armoire. Coat hangers dangled from a rail across the top, while a couple of blankets and a spare pillow lay in the bottom. After squeezing back, she slumped onto the bed. The springs in the mattress creaked loudly. Shifting only slightly prompted another loud creak. She rolled her eyes and hoped whoever was in the next room wasn't feeling horny.

Tess didn't mind slumming it in the hostel. The location was ideal because it was within walking distance of almost everywhere, even the mountain. Not that she'd have time for sightseeing. More importantly, however, it was inconspicuous, like taking the bus as one of many passengers instead of hiring a cab as just one. After all, which self-respecting criminal would choose to live in a dump? Not to mention security checks were less stringent, especially for cash payers, which was useful when traveling under a false name.

Most importantly, however, was the staffing level. Or lack thereof. To offer budget accommodation, many such hostels weren't staffed after dark to cut costs. To hide any late-night comings and goings she might have, Tess had specifically chosen a place that was only staffed from early morning until midevening, so her activities wouldn't arouse any suspicion. Yep, this place was ideal.

Accompanied by creaking, Tess swung her legs around so she could lie down.

It was already too dark to be able to properly scout out the location Bomb had found, and she'd eaten umpteen meals on the flight to London, then more on the connection here, so there was little for her to do but relax now. She took out her phone, entered the Wi-Fi password the cheerful woman had given her, then logged onto the VPN account Bomb had set up for her that masked all her

123

online activity. Not wanting to push what appeared to be a shaky Wi-Fi signal, she placed a voice-only call.

"Yo, Tess," said Bomb.

"Hey. All's fine so far, so we're looking at a go tomorrow. Have you got any updates?"

"I've uploaded the location's floorplan to your space and some other bits and pieces, but I'm still struggling to find out who's behind that shell company WestLine. According to the city's records, the property owner is a Joan Claasen, but she sure as hell ain't who we're looking for."

"How can you be so sure?"

"Well, apart from being 82 years old, which don't exactly fit the profile for a Deep Web entrepreneur, dear old Joan fell off the perch five months back."

"She's dead? So is someone using her identity?"

"Not as far as I can tell. Looks like city hall just ain't gotten around to updating its database yet. But I'll keep digging."

"Okay, thanks. But how about WestLine's system? If they replied to your email, didn't that give you a back door?" Bomb had various pieces of software that would automatically download onto a device if an unsuspecting user simply clicked a link in an email or on a fake website.

"My kit bought it, the same as old Joan. I figure they're using a sandbox to protect their gear from all the Deep Web crazies and scammers. I'm testing other options, but this ain't gonna be easy."

Tess sighed. "And the shell company is a complete dead end?"

"Man, that's a real bitch. Whoever put it together sure knew what they were doing. Are you sure you don't want me to reach out and—"

"No. No one else. I'll get what we need. One way or the other."

"Okay. Ciao, Tess. Good hunting."

"Good night, Bomb."

Tess left her room and tramped down the gloomy pale green corridor toward the communal bathroom. Pop music came from one room and a hairdryer blew in another. As Tess neared the bottle-green bathroom door, each step pushed her heart to beat that little bit faster, that little bit harder.

Taking a gulp of air, she reached for the silver handle, but her hand froze and hovered a couple of inches before it. She chickened out and pulled back. Rubbing her brow, she stared at the handle. It was just a handle, for crying out loud. A handle couldn't hurt her.

She ripped the door open.

Inside, three shower cubicles with lockable wooden doors greeted her. She rubbed a hand over her mouth. The journey had taken the best part of a full day, so a shower would normally be an absolute delight. She opened the door to the nearest cubicle. Many of the blue tiles were cracked, the chrome soap dish had a pink disposable razor lodged between its bars, and an empty bottle of shampoo lay over the plughole. This late in the day, that was actually pretty clean for a place like this.

Tess stood in the shower doorway. Frozen, she glowered at the cubicle, sweating so heavily her clammy T-shirt stuck to her. Her breathing came ever harder, ever faster.

She stared at the showerhead. At a droplet of water clinging to the grimy rim. She felt dirty. Absolutely filthy. So filthy she could scrape the grunge off with a knife. But she knew no matter how much she scraped, how deep she dug the blade, she would never feel clean.

Like a junkie seeing a wrap of coke lying on the sidewalk, she ached to leap into the shower and sate her need.

She slammed the shower door shut, spun away, and collapsed over one of the six green washbasins. Her head on her arms, she gasped as if she'd run a marathon.

The locking bolt scraped open on the door of one of the other shower cubicles.

Tess glanced in the mirror as the door banged open, revealing a young, pimply-faced woman with a pink towel wrapped around her body and a blue one around her head.

Pushing up off the basin, Tess drew a broken breath and tried to act as if her world hadn't crashed around her. She wiped away the tears that had welled in her eyes.

Pimply Girl spoke with a British accent. "Are you okay?"

"Hmm? Yeah, fine, thanks." Tess forced a feeble smile.

"Don't tell me – a fella, right?"

With a shrug, Tess said, "Kind of."

The young woman shook her head. "Doesn't matter where you go, you know, they're all the same – complete a-holes."

"You're not wrong there."

"Tell you what, if you're up for a girls' night, me and my mate are having a few cocktails at Grand

126

Daddy's, then hitting a bar for a boogie. You're welcome to tag along. A good laugh will cheer you right up."

Tess had seen that boutique hotel a block or so down Long Street. "Thanks, but it's been a hell of a long day, so I'm just having a quiet night tonight."

As the woman left, her flip-flops slapping on the floor, she said, "If you change your mind, we're in room six, just here." She pointed out of the open door.

"Okay, thanks."

Once the door closed behind the woman, Tess leaned back down over the basin.

After a minute or so, she pushed up and studied her reflection in the mirror above the basin. She barely knew the person staring back. That person used to be so strong. Invulnerable. Unstoppable. What the hell had happened to her?

Tess reached to turn on the cold water, but the sink had a crack so deep into the green porcelain that she couldn't see any way it could be watertight. She moved along to the next one and splashed water on her face. Slightly refreshed, she then brushed her teeth.

She yanked the bathroom door open to leave, but stopped. She turned. Stared at the shower cubicle again. The sweating started almost immediately.

She lurched out and slammed the door closed behind her.

In her room, she smoothed a little manuka honey onto the two small burns on her back where the stun gun had zapped her with 50,000 volts. They were healing nicely, thanks to the honey's debriding action and anti-inflammatory properties.

Lying on her back in her bed in just a clean T-shirt and panties, she gazed up at the ceiling. The room was surprisingly quiet considering the number of bars and restaurants on the street. Not that she expected to get any sleep – whenever she closed her eyes, she just couldn't block out what had happened to her in the van. And some warped image of Dracula rearing over her.

All the same, she closed her eyes and rolled onto her side. If only she could calm her mind and get some decent rest, she was sure she'd start to feel more like her old self. She pictured the mountain valley in Rishikesh. Pictured sitting on a boulder in the middle of that lazy stream. Pictured the water babbling around her feet, the ripples casting swirling shadows beneath the Indian sun. And all the while, the water gurgled. And gurgled. And gurgled. And...

In the dead of night, a loud clattering woke her. She bolted upright. Breath held. Eyes wide. Fists clenched.

Chapter 21

THE PIMPLY-FACED YOUNG woman from the bathroom stood in the murkily lit corridor outside Tess's room, tears streaming her cheeks. "W-why would they do that? All I said was 'C-could you keep the noise down, please?'" Her hand trembled as she wiped away her tears.

A young woman with thick-lensed glasses dabbed at Pimply Girl's curly red hair with a paper tissue. "I think I've got it all out now."

Her arms folded, Tess said, "And they spat at you? A whole group of them?"

"I don't know h-how many. I–I was trying t–to get away."

"And one of them threatened you with a knife?"

"A fat guy, yeah. Well, no. I mean, I–I don't know. He was flicking it around in his hand like a, like a gangster or something, you know."

Laughter erupted from the floor below. Shouts came in a strange language. It was not any of the European, American, or Asian languages of which Tess had some knowledge. Was it one of the African languages? Maybe Afrikaans?

Tess glanced at the stairs down. "You're sure they aren't staying here?"

Thick Glasses said, "It sounds like the same bunch who were here last night till after three. We complained to reception this morning, but the woman just shrugged and said locals often sneak in to party if someone doesn't shut the front door properly. She said it was some guest's fault for ignoring that sign on the intercom, so there was nothing she could do."

"It is. It's the same group," said a guy with dreadlocks and a German accent, peeking out through his partially open door.

Tess heaved a breath. She couldn't risk getting involved in a situation like this. While she might go down and resolve things in just a matter of seconds, in a strange country, with strange customs and attitudes, things could go sideways in a heartbeat. No, she couldn't risk that. Not even though the woman had been kind to her earlier. She was here to do a job, not resolve petty squabbles between tourists and locals.

Pimply Girl burst out crying again. "I don't know what we're going to do. We've already paid for a full week here, so we can't afford to move anywhere else."

Under her breath, Tess said, "Goddamnit."

Once more she glanced at the stairs down to the main floor. Not get involved? Who was she trying to kid? Like she'd ever been able to walk away from someone in need like this.

Tess gently rested her hand on Pimply Girl's arm. "Go to your room. Both of you. And don't come out no matter what you hear. Okay?"

Teary-eyed, she looked questioningly at Tess. "Why? What are you—"

Tess squeezed her arm. The sympathy drained from her voice and was replaced by stern authority. "Just do it. Now."

The young woman suddenly looked as frightened of Tess as she did of the men downstairs. She backed away. "Yeah. O–okay."

Tess watched them go to their room and then heard the door lock. Something heavy slid across the floor, as if they were barricading themselves in.

Tess went to her room too. But she did not barricade her door. She pulled on her jeans, then reached for her backpack and her armor. She velcroed her seven-inch-long titanium-alloy guards to her shins and the outer edge of each forearm. Ergonomically contoured and less than one inch wide, the three-sided strips of metal hugged her perfectly, enabling her to fend off blades and bats or, when used offensively, to break bones.

Finally, she slung on her black leather jacket. Her titanium armor was so discreetly designed and manufactured, it was invisible under such a heavy garment.

She caught a glimpse of herself in the mirror next to the door. Finally, she saw someone she recognized. Tonight, those assholes downstairs had merely threatened a woman with a knife, but if that went unchecked, what would they think they could get away with tomorrow? Abducting innocent women off the street, maybe?

"Like hell."

Heading for the stairs, she pulled on her armored gloves. The one-tenth-of-an-inch-thick titanium-alloy inserts cocooned her knuckles and palms. She flexed her fingers and clenched her fists to make sure the inserts hinged properly and didn't impede any movement.

131

Lighter than steel, but even tougher, the armor not only protected her hands but gave her punches the stopping power of a hammer.

"Let's see you pull a knife on me."

Chapter 22

TESS STALKED DOWN the stairs. With each step, her adrenaline spiked higher and higher. To help her handle the hormonal rush, she breathed in slowly for four seconds, held it for four, then breathed out equally slowly. The reduced oxygen intake enabled her to maintain a sense of equilibrium, combating her fight-or-flight response. Being able to control her physical reactions through her breathing gave her an edge, sharpened her mind, and powered her reflexes. It was a devastatingly simple technique and yet had probably done more to keep her alive than any death blow she'd ever dealt.

The communal area was shrouded in darkness. As was the kitchen. But light shone from the open doorway of the game room.

Pool balls clattered into each other, and one made the unmistakable sound of being potted. A number of voices cheered while others shouted in annoyance.

Hanging back in the shadows, Tess stole across the communal room. She crept parallel to the game room doorway, so as her viewing angle changed, she saw much of what was happening inside.

133

Pimply Girl had said there were six young black people: four guys and two women. Tess could see all but one girl and one man. From the design of the room, Tess guessed the missing two were somewhere immediately to the left of the doorway.

Of the others, a rotund girl with a huge afro slouched in a chair at the far end near the window, her massive breasts all but bursting out of a tiny red top. Nearby, a fat guy leaned against the soft drinks machine swigging from a bottle of beer, while a tall guy and a muscly dude played pool. Smoke hung heavy in the room, and the scent of cannabis wafted on the air.

Tess swallowed hard. Her mouth dry, her tongue dragged along her lips when she tried to lick them. Yet strangely, a warm glow welled up from inside her.

It had felt so good to pound on those two guys in the bar back home. So unbelievably good. Positively cathartic. So, if that was what she had to do to... to feel 'normal' once more, bring it on.

Her glare drilled into the room. This was what she did. This was what she excelled at. This... was who she was.

She drew one last energizing, deep breath, then slunk into the room.

Muscly Dude hit the ball hard. It flew across the table and slammed into another, which ricocheted around but didn't fall into a pocket.

"Ahhh!" He banged his cue down on the edge of the table, then frowned when he noticed no one was watching. He followed everyone else's eyeline.

They all stared at Tess.

She said nothing, but strolled straight past them to the snack-filled vending machine and pretended to study what was on offer. In the machine's glass, she saw the reflection of a sleeping woman wedged into the corner of the room on a barstool, and next to her, a guy rolling something way too long to be a cigarette.

Fat Guy swaggered closer. With a thick South African accent, he said, "Ever had a black man, baby? You'll never want white dick again, believe me." He smirked as if he'd said something incredibly profound.

Muscly Dude said something in that strange language, and everybody laughed.

They all watched Tess, waiting for her to either fall to pieces or fly into a disgusted rage. Tess turned around to face them but merely glanced at each of them, completely impassive.

They met her gaze, but then looked to each other when there was no reaction from their new victim.

Tess's fists clenched tighter. Though her heart hammered and her lungs burned to gulp in air, she forced herself to breathe slowly, forced her body to take in less oxygen and so control her fight-or-flight response through sheer strength of will.

"Maybe she's deaf," said Tall Guy.

"Or retarded," said Smoker.

"Or she's seen the size of your cock, Lonwabo!" Muscly Dude wiggled his pinkie at him. Everyone laughed except Fat Guy. And Tess, who didn't flinch.

Fat Guy stabbed his beer bottle at his friend. "Fuck you, Musa."

The laughter subsided and they all focused on Tess again.

Still Tess said and did nothing. Just looked at them with an eerie calmness. The kind of eerie calmness in a crocodile's gaze as its eyes poke above the water's surface and effortlessly glide closer and closer to a drinking wildebeest.

Anxious glances shot around the room. More was said in their strange language, but the subsequent laughter was tinged with unease.

As if he believed he had something to prove after his manhood had been challenged, Fat Guy stepped closer. He looked her up and down in an exaggerated fashion and then nodded. He said something she didn't understand, and everyone laughed again.

Finally, he reached out and squeezed her left breast.

Tess still didn't flinch.

With the nonchalance of checking her watch, she glanced down at his hand. Then she looked up into his grinning face.

The image of the guy in the back of the van shot into her mind. The image of him groping her. Of him ripping away her clothes. Of him... Her fists balled all the tighter.

Tess smiled back at Fat Guy.

His eyebrows rose with delight. "Ohhhh, boy! It's pussy time for old Lonwabo tonight."

Tess grabbed a finger of the hand groping her and wrenched it back, snapping it. He howled with pain.

Her other hand slammed into the side of his head and pounded it into the vending machine, breaking the glass with a loud crunch.

She stamped on his knee.

His leg bent at an unnatural angle.

Fat Guy slumped to the floor. Motionless. Blood oozing from his head.

Tess looked up at the others with not a flicker of emotion.

She said, "You have five seconds to leave." She didn't even bother counting. There was no point. She knew exactly how this was going to go down.

While Afro Girl struggled to push herself up out of the chair to Tess's right, Muscly Dude dashed at her, swinging his pool cue.

Tess caught the cue with one hand, the armor across her palm spreading the impact so it didn't break her bones. Her other hand punched through the cue's middle, breaking it in half.

Still holding the thicker part of the cue, Tess spun around backwards. Smashed the cue into Muscly Dude's head.

He fell sideways. Crashed to the floor.

Tess turned just as Afro Girl screamed and swung her arm to clobber her.

Tess blocked it with the cue. In the same movement, she speared the woman in the left breast with the splintered end of the cue, then headbutted her in the face.

The woman staggered back.

Tess kicked her in the stomach.

Wailing, the woman reeled away and slammed into the wall. Clutching her bloody wound, she crumpled to the floor.

Tall Guy had run around from the far end of the table. He swung his cue at Tess.

Instead of moving away, or trying to block his strike, Tess moved in. As he swung, she grabbed him and twisted around, shoving her butt hard against him. She threw him over her hip.

He flipped head over heels and smashed into the other vending machine upside down. The glass shattered as he crashed right into the workings to end in a tangled heap, legs inside, body hanging out onto the floor. Candy bars and bags of chips cascaded onto him.

Before Tall Guy had time to think, Tess hammered her pool cue down into his crotch.

He twisted onto his side, retching with the pain.

Barely breathing hard, Tess turned. Slowly eased into a fighting stance. Glared at Smoker.

He stood at the back of the room, eyes so wide his irises were small brown disks in a sea of white. Beside him, the woman on the barstool was still fast asleep.

Tess's voice calm and steady, she said, "Get them out. Never come back."

Bleeding, hobbling, and whimpering, the gang left.

Tess returned to her room. Cathartic? Damn right. She felt more alive, more like her real self than she had for days. She wished there'd been another four or five looking for trouble.

Her heart still pounding, she lay down to sleep.

But the moment she closed her eyes, she felt that hand on her breast again. She winced and tried to shake it off. But then she pictured the man rearing over her in the back of the van. Felt him touching her. Felt him...

She curled into a ball.

Buried her head in her pillow.

And sobbed.

Chapter 23

A BEAUTIFUL FALL dawn greeted Tess when she woke to the alarm on her phone at 6:30 a.m. It seemed strange that she'd left Manhattan in springtime, just two days ago, and yet now the seasons had moved on six months. Or gone back six months. Or... Well, like it mattered. If she hadn't been so stressed, she'd probably have gotten a kick out of being the other side of the equator, but as it was, it would just be yet another day of hassle-filled crap she would have to deal with.

She groaned as she got out of bed. Almost as loudly as the bed's creaky mattress did.

Entering the bathroom, she looked at the floor to avoid seeing the showers. In case she had to get close enough to talk to someone today, however, she removed her T-shirt and washed her armpits in one of the basins. Brushing her teeth, she looked in a mirror mottled by yesterday's splashes – her hair hung lank and greasy. She ignored it. She was on a job, not a date.

Tess pulled her shirt back on and left.

Outside, Long Street was busying itself getting ready for another onslaught from expectant tourists. The covered sidewalks with balconies looked even prettier in the sharp morning light, a few having people sitting at tables enjoying an early-morning breakfast.

Tess gazed up at a young couple. Arm in arm, they leaned against the balcony, people watching. Was that what it was like to be ordinary?

She studied them closer. The woman stroked the man's hand, yet was obviously doing it subconsciously, as if it was the most natural thing in the world.

Tess wondered if she could ever be like that. Be blissfully unaware of the true darkness in the world. Simply show up to a nine-to-five, then enjoy pizza in front of her favorite soap with her 'soul mate' before finally having a quick fumble in bed and going to sleep believing she was content and fulfilled. Could she ever live that life? Or would it be as awful as it sounded?

Dumb question. Like she'd ever get that opportunity anyway.

Tess looked down at the fold-out map she'd picked up at the airport. The location Bomb had found was only around a half hour's walk and looked pretty easy to get to – along Long Street to the intersection at the end, turn right, then turn left onto the first major road she came across. Easy.

Tess strode along the street, checking out the architecture and peering into the stores. Not like a tourist looking for the perfect photo op or the ideal souvenir, but like a covert operative researching places to hide, escape routes, from where possible threats might come…

When she realized what she was doing, a smile flickered across her face for the briefest of moments as she thought about Shanghai and Sergei, the ex-Spetsnaz Russian who'd taught her the finer points of shooting, and about urban warfare and tradecraft. She idly wondered what he was doing now. They'd stayed in touch for a while after she'd left China, but she hadn't heard from him now for going on two years or so. Once all this was over, she'd have to reach out. Maybe even visit him – a change of scenery with an old friend might be just what she needed to kick-start the healing process.

The smell of freshly baked bread wafted down the street on the light breeze. Tess's mouth watered. Not surprising since she'd had no breakfast. Since the van incident, her days had had no real routine, and things like mealtimes slipped by without a thought. When she did eat, it was either only because she had food presented to her, like on the flights, or because intellectually, she knew she needed to eat, so she forced something down. That fresh-bread smell, though...

Tess stopped and looked into the bakery. Should she get something now or later?

A white guy in a dark blue suit and carrying a paper bag sauntered out past her and got into a white BMW parked outside. Two other people stood at the counter placing orders.

Tess went in. A middle-aged black woman with a cheerful face sold her a coffee, a couple of fresh croissants, and a tuna fish sandwich. Outside, Tess stuffed the sandwich into her backpack and then dug into the croissants. Crumbs fell down her chest and gathered on her black T-shirt as she strode up the street like a real tourist.

Having taken a right, Tess hung a left onto Kloof Nek Road, which climbed steadily uphill. She crossed the wide two-lane street and started up it on the right-hand side. The road cut up a hillside, so the buildings on the right climbed up a slope, while those on the left followed the slope down into the valley. In this area, the stores were ordinary community stores rather than food joints and boutiques aimed at the tourist market, while the buildings were generally smaller, being mostly residential.

There were also a few hotels she could have stayed in that were closer to her target, but they wouldn't have provided the anonymity she gained from being in the heart of the bustling tourist area.

Tess continued up the street.

Ahead on the right, behind the buildings, lay an enormous grass-covered hill with an oddly shaped rocky outcropping on the top. Her guidebook said it was a mountain called Lion's Head. Though it was a struggle, she could kind of see a head, but unless she was at the wrong angle, the name was somewhat fanciful.

On the left, however, the view was as dramatic as any she'd ever seen. Rearing over the city like an oncoming storm stood the huge gray mass of Table Mountain. The crisp fall sunshine streaked its cliff face with deep, dark shadows.

The road headed directly between these two giants. With world-class views like these, the properties would be highly desirable.

Tess approached a house almost obscured by a large white garden wall. As if the wall wasn't deterrent enough, six layers of wires were suspended across its top from posts about two feet tall. A small yellow sign hanging on one of the wires showed a lightning bolt hitting a hand and read: 'WARNING: Electric Fence.'

As she got closer, she heard a faint but unmistakable click-click-click emanating from the fence. That suggested a short circuit somewhere, which meant if someone tampered with it, the alarm might not be activated. The problem was that there was no way to tell without actually trying to set off the alarm.

Looking at the warning sign, she rubbed a hand over her mouth, hoping that this property belonged to a particularly paranoid owner and wasn't representative of the security precautions homeowners took in this area.

A little further along the road, another large house hid behind another large wall with another sign: 'Property protected by West Cape Security. ARMED RESPONSE.'

Oh, boy. And she'd thought an electric fence was bad news. At least that would only jolt her arm, not slam a slug into her back.

The guidebook had warned that violent crime was prevalent in South Africa's major cities, but she hadn't expected to have to contend with obstacles like these.

As she got further along the road, she came upon more and more large residential properties. Each had some sort of security measure in place, sometimes more than one. That did not bode well.

Finally, she spotted the house she was looking for on the opposite side of the street. She checked the time: 7:24 a.m. She crouched down and retied her shoelace while looking across at the building. The blue garden wall was around seven feet tall with a small fence running around the top consisting of five parallel rows of wires a few inches apart. One wire had a small yellow sign hanging from it. Even though she couldn't read it at this distance, Tess knew exactly what the sign said.

Standing up, Tess set off again but immediately took out her phone and pretended to take a call while idly turning this way and that on the spot.

From what she could see over the blue boundary wall, the two-story house had been painted the same blue, while red terracotta tiles formed a pyramid-shaped roof. Below one of the large upstairs windows, a floodlight was angled down at the garden. That was probably part of the security system and would be activated by either a motion or heat sensor.

With the house positioned atop a slope, the upper rooms would have fabulous views of both Lion Head and Table Mountain. This was prime real estate. An owner would have to have a very high-powered job to afford a place like this. Or a substantial income that they didn't declare.

A side street curved away from Kloof Nek Road immediately after the house. Tess crossed the road. As she neared, she checked the signs on the wall. One showed a picture of a snarling German shepherd and read: 'Beware of the DOGS.' On the same sign beneath that, in smaller lettering, it said, 'Tshaba Mpsa Tshaba Mpyana.' Tess guessed that was probably the same warning in a local language.

Made to draw the eye, another sign was bright yellow and about eighteen inches high. It read: 'CapeCore Armed Response,' below which was a phone number. The sign wasn't cracked or chipped but in excellent condition, as was the fence.

So the place had guard dogs, floodlights, an electric fence, and an alarm system monitored by an armed response unit. All in seemingly pristine condition. Just fantastic. She blew out a weary breath. While she hadn't pictured just moseying on in, neither had she imagined Fort Knox.

144

With the level of violent crime so high in the city, she wondered how many questions an armed response unit would ask before guns started blazing.

She meandered down the side street, casually trying to get a better view of the house, but most of it was secreted behind that enormous wall. And the security measures continued – even the gate for the car to reach the garage had been electrified across the top.

Now closer to the fence, Tess could read the warning sign. Or more importantly, read the manufacturer's name: Aarronson Electrics SA.

She walked alongside the wall, listening intently for the tiniest clicking sound coming from the fence. Silence. That suggested it was functioning perfectly. Great.

Tess wandered back up to the main street. She bought a soft drink at a nearby store, then crossed the road again and sauntered back to where she'd pretended to take the phone call. A few yards higher up, she took a seat inside a gray bus shelter, sitting next to an advertisement for a spicy chicken burger. The roof put her in the shade, making her harder to see from a distance, which was ideal.

She looked up at the bus stop itself, which consisted of two red metal poles angled upward, between which was a triangular sign giving the location of the stop and a handful of bus numbers it serviced. With so many buses to choose from, it meant Tess could legitimately be seen waiting there for quite some time as anyone seeing her would assume her particular bus hadn't yet shown up.

After checking up and down the street to ensure there was no one approaching the bus stop, she called

Bomb. Though it was still the early hours of the morning back in Manhattan, he sounded as alert as ever.

Tess reported her findings. "The property has security I need to get around, at least two elements. First, a five-strand electric fence by Aarronson Electrics SA. That's double A, double R."

Clicking came from the other end of the phone as he typed the information into his system. "I'm only guessing, but that fence is probably a self-contained unit, which means I can't do squat from here."

Tess scanned the vicinity again. Though there was the odd tree along the sidewalk and some in the garden, any branches that had extended over the boundary wall had been lopped off. That meant she'd have no option but to find a way to physically negotiate the fence.

"Okay. The second element is an armed response security service provided by CapeCore. That's all one word."

"Yeah, I know." More typing. "I figured we'd need background info on security companies, so I've already been putting a list together."

She said, "Cool."

"Okay, I'll dig around," said Bomb. "CapeCore ain't a national company with unlimited resources to throw at their security, so I figure finding a vulnerability to get into their system shouldn't be a problem. Take it that alarm's as good as burned."

"Great. Let me know what else you come up with. Thanks, Bomb."

"Will do. Ciao, Tess. Good hunting."

Tess made herself as comfortable as she could on the curved metal seat, then put in her earphones. From her vantage point, she could see the door in the boundary wall, the upstairs windows on two sides, and the exit from the garage. She leaned back, hit Play, and bathed in a post-rock instrumental.

With the time approaching 9:00 a.m., Tess stood and stretched her legs. No one had come out of or gone into the property, and she'd witnessed no activity through any of the windows she could see. If the occupant had a job, surely they'd have needed to leave by now. And if they really had dogs, they would've needed walking. Maybe there was no one there, or they'd left the house before she'd arrived. Whatever the reason, she wasn't getting anywhere by just sitting and hoping.

She stared at the house and drew a long slow breath. She couldn't rush in there blind, no matter how much she ached to get at the person responsible for sharing that video online. No, she needed to know who or what she was facing. Time to shake the tree.

A middle-aged woman wearing a white tracksuit and walking a white poodle sauntered down the street while gazing at her phone. Walking a dog suggested she was a local resident.

Tess said, "Excuse me."

The woman looked up from her phone and smiled. "Yes?"

"Do you happen to know where the van Cleef residence is, please?"

"Van Cleef?" She frowned. "Oh, you've got me there."

Tess looked at a piece of paper in her hand, angled so the woman couldn't see it. "I've got it down as Cedarberg House, Kloof Nek Road, if that helps?"

"Oh, Cedarberg House? Well, that's there" – she pointed to the blue house – "but I don't know who it is that lives there now."

"Now?"

"Mrs. Claasen died, and there's a new owner."

"Oh? Is it a family? A single man?"

She shrugged. "Couldn't say. Sorry."

"Okay, thanks."

Tess let the woman disappear around a corner, then crossed the road again and walked along to the house just below the one she was surveilling. She ambled beside its six-foot-high garden wall until she reached the gate. A security camera stood on a pole, angled down at the entrance. She couldn't pull a decent scam if they could see her, so she moved on.

The next house had a wooden door in its boundary wall with a small intercom system to its left. Tess couldn't see any camera, so she pressed the button on the intercom.

After a few moments, a gruff male voice said, "Yes?"

Tess figured a different tack might offer a different result.

"Hi, I'm looking for a company called WestLine. Is this the right place, please?"

"Who?"

"WestLine? This is, uh, Cedarberg House, Kloof Nek Road, right?"

"No."

"Excuse me?"

"No, it's not Cedarberg House. That's a couple of doors up."

"Oh, I'm so sorry. So WestLine is two houses up, yes?"

"I wouldn't know. I've never heard of them."

"Oh, fudge. Don't tell me I wrote down the wrong company. I don't suppose you know who I can ask for up there to help me clear this up, do you?"

"Sorry, but who are you?"

"I have a package to deliver."

"I don't see a package."

Oh hell. So there was a camera. But where? Her gaze darted all around the entrance.

"It's in my car." She smiled, hoping to appear both friendly and vulnerable to whoever was looking at her.

"Hold your ID up to the camera."

"ID?" This was quickly going sideways. But when all the nearby properties were so well protected, was it any real surprise that people were suspicious of unexpected visitors who asked strange questions? For all the occupant knew, Tess could be casing the joint and looking for a weakness.

The voice said, "Hold it up to the small lens on the intercom."

Tess leaned closer and scrutinized the panel. Sure enough, below the speaker grille was a tiny glass disk.

Damnit, she never missed things like that, so how the devil had it happened today? Maybe it was jet lag. Yeah, jet lag. Had to be. It sure as hell wasn't that Bomb was right and she was unfit for to take on a job like this.

With a chirpy tone, she said, "I'll just go get it from my car."

She meandered away, using all her strength to resist the urge to run like hell. Her heart pounded as she forced herself to walk slowly. So slowly it felt like she was walking in slow motion.

The guy was already suspicious. For all she knew, he'd had his finger on a panic button the whole time he was talking to her, and her failure to provide ID had pushed him to pound on it like crazy.

She peered up and down the street, praying an armed response unit wouldn't come barreling along at any second.

Chapter 24

TESS SCOOTED UP the street as quickly as she could without looking shady to any onlookers.

She wouldn't be returning with her ID, so if that guy was too freaked, he might warn all his neighbors that there was a suspicious character in the area. If an armed unit wasn't on their way now, they sure as hell would be if she approached another resident. That left her only one option – time to abort.

Partly as a safety precaution and partly as a surveillance tactic, Tess continued up Kloof Nek Road. Should any nosy do-gooders raise the alarm, any reported sighting of her would have her going in the opposite direction from where she was staying in the city, making it harder for anyone to track her down. But more importantly, higher ground would give her a line-of-sight advantage.

After another few minutes' walk, she turned left onto Tafelberg Road, a narrow two-lane road that wound its way up to the cable car station. From here, Table Mountain towered over Tess. A bank of white clouds was slowly tipping over its gigantic rocky face like a huge foaming wave breaking in slow motion.

Tess ambled a little further to where the sidewalk gave way to waste ground and the sidewalk was replaced by a dirt path. She stood among the few trees and gazed out at the city splayed before her as it crawled to the sea. She took a small pair of binoculars from her backpack and, tracing her route back down the hill, came to a blue house with a red pyramid-shaped roof. A seven-foot-high wall was a hell of an obstacle from the sidewalk, but from the side of a mountain...

No one moved around the yard. No dogs played on the lawn. No activity came from the property. The sun glare on the window glass made it impossible for Tess to be sure, but it appeared no one was actually in the house. Maybe the new owner hadn't yet moved in. Then why had Bomb traced the Internet connection back to this place? No, someone was there. Somewhere.

Tess sat on the grass on the slope of the hillside. She pulled her knees up and rested on them so she could watch the house through her binoculars as comfortably as possible. With no buildings on Tafelberg and the only passers-by appearing to be tourists looking to hike up one of the mountain trails, there was no chance of her arousing suspicion – she'd merely appear to be just another tourist admiring the view of Cape Town. She put her earphones back in again and hit Play. Rock music blasted her eardrums.

Around noon, she ate her tuna fish sandwich one-handed so she could continue holding up her binoculars with her other. Unfortunately, nothing had yet happened at the house.

Another hour went by.

And another.

With her butt numb and her eyes aching from focusing so intently on the same thing for so long, Tess pushed up to her feet. Light-headed with the sudden rush, she swayed for a moment, then steadied herself. She took a few steps to stretch her legs while swinging her arms. Rubbing her aching neck, she glanced up at the mountain. Or at least where the mountain had been. The top had been engulfed by thick white clouds, making it impossible to discern its true shape.

Tess tapped a root extending from one of the nearby trees with her foot. Yet another decent plan had failed. Time to try something else. Again.

She picked up her backpack and headed back the way she'd come. Walking downhill, she quickly reached the bus shelter again, so she took a seat to watch the other side of the street once more.

But movement lower down caught her eye.

A tall man in a blue shirt and jeans left the house at which she'd pretended to be a delivery person. If it was the same man and he saw her loitering in the area still, not only might he call the cops, but he might go to Cedarberg House and warn the occupant that someone suspicious had been asking about them. That could ruin everything. If the occupant got spooked, they could run and Tess would never find them. Or they could hole up with their own private arsenal and wait for her to poke her head above their garden wall...

A white single-decker bus appeared, heading down the street toward Tess, its light blue bumper set off by a streak of red. Turning her back, she knelt to tie her shoelace again, so she could hide without appearing to be hiding.

She watched the bus near.

At the last minute, she shot up and waved for it to stop. It did so and she boarded. As she walked down the aisle to take a seat, she glanced out the window at the blue house.

Tess's jaw dropped.

A shadow moved across one of the upstairs windows.

Chapter 25

TESS SCOOTED ALONG the bus's aisle, bending over to better see through the windows. But the vehicle sped away and the house quickly became just a distant speck of blue out the rear window.

She slumped down onto one of the blue-gray seats. Well, at least she knew there was someone there. If only she knew who.

The bus dropped her off in the center of Cape Town. With time to kill, and not wanting to risk being spotted on Kloof Nek Road again, she meandered around the shopping area and came upon Greenmarket Square in the heart of the city. Awash with color, the stalls sold African masks, paintings, wooden sculptures, clothes, ornaments, tribal drums... a souvenir for every taste and every pocketbook. Very bright. Very welcoming.

Two guys played guitar and sang below one of the trees that dotted the area, adding to the easy-going vacation atmosphere. A vinyl guitar bag in front of them had a selection of coins and small notes.

Tess ambled through, checking out the wares.

A grimy middle-aged man shook a battered metal cup at her, his front teeth missing and his clothes tattered.

Tess gave a slight shake of her head without making eye contact and walked past.

A white couple in their midtwenties stared up at the fifty or so carved wooden masks that hung across the back of one stall. Both wore designer sunglasses, though the afternoon was now quite overcast. They talked loudly, comparing the faces of the masks to their acquaintances and laughing loudly.

Behind them, a scruffy young black boy stood, innocently sipping from a bottle of water. After checking that no one was watching and that the couple were still engrossed in the artwork, he eased his hand into the open bag the woman had slung over her shoulder. With great care, he slipped out a cell phone.

Tess lightly tapped him on the shoulder.

His head snapped around to her. Wide eyes stared up in surprise and fear.

She shook her head, then gestured with a tip of her head for him to put the phone back.

The boy delicately eased the phone back in, then looked anxiously up at Tess. He was probably imagining being hauled away by the police.

Tess looked him up and down.

Though he was only around nine or ten years old, that didn't mean he wasn't stealing to buy drugs. However, despite his green T-shirt being faded and his sneakers coming apart at the seams, he looked like just a normal kid. Maybe he was stealing for drugs; maybe for food; maybe for a sick relative.

Tess held out a 200 rand note, about sixteen bucks.

Warily, he reached for it, his eyes flicking from the note to Tess to the note and back to Tess. When he finally

156

grasped it and she let go, he looked up at her as if asking what he now had to do for such payment.

Tess winked at him, then nodded toward the end of the market aisle where it turned left. The kid turned and ran, quickly disappearing among the tourists and sellers.

The designer couple were still joking about the masks, none the wiser about what had happened directly behind them. Tess tapped the woman on the shoulder. She turned.

Gesturing to the bag, Tess said, "There are quite a few pickpockets around here, so if I were you, I'd either hold that in front of you or buy one you can fasten."

The woman thanked Tess and pulled her bag around to sandwich it between her arm and her side.

Leaving the market, Tess wandered further. Through the buildings she saw greenery. A lot of greenery. She quickened her pace. The street opened out onto Company's Gardens. It wasn't her special place beside her lake back home, but it was no less a sanctuary in a crime-addled, bustling metropolis.

Tess ambled along a tree-lined avenue of towering oaks, many of their leaves still green but a lot showing the rich reds, vibrant yellows, and earthy browns of fall. Squirrels scampered through the vegetation, the more daring taking treats from overjoyed tourists who frantically clicked with phones and cameras.

She turned onto a red brick path between manicured lawns. Atop a ring of stone columns stood a sculpture of a man standing with a horse, while in the background, Table Mountain reared over the city as if shielding it from the rest of the continent.

In one of the quieter areas, Tess passed a small ornate pond where a gray-haired black guy in green

157

coveralls was scooping dead leaves out of the water with a net on the end of a metal pole. Nearby, she found a wooden bench beside a tree. With a dangerous and traumatic night ahead of her, this was just what she needed.

She pulled her feet up to sit cross-legged. Closed her eyes. Focused on the in and out of her breathing. And let peace wash over her.

When she next opened her eyes, a squirrel was sitting on the bench beside her, casually brushing its fluffy tail with the claws of its front paws. It looked up at her as if to say, 'I'm okay with this if you are.'

She was. Tess watched the little creature groom itself. The care it took, the way its tiny handlike paws worked, the way it combed its fur with its teeth ... Tess found it wonderfully calming, soothing, bonding.

A small fat kid sporting a 'I ♥ Cape Town' baseball cap appeared from around some bushes. He saw the animal and tore toward the bench shouting, "A squirrel, a squirrel, a squirrel!"

The animal leapt away and scurried up the tree trunk. It was out of sight in an instant.

Following the boy, a squat woman in a matching cap carried a tablet in front of her as a camera. In a New Jersey accent, she said, "Never mind, PJ, we'll find you another one, baby."

"But I want that one," he said in a whiny voice.

He picked up a small stone and hurled it up into the tree. "Squirrel?"

Tess leaned forward. "Excuse me, please don't do that."

The boy ignored her and tossed another stone.

Tess added a serious edge to her voice. "I said, please don't do that."

Scowling, the woman approached Tess. "Excuse me. It's not your place to tell my child how to behave."

"No, it's yours. So would you mind doing it?"

"What? He ain't doing any harm."

"No? That's a small stone to you and me, but to that squirrel, it's a damn big rock. If your son hits it, he could kill it."

The woman put her hands on her hips as though she meant business. "I don't care for your tone."

"Then control your kid and you won't have to hear another damn word."

The woman's scowl darkened. "I'll thank you not to blaspheme in front of my son."

There was only one kind of person who objected to such minor curse words. Tess had no time for such weak-willed, easily led bigots.

She stood and nonchalantly closed the gap between them. "Revelation 11:18. Ring any bells?"

The woman frowned as if struggling to recollect that particular Bible verse.

Being five foot seven, Tess towered over the chubby woman and stared down into her face.

"No? 'Now the time of your wrath has come. It is time to destroy all who have caused destruction on the earth.' Now, I'm no angel, but I didn't just try to hurt one of God's creations. So, if I were you, I'd check the label in those lovely hats of yours, see if they're fire-retardant – somehow, I don't think your travel insurance will cover where you're going."

The woman shuffled backward, warily eyeing Tess up and down. Then, her jaw set, she pushed past Tess, even though there was ample room on the path. She sneered. "You do know a squirrel is little more than a rat."

"And you do know you're little more than an ape. Or to graduate from your high school, did you just have to superglue your knees together and chant 'Darwin is the Antichrist' three times?"

The woman put her arm around her son's shoulders and steered him away. "Come on, PJ, we'll find someplace a little more civil to take your picture, baby."

He looked up at her. "Mom, is an ape a monkey?"

She ruffled his hair. "Well, ain't you a clever little thing."

"So, if you're a monkey, am I a monkey, too?"

"Take no notice of that lady, PJ. Some people are just plain wicked."

Tess shook her head. What kind of a future would that poor kid have?

But that was a battle for another day. For now, with her batteries recharged, it was time to prepare for the fight to come. After double-checking her tourist map for the route to take to collect everything she needed for tonight, she left the park.

Once she'd gotten it all, she'd check in with Bomb. She hoped he'd have good news for her and that she wouldn't be going into this battle as good as blind. But....

Chapter 26

TESS WOKE UP. Mired in dense gloom. Groggy, she made out the interior of a van. Her heart pounded and a wave of panic hit her as she envisioned the gang of rapists rearing over her, pinning her down, their hands crawling all over her.

Gasping for breath, she jerked off the van floor to sit upright. Her clothing clammy on her back.

She was safe. One hundred percent safe.

Blanking her memories as much as she could, she focused on her breathing. In and out. In and out. In and out.

Gradually, her heart stopped racing and the tension drained from her body.

She moved gently so as to make as little noise as possible and pushed the blanket off her, then pulled over her backpack. Kneeling on the hostel's comforter, which was now doubling as a mattress, she hitched her panties partway down, eased her slender polypropylene funnel into place, and then peed into an empty water bottle.

One of the body's natural preservation processes in a fight-or-flight situation was to rid itself of waste, which was why some people wet themselves when frightened.

There was no point in her going into a confrontation with anything but an empty bladder if she didn't have to.

After securing the cap on the bottle and putting it at the opposite side of the van from her drinking water, she shook the funnel, wrapped it in a paper tissue, and replaced it in her bag to be washed later.

She checked her watch: 2:23 a.m. Thirty-seven minutes to go-time.

After turning off the alarm on her phone because she wouldn't need it during the incursion, she sat in the lotus position so she could relax, but stay alert.

After she'd rented the van and driven back to the hostel, she'd enjoyed a meal at a nearby restaurant, grabbing two servings of steak and fries, and then finally spoken with Bomb. Again, he'd had good and bad news. The good could have been better, but the bad could have been worse, so all in all, she couldn't complain. Now, it was simply a case of waiting.

Not that there was anything simple about it. Nothing was worse than waiting.

The anxiety of being discovered.

The stress of an impending confrontation.

The fear of the unknown.

They were all intangible. All horrors her own psyche created. All things she had to conquer to ensure she could go into battle as calm and rational as possible. But controlling them was never easy. Give her a battle against a real opponent over a battle in her mind any day.

However, this job was even worse than usual. Without knowing who or what she was facing, she couldn't use many of her visualization techniques. How could she visualize beating an 'invisible' foe?

Instead, Tess focused on herself. Focused on sensing each part of her body. On her fingers. Then on her forearms. Then upper arms. Shoulders. Back. She traveled the length of her body, reconnecting with each tiny part on the most intimate of levels.

Her goal was to be able to move without 'moving.' To be so in tune with her body and her abilities that something such as punching someone when an opening occurred would happen automatically, without any conscious effort, as though the punch 'punched' itself. To achieve that, her mind and body had to be in perfect sync. Stress, fear, and anxiety blocked that. If she was to leave Africa in anything but a body bag, she needed to unblock it.

Tess completed her meditation, instinctively knowing how long such a session required.

She opened her eyes.

It was time.

After taking her armor from her backpack, out of force of habit, she ran a finger along each of her seven-inch-long metal guards to check for damage before velcroing them in place.

Next, she put on her Threat Level IIIA body armor, followed by her leather jacket. The thousand-dollar armor was so slimline it was virtually invisible under her jacket, yet was bullet- and knife-proof.

Finally, she pulled on her gloves. She clenched and unclenched her fists to ensure the hinged titanium-alloy inserts responded correctly to her movements. They did.

She was ready.

She checked the street through the front windshield and then the side mirrors.

Deathly still.

Crouching next to the side door as the clock on her phone hit 3:00 a.m., she phoned Bomb.

He answered immediately and said just one word: "Now?"

"Now." She hung up and slowly eased the side door open. Metal scraped along metal but, because of the care she took, way too quietly for anyone in the nearby homes to hear.

Tess crept out. Standing beneath a small palm tree, she double-checked up and down the small side street.

Still clear.

She strained to hear the faintest click-click-click coming from the fence, praying the device had shorted and was malfunctioning.

Silence.

She heaved a breath.

Delicately, she eased the aluminum stepladder she'd bought out of the back of the van and set it beside the wall, then reached in for the incontinence sheet. Quietly, she closed the door and locked it manually with the key so it wouldn't beep.

She'd have liked to have stayed at the hostel for as long as possible and only come here at the last minute. However, she couldn't risk waiting only to find this parking space had been taken, because it offered the most cover of any that surrounded the blue house. The van was tall enough to hide her using the ladder against the wall, but once she reached the top, it simply wasn't big enough. To obscure her negotiating the fence, she needed something far bigger – that was where the palm tree came in.

Tess eased open the ladder as close to the wall as possible, put the loop of the rope she'd tied to it over her wrist, and then climbed onto it. The metal ladder rattled.

Cringing, Tess froze.

She placed her other foot far more carefully and the ladder was quieter.

Gingerly, she continued up as softly as she could.

Halfway up, she checked that the van and the tree hid her from view from all but anyone walking along that sidewalk.

A car engine rumbled in the distance.

She looked up at the intersection to the main road just a few yards away. If the car turned down here, or the driver looked out, they'd see her and probably raise the alarm.

She leapt off the ladder and squashed herself and it against the far side of the tree trunk.

Tess froze.

Though she was hidden, she couldn't help but hold her breath. Her heart thumped like she was running full tilt up a hill.

The car roared along the main road and sailed straight past the intersection. False alarm. And even if she'd been up the ladder and they'd been looking, she doubted they'd have seen anything at the speed they were traveling. Maybe she was being overcautious.

Again, she opened the ladder and crept up it.

Above her, the electric fence was completely silent. Not the tiniest of clicking sounds came from it, which meant one of two things: either it was not active, or it was working perfectly. Not that she could check. If she touched it and it was active, she'd be shocked, fall off

165

the wall, and possibly be seriously hurt. Plus, the alarm would sound, warning the occupant.

That would be game over.

Finally standing on the top of the ladder, she checked one last time to ensure the street was clear. This was the riskiest point, so any interruption now could end in either serious injury or seeing the inside of a police cell. Or both.

An image flashed into her mind. She pictured herself locked up in some filthy prison, her leg in a cast, and thugs with shanks taking advantage of her incapacity. Her concentration broken, the ladder wobbled.

She swayed. Almost toppled.

The ladder creaked loudly.

Tess crouched and clung to the ladder to steady herself. She closed her eyes for a moment to center herself.

She could do this. Bomb was wrong. She could handle this job just fine. This was what she did.

He was wrong.

Period.

After cowering on top of the ladder in the cover of the palm for a few seconds, she'd cleared her mind so stood up again.

She checked the sidewalk, once more.

Nothing stirred up or down the street. No engine noise drifted through the night from the main road.

Because of the electric fence's design, Bomb had been unable to do anything about it from off-site. Luckily, that was a minor inconvenience as opposed to a major problem.

Holding the rubber incontinence sheet out wide, she delicately draped it over the top wire of the electric fence so it hung down over both sides and covered all five wires. She'd once used the rubber mat from a car but, being far thicker, it hadn't draped properly and the weight of it had compressed the fence so much that the wires had touched, which had set off the alarm. She'd had to abort that job. But she had learned from it – a thin rubber sheet was ideal. Thank God for bedwetters.

Protected from being shocked by the insulating sheet, Tess placed one foot on top of the wall and raised herself up onto it. Unfortunately, the top of the wall wasn't flat as she'd expected but sloped down to either side. She shifted her foot around, struggling to get the best grip.

Confident her grip was secure, she then lifted the other foot off the ladder to stand completely on the wall. Slowly, she raised it to clear the eighteen-inch-high fence.

But she teetered.

She flung her arms out like a tightrope walker, bending this way and that, struggling to regain her balance. If she fell and caught the fence so the wires touched, even with the rubber over it, the alarm would sound and this job would be dead in the water. And falling from this height, she might be dead on the sidewalk.

Her foot skidded an inch or so on the sloping wall.

Tess tipped forward.

She felt herself falling.

But at the last moment, she caught herself.

Swaying, she straightened up. After a second or two, she was stable, balancing on one leg.

She drew a couple of deep, calming breaths to steady herself, then lifted her foot again. This time, she got it over the wall and down onto the other half of the top to straddle the electric fence. Now with a solid stance, she hoisted the ladder up with the rope she'd looped around her wrist.

Taking the utmost care, she swung the ladder over the wall and lowered it so it lay flat on the lawn. She dropped the rope, then leapt down into the yard.

She was in. Kind of.

In case she had to make a break for it, instead of opening the stepladder out, she simply rested it below the rubber sheet – a few bounds and she'd be up and over the wall.

Tess scrutinized the darkened house. If she'd made a mistake negotiating that fence, an alarm would have sounded in the house to warn the occupants. If they put a light on, she'd have to run. But even if the house remained in darkness, it didn't mean she was safe, because many homeowners owned guns – she might take a bullet from someone she didn't even see.

Crouched on the ground, she froze. Her heart pounded as she listened and studied the house for any sign of activity.

Any moment, a gun could poke out of a window and find her as the proverbial sitting target.

Any moment could be her last.

She waited.

Ten seconds passed.

She strained to catch the tiniest of sounds.

Twenty seconds.

She squinted to spot the smallest of movements.

The seconds crawled by like hours. Torturous, unending hours.

Thirty seconds.

Everything remained deathly still.

She was clear. So far.

Tess stood up.

Bomb had hacked CapeCore and, on her command, had deactivated the intruder alarm's motion sensors and the devices that secured the property's windows and doors. Unfortunately, that still left the most unpredictable and potentially most dangerous of the security measures to be dealt with – the guard dogs.

In the moonlight, she scanned the lawn for dog mess. The 'Beware of the Dog' sign was either a ruse or a legitimate warning. Unfortunately, having no background on who owned the house, she had no idea which was the case. There didn't appear to be any dog mess or toys on the lawn, which was encouraging as it suggested there was no dog. However, it could just as easily mean that the owner was fastidious about keeping a clean and tidy yard. The only thing she was sure of was she hadn't been savaged by a Rottweiler. Yet. That could change once she gained entry. If there was a canine threat, that was where it was waiting to strike.

Keeping low to the ground, she crept across the lawn toward the house. Once in, she'd check the kitchen for food bowls.

The floodlights remained off as she crossed. Bomb had done his job well.

One of the rooms upstairs had a small balcony, just large enough for a couple of chairs and a small table. It would be perfect for a morning coffee while admiring Table Mountain. She'd studied the floor plan Bomb had obtained to know that was the master bedroom. That was likely her ultimate target.

Tess made for a decked area with wooden benches and a rectangular table with an umbrella, a shadowy door to the house visible behind them.

As she approached the door, Tess saw a security camera pointing directly at her. The floodlights and alarm were all off, so she hoped that was disabled too.

She glanced in through a window. Where she'd imagined a dining room would be, there was an open space piled high with storage boxes.

Though she might be completely wrong, this didn't look at all like a gang headquarters. On the contrary, it looked like a house a family had recently moved into. Could it be that Bomb was wrong and that this was not the sordid lair of the pornographic movie distributor?

Tess tapped lightly on the window. If there was a big dog, she'd rather see it from this side of the glass.

No slavering jaws appeared, teeth bared.

She reached the back door and unslung her backpack, crouching down. After taking out her lock-picking kit, she selected two tools. Inserting one to jimmy the mechanism inside and one to ease the lock around as she did so, she patiently teased the lock's tumblers up into the open position one by one. After a few seconds, the door clicked unlocked.

Tess gently swung the backdoor open. Her hands sweated inside her gloves, yet her mouth was so dry she could barely swallow. For a few seconds, she closed her eyes and focused on breathing slowly to calm her racing heart. Finally, she stepped into the doorway of the darkened hallway.

She was in.

But who was in there with her?

Chapter 27

THE FAINT BEAM from Tess's tiny flashlight illuminated just enough for her to navigate the house but revealed little detail of anything. Moonlight through the windows revealed a little more. At head height on the hallway walls were rectangular patches where artwork had long hung but had since been removed, further suggesting new ownership. The floor was a parquet checkerboard pattern.

Tess lifted her right foot off the rubberized doormat and placed it on the parquet. As she increased her weight, the wood creaked. She moved her foot six inches to the left and tried again. Silence. She put her weight on that foot and then repeated the process with her left foot. For each footstep, Tess tested it to ensure that spot wouldn't creak. If it made the slightest noise, she shifted one way or the other until she found somewhere solid and silent.

Thus, she crept on. Painstakingly slowly. But she couldn't risk alerting someone to her presence. Because she was going in blind, the element of surprise was vital to not getting caught. Or more crucially, to not getting her head blown off.

However, the more she saw of the house, the more she thought Bomb had made a terrible mistake and no one was yet living there.

The hallway opened out into a large living area. Amid more boxes, two large couches sat in a L-shape with a coffee table nestled between them, while a TV hung on the wall, but there were no photographs, no paintings, no knickknacks. It looked like someone might be in the process of moving their belongings in, but wasn't actually living here.

She swung her light around, looking for a clue as to who she was going to have to face, have to fight, potentially have to kill.

Against the main wall, as if the room's centerpiece, stood an eight-foot-long oak display unit with different-sized glass shelves forming compartments. The unit housed a collection of porcelain dogs. Thirty or more. Was this the closest thing to a canine threat she was going to find?

Some of the compartments were still empty, so Tess peered into a nearby box. Inside were objects wrapped in bubble wrap. It seemed someone did live here, but that they were unpacking very slowly, starting with items so precious that they couldn't live without them.

Tess crept toward the staircase, which curved around in a wide arc to the upper level.

At the first step, Tess placed her foot down and gradually lowered more weight onto it. She waited for a creak. It didn't come. She repeated the process with the next step. That was firm and silent too. Maybe this was going to be easier than she'd thought.

Tess looked up to the top of the stairs. The moonlight illuminated some of it, but the upper floor was drenched in shadows.

Still, at least it was all clear.

She took another step. But pulled up. Froze. She held her breath, listening intently.

Was that…? Was that a noise from upstairs?

If it wasn't and she raced up to repel a nonexistent assailant, her heavy footfalls would warn everyone of her presence. Instead, she crouched down beside the wall, making herself as small as possible and clinging to the blackness. Maybe it was just someone going to the bathroom for a glass of water.

Or maybe she'd imagined it and was freaking herself out over nothing.

She strained to hear something, but prayed to hear nothing.

Deathly silence.

Then…

There it was.

A barely audible tap tap tap tap squeak, tap tap tap tap squeak.

What the hell was that?

Whatever it was, it was getting closer.

Tess's gaze drilled into the shadows at the top of the stairs.

Waiting. Heart pounding.

Tap tap tap tap squeak.

What the hell?

Aware she was focusing all her attention on one tiny area, Tess scanned the room and hallway downstairs. Realistically, a threat could come from any direction. Especially if Bomb's deactivation of the electronic

173

security had somehow failed or, worse yet, been discovered and CapeCore had rebooted the system.

But everything downstairs was still.

Tap tap tap tap squeak.

Tess glanced back to the top of the staircase.

A little face stared back at her. A little furry face. The kind of cute little furry face that a person couldn't resist hugging and letting lick them. But also the kind of face that, at any moment, could bark loud enough to raise the dead.

Goddamnit. She'd intended to look in the kitchen for food bowls to confirm whether or not there was a dog. How the hell had she been so sloppy? Maybe Bomb was right. Maybe she wasn't up to the job. But whether she was or not, it was way too late to debate that now.

Tess held her open hands out toward the dog and whispered. "Shhh, little buddy. Everything's fine. Shhh."

Moving in slow motion so as not to spook the dog, she unslung her backpack and then reached inside. She took out the piece of steak from the second serving she'd ordered just in case she ran into any sort of hound tonight.

Offering the meat, Tess said, "Come on. Come get your treat."

The dog tilted its head to one side and stared at her.

"That's it. Good boy."

Even more slowly than before, Tess lifted her foot and gingerly placed it down on the next step up.

The dog barked. And barked. And barked.

"Goddamnit." Tess ran. If she was quick enough, she'd reach the dog owner before they were fully awake and able to fight or raise the alarm.

But before she made it halfway up the stairs, a middle-aged white woman with wild hair and a white nightgown appeared at the top. A woman who must have been disturbed when her dog left her side, so she had gotten up to investigate. A woman with a double-barrel shotgun.

Chapter 28

THE WIDE SPREAD of a shotgun meant aiming wasn't that much of an issue compared to a handgun. Tess couldn't fight such a weapon head-on.

She leapt over the handrail and over the side of the staircase.

The gun thundered.

Two spindles in the balustrade blasted apart.

The dog yelped at the noise, its claws tapping on the wood floor as it ran away.

Tess rolled across the floor and straight up to her feet. She dove for cover behind one of the couches just as the gun blasted again.

The shot tore into the display unit. Two large glass shelves shattered, and porcelain dogs exploded. The debris fell onto other shelves and sculptures, shattering them.

The woman on the stairs screeched. "No!"

Tess leaped to her feet and tore across the room toward the staircase. That was both cartridges used, so the shotgun was empty. She had to reach the woman before she had time to reload.

Aghast at the damage she'd done, the woman stared with her hand clasped over her mouth. Her eyes widened as Tess stormed up the stairs toward her. She shrieked and fled.

Tess raced up the stairs. At the top, she turned left. Ahead, the woman dashed into the master bedroom and slammed the door.

Tess stormed after her down the shadowy corridor. Light bled around the edges of the door.

Reaching the bedroom, she yanked on the door handle. Locked.

She took one wide step back, then spun around and launched a massive sidekick at the door. It crashed open, the jamb splintering.

Whimpering, the woman stood at the opposite side of a queen-sized bed before an open drawer in a nightstand. Her hands shaking, she struggled to insert fresh shells into the shotgun.

Tess tore into the room.

Ran straight at the bed.

Leapt.

She sailed through the air with her legs pulled up, body angled sideways. At the last moment, she shot her right leg out straight.

A flying sidekick hammered the woman in the side.

The woman reeled away.

She careened into the wall.

Crashed to the floor.

Tess jumped on top of her. Straddled her. Unleashed her pent-up fury.

She rained down blows. The woman feebly tried to shield herself with her arms but obviously had no fighting experience, so Tess pounded in shot after shot.

Finally, with the woman suitably softened up, Tess grabbed one of her arms and spun around to sandwich it and the woman's neck between her thighs. Tess clamped her legs and leaned back, still gripping the arm.

The armlock strained the woman's elbow and shoulder joints, while the leg lock crushed the carotid artery in her neck, cutting off the supply of blood to her brain. Tess remembered all too well from her training with Ayumi just how excruciating the pain was from this strangulation technique.

The woman spluttered, struggling to breathe. She squirmed. Clawed with her free hand. Heaved to try to break free.

It was impossible.

Tess squeezed tighter. Crushing the woman's neck. Wrenching the arm joints apart.

She wanted the woman to feel totally helpless. To know she was completely at Tess's mercy. To know she was going to die.

The woman's kicking subsided and the strength in her arms started to fail. That was a sign she was passing out from oxygen deprivation. If Tess didn't relax the hold, she'd kill the woman. And she didn't want that. Yet.

Tess eased up on the pressure for a moment.

The woman spluttered, choking as she fought to gasp air through a damaged windpipe.

Tess said, "Tell me who supplies the *Monster Bang* videos."

Still spluttering, the woman said, "What?"

178

"*Monster Bang.* Who is it?"

"I" – she coughed – "I" – she coughed again – "don't know."

Tess tightened her grip again. Literally squeezing the life out of the woman.

"Who is it?"

Between Tess's crushing thighs, the woman struggled to shake her head.

Tess shouted, "Tell me!"

From under the bed, the cute little dog dashed out. Tess had only seen its head before over the top step. Now she saw the whole animal. It had gray, shaggy fur with white flashes. But its coloring wasn't its defining feature.

It dashed to Tess and chomped down on the leg of her jeans. With all its might, it heaved back, to try to free its beloved mistress.

But it couldn't pull because it couldn't get sufficient purchase on the cream carpet with only two paws. Due either to injury or illness, its back legs hung limp in a harness between two eight-inch wheels. Wheels that obviously needed lubricating to stop them from squeaking.

The little dog yanked and yanked on Tess's jeans. Snarling with each tug.

The woman's wild eyes turned from Tess to her dog.

Tess relaxed her lock around the woman's neck so she could shake the dog loose.

The woman cried out, "No! No!" She tried to reach with her free hand to push the dog away. "Run, Coco. Run!"

Tess grabbed Coco by the harness and heaved him over.

The woman's voice croaked as she spoke. "No. Please. No. Take anything. Anything you want. Just don't hurt Coco."

There was no need to torture her any more. Getting the information she needed had just gotten a whole lot easier. Tess lodged her foot against the woman's ribs and shoved. The woman flopped over and away. Tess leapt to her feet.

The woman clambered up onto all fours. Her face flushed and sweaty, she stared at Tess, her bushy hair even wilder than it had been before. She reached out toward Coco, but Tess held him away.

"Tell me where you sourced those videos."

Her head hanging down, the woman clutched her throat and gasped for air. She nodded.

"So tell me."

"I–I don't have a n–name."

The woman collapsed onto her elbows, still wheezing for air after all the stress and pain.

But after the torment this woman had caused her, no way was Tess letting her take one more breath than was necessary to get the information she needed. She dangled Coco by his harness.

Tess said, "You better have something, or you better pray Coco's fire-proof."

180

Chapter 29

"NO! PLEASE," **SAID** the woman, her eyes wide, hands clutching her mouth. "Everything's on my computer. You can have it all. Just don't hurt Coco. Please!"

Gasping and holding her throat, the woman clambered to her feet. She swayed a little, then, once steady, she led Tess out of the room.

In another of the bedrooms, a gray metal filing cabinet stood against one wall beside a desk made of cheap ash-effect wood composite. A printer and two monitors sat side-by-side on the desk, while a computer tower sat on the floor underneath. More unpacked boxes lay strewn about on the floor.

The woman turned on her computer and a Microsoft boot-up screen appeared. She logged in using a six-character password, which she tried surreptitiously to shield. Tess didn't even bother trying to see it.

Instead, Tess phoned Bomb, still holding Coco under one arm.

"Yo, Tess. We good?"

"Almost. I'm about to plug you in now. Looks like the latest Windows OS. I need you to analyze the drive and any cloud storage."

"Got it."

Tess put her phone down on the desk, then pointed to a space on the floor between some boxes next to the wall. "Sit there. Facing the wall."

"But I—"

Tess narrowed her eyes.

The woman jumped, then scurried over to the space. Facing the wall, she sat blubbering.

With the woman no immediate threat, Tess crouched and pushed a memory stick into the computer's USB port. Computer code flashed up on the monitors as Bomb's malware took control of the system, thus granting him remote access.

"Where do you keep your passwords?" asked Tess.

The woman didn't answer.

Tess waited, but the woman was not forthcoming.

"Passwords?" Tess gave the dog the gentlest nip she thought she could that wouldn't hurt too much but would elicit a yelp. Coco obliged.

The woman jumped. She flung an arm back, pointing at the top of the filing cabinet. "There. In there. A blue notebook in the fifth folder."

Tess pulled the drawer open.

"Please…" said the woman, tears streaming her face. "Please, don't hurt him."

Flicking through the folders, Tess found the fifth one. It did have a notebook in it. Inside was what appeared to be a comprehensive list of passwords.

"How do I find *Monster Bang*?"

"All I've got is an email address. That's where I send the payment using PayPal." She pointed behind her in Tess's general direction. "It's in there too."

Tess had hoped for more. But deep down, she'd always suspected they wouldn't get anything spectacular like a name or physical location, but that she'd probably have to make do with just an email address. This was only a tiny step forward, but it was a step, all the same.

With it looking like they had everything they were going to get here, she picked up her phone. "How are we doing?"

"We got passwords?"

"Yeah."

"Then we're good. Just leave the computer running for a full scan."

She glanced at the woman. The woman's back was juddering while she cried.

Tess said, "Check in in thirty. I'm moving just as soon as I clean up here." She hung up.

The woman tensed noticeably and whimpered. Tess could imagine the thoughts going through her mind, knowing she was about to die.

Tess looked at Coco.

She exhaled sharply. Then set the dog on the floor. It ran to its mistress.

The woman sobbed with happiness and whisked her little dog up into her arms. She cradled it, burying her head in its shaggy fur, which muffled her crying.

Tess stared at the pair of them, hatred in her eyes, fury in her heart.

This woman fed off the most extreme suffering any woman had ever had to endure. By selling such videos, she helped to maintain the demand for them. Removing her wouldn't eradicate the problem, but it would kill one distribution channel, making it just that tiny bit harder to deal in such filth.

Over the woman's shoulder, Coco's big brown eyes stared at Tess.

Tess slumped and breathed a mighty sigh.

Many pet owners would have taken the easy option and had a dog with such a disability put to sleep. They wouldn't have gone to all the expense of having a custom harness and wheels made. Let alone coped with all the extra care needed, particularly when it came to toileting a dog that couldn't stand by itself.

If the woman was gone, what kind of a life would Coco have?

Tess said, "We own your computer now. We know everything you do on it. If you try to remove our software, we'll know. Change your passwords, we'll know. Use any account on another computer, we'll know. Understand?"

Her voice shaky, the woman said, "Yes."

"Continue selling this filth and we'll take everything. Your money. Your house. Your dog. Understand?"

That was the beauty of the Internet. Once you had someone's passwords, you had control of their entire life.

"Yes." She sniffled away tears. "Yes, I understand."

Tess stood looking at the woman and her dog. Was this the right move?

"And oil his damn wheels, for God's sake." She marched out of the room and didn't look back.

In the van driving back to Long Street, Tess struggled with her decision to let the woman live, but consoled herself with the fact they had a decent lead at last. If Bomb could just work his magic once more, that entire gang would be bleeding out this time tomorrow.

Tess parked the van outside the rental company's office. Her flight was far too early in the morning for her to return it during business hours, so her bank account would have to suffer any penalties. She stuffed the keys through the slot and then trudged back to her hostel with the bedding under her arm.

As she lumbered along the dark streets, her feet dragged and her shoulders slumped. The daylong journey, the daylong surveillance, and then the nighttime incursion had wracked her body with aches and pains. Still, at least she'd be able to enjoy some peaceful sleep on the plane in just a few hours.

At the hostel's front door, she input the code into the keypad below the intercom and entered. Feeling like she was climbing up Table Mountain, she tramped up the stairs into the silent, shadowy communal TV area and toward the staircase at the back.

Something hit her over the back of the head. Everything went black.

Chapter 30

THE COARSE CLOTH bag over Tess's head smelled of vegetables and dirt, while the rag in her mouth tasted of oil, as if it had been used to wipe car parts.

She sniffed. Burning. She could smell burning. Not wood. Not gas. Something else. Something more rudimentary. Something she couldn't put her finger on.

The bag completely opaque, she couldn't see a thing, but she felt no air movement on her hands, suggesting she was inside. She could hear talk and laughter coming from quite close by too. Not the same room. Not so distinct. More distant. Possibly the far side of the next room. It sounded like that same strange language she'd heard last night in the pool room. She strained to hear, to count the different voices so she'd know how many thugs she would have to battle. Four. Maybe five. The distance and structures between her and them made it impossible to tell.

Her wooden chair rocked a little as she shifted her weight, suggesting either it had one leg shorter than the others or the floor was uneven.

She lifted her left heel and carefully pivoted on the ball of her foot. Nothing tugged at her ankle – it wasn't bound to the chair leg. Neither was her right.

Behind her back, she flexed her muscles to pull her arms apart. Impossible. Something bound her wrists. From the feel, strength, and flexibility, she guessed it was duct tape.

With the bag over her head, she didn't know if someone was guarding her, so she couldn't risk moving more. Instead, she focused on breathing slowly, steadily, to maintain her composure so she'd be ready for the hell that would undoubtedly come.

A burst of laughter came from the room beyond where she was, and then a door creaked open. Multiple footfalls on wood sounded in her room.

Tess's heart hammered.

She'd no idea who was there. How many of them. What they wanted. What weapons they had.

As disadvantages went, those were doozies.

In Shanghai, Tang Lung had taught her Wing Chun, with particular emphasis on Chi Sau, mastery of which now enabled her to fight, to a degree, while blindfolded. But not against an unknown number of assailants, any of whom could drop her with a single shot.

No, for now, she'd just have to wait and see how things played out.

Someone approached her, their heavy feet pounding on the wooden floor. Tess braced herself. The air inside the bag was hot, stale. She couldn't breathe. Panic started to overtake her. She held her breath. Forced herself as calm as she could.

She tensed every muscle possible. And waited for the inevitable pain.

187

Something slapped her across the face.

She didn't respond.

Another slap.

Still, she remained silent.

If she appeared unresponsive, they might take the bag off to take a closer look at her.

Someone snatched the bag off her head.

She pulled away, blinking in the half-light of a kerosene lamp sitting on a crate. The yellowy light cast an eerie glow over the corrugated metal walls of the room. Her backpack lay on the crate, much of its contents emptied out.

A cigarette-smoking black guy slouched in the far corner in a deck chair. Anyone else was blocked by the big brute standing in front of her, holding the vegetable bag in his beefy hand. He stared down at her, the whites of his eyes gleaming almost as much as the stainless-steel Smith and Wesson revolver stuck inside the waistband of his jeans.

He ripped the rag from her mouth and tossed it on the floor, then held up the ATM card that had been in her backpack.

With a thick South African accent, he said, "How much money is in this account?"

So that's what this was? A simple case of abducting a tourist to clean them out? Okay, this was going to be easier than she'd thought – she'd palm them off with a few hundred bucks, and before she knew it, she'd be relaxing on her plane with the flight attendant serving her breakfast.

She feigned a waver in her voice – she wanted them to think she was weak, frightened, compliant.

"About 1,200 bucks. Take it. Please. I'll give you the PIN."

"You have family?"

"Why? I can give—"

He slapped her across the face.

Her head swung sideways under the force of the strike. Her cheek stinging, she turned back and gazed up with big sad eyes. She made her bottom lip quiver.

"Yes," said Tess with a weak voice. "Yes, my mom and my little brother." There was no one, but she wanted to humanize herself as much as possible.

"How much will they pay to get you back?" The glare from his white eyes drilled into her.

Uh-oh. Now this she hadn't expected. Bomb had access to her offshore bank accounts for emergency use, so money wasn't actually a problem. No, the problem was how long a situation like this could drag on. Not least because she'd bet that every time Bomb paid a ransom, no matter how much he handed over, it would never be quite enough.

"They're broke. My mom mops floors and cleans toilets at the local YMCA."

He nodded, though it was clear he was not satisfied with her answers.

"Please, I–I'll give you everything…" She sniffled and screwed up her face as if struggling to contain her tears. "Everything I have."

She was weak. A pathetically soft tourist from a pathetically soft country. She whimpered. "Please."

White Eyes turned sideways. "Did you do this?" He pointed. At the far end of the room was a guy in a Nike vest with dreadful acne and a guy with razor-sharp cheekbones. Between these two stood the fat guy from the pool room, now propping himself up on crutches, his leg in a cast. He had a bandage around his head, and two of his fingers were taped together and splinted.

Oh, crap. And she'd thought she might have been getting somewhere with her act.

There was little point in continuing the frightened-little-girl routine, so she spoke normally. "I'm sorry. Believe me. Look, how much do you want to make up for it? My PIN is 6-6-3-9. Take everything. Then, give me my phone. It's right there" – she nodded to her phone on the crate – "and I'll call my mom and they'll send, I don't know, maybe another seven or eight hundred bucks. That's two thousand US. That has to be a good deal, right?"

He ignored her, passed the ATM card to the guy with the cheekbones, and said something in their language.

White Eyes looked back at Tess. He leaned right down into her face. His breath stank of cheap cigarettes. "If you're lying, I'll send your mother an ear."

She shrank back from him as far as she could. "6-6-3-9. Just try it. 6-6-3-9."

White Eyes nodded to the other guy, who then left. He turned back to Tess. "We'll talk more later."

Instead of putting the bag completely over her head, he merely threw it over her so it draped over her face.

Tess heard him clomp away. The door creaked, then banged shut. The room fell silent again.

She couldn't believe they'd left her unguarded, so she didn't move. She strained to hear breathing, or shuffling, or breaking wind... anything to tell her someone was there.

Silence.

Maybe they had left her alone. If they had, this was the optimum time to make a break for it, hands tied or not.

She hung her head forward and shook the bag off.

The guy in the deck chair was staring directly at her. He didn't say a word, but instead raised a Glock semiautomatic. When she didn't move, he put the Glock in his lap, put his head back and gazed up at the ceiling in silence.

Great. Like it was ever going to be so easy.

The room was about thirty feet long by twenty across. Other than the door, there was a window on the wall to her right, which appeared to have some kind of metal mesh covering it. Instead of glass, plastic sheeting had been used that was so dirty and scuffed, nothing was visible.

The floor, if it could be called a floor, was uneven and plastered with muddy footprints, being formed from wooden panels laid out checkerboard-fashion on the ground. Dirt squeezed up between some of the joints.

She looked at the door. That was her only way out.

Tess's titanium armor was custom-made, designed not just to be light and incredibly strong, but also discreet. Because it was a cool night, she'd kept her leather jacket zipped up, so they hadn't discovered her bulletproof vest or shin and forearm guards.

So, the good news was she was all geared up for battle.

The bad news?

Her hands were bound behind her back. She didn't have a clue where she was. And there could be a whole army of thugs sitting just beyond that door, each one polishing a bigger gun than the next.

As good-news-bad-news scenarios went, this one seemed hellishly lopsided.

She drew a long, calming breath as she studied her options. As far as she could figure, she had just three.

The easiest choice was for her to sit it out and hope a reasonable ransom was enough to get her back to the States. Alternatively, she could fight her way out using just her feet. Finally, she could use an old standby to somehow turn the tables – sex.

Each had its pros and cons, but which gave the best overall odds of success?

With her head bowed, she stole a crafty look at the guy in the deck chair. Completely expressionless, he stuck a finger up his right nostril and had a good dig around.

Tess could disembowel a target with her bare hands, but seeing someone with a finger up their nose turned her stomach. She looked away, cringing at the thought of what other filthy habits he might have.

According to her guidebook, AIDS was still rife in Africa. The book recommended abstaining from sex with strangers or indulging only with the utmost care and quality protection. Thanks to poverty, arrogance, and ignorance, nearly twenty percent of the adult population had the illness. That meant of the five guys who had been in the room, statistically, one of them was infected.

The problem was that the longer she was here, the more her captors would look on her not as a person, but as something they owned. She might become nothing but a sex toy to them, something they'd come and bang whenever they were bored and had nothing better to do. Would they use the 'utmost care and quality protection'?

She had to get out.

Get out now.

Get out whatever it took.

She looked at Nose-Picker. *Whatever* it took.

Chapter 31

SOMEWHERE CLOSE BY outside the room in which Tess was bound, someone kick-started a motorcycle and then roared away. That was probably the guy with her ATM card. Great, now even if she got out, she had no funds to be able to get anywhere safe.

Nose-Picker still slouched in his chair, finger digging away.

Tess said, "Excuse me."

Nose-Picker didn't respond in any way.

"Could I get some water, please?"

Nose-Picker said nothing. Didn't even look at her. Instead, he picked his Glock back up with his free hand and, resting it on his thigh, aimed it directly at her.

Tess didn't give up. "I'll make it worth your while."

His head slowly moved so he could look at her. He stared, expressionless, as though there was absolutely nothing behind his eyes.

Tess winked at him, then slowly spread her legs wide apart, so there could be no misinterpretation.

He didn't move. Just froze with his finger still up his nose. But his gaze flicked to her crotch.

Finally removing his finger from his nostril, he looked around at the door and listened for a moment. No footsteps approached and the voices still seemed yards away. He pushed up out of his deck chair, then tucked his gun into the back of his waistband under his red soccer shirt, as he sauntered toward her.

He reached out his right hand and combed his fingers through her hair. The same fingers with which he'd picked his nose. Tess nuzzled against this hand. Her stomach churned, but outwardly, she tried to smile as best she could.

She eyed his crotch, making sure he could see her doing it, then she licked her lips.

He smirked, then tossed his Glock onto the deck chair.

Talk about dumb. Hell, sometimes it was almost too easy.

This guy had obviously been told how she had torn three of his friends apart with her bare hands, but he must have figured he was perfectly safe. After all, what danger could one scrawny chick be to a hard man like him? Especially a chick who was tied up? And with all his gun-toting buddies just feet away? How much safer could he possibly be?

After a quick glance back at the door to double-check that no one was coming, he unfastened his jeans and let them drop to the floor. He then hoisted up his red soccer shirt. There was a pronounced mound in the front of his gray shorts next to what looked like a urine stain. Sadly for his ego, the stain drew the eye far more than the mound. So much for the urban myth about black guys.

Looking up into his eyes, she whispered, "My hands."

He didn't say a word, but merely sneered.

Okay, this guy was dumb, but even his stupidity had limits.

He stuck his hand down his shorts and eased out his dick.

Tess wished she could have the oily rag stuffed back in her mouth to deaden the smell of stale sweat, dried urine, and spent semen – he really was every girl's dream guy. She ached to pull away. To breathe clean, fresh air. To brush her teeth and gargle with mouthwash... But if she was ever to get out of here, she was going to have to see this through. One way or the other.

Trying to breathe as shallowly as possible, while struggling not to hurl, she smiled up at him.

He stared down at her with a stupid smug grin.

Yep, this guy thought he was in complete control. Moron.

But then he grabbed the back of her head to pull her toward his crotch.

Tess flinched at being manhandled. She pictured the van. Saw the gang rearing over her. Felt pawing hands.

Her heart rate skyrocketed in an instant. She wanted to break away. Run. Run like hell and never look back.

But she stayed rooted to the chair. She clenched her mind as she would her fist. Made it hard enough to smash down any barrier. Used her will to overpower her animal instincts.

Run?

Run where? How?

No, she had one option. And the only way she was going to survive this was to play it out.

For just a moment, she screwed her eyes closed and thought of her tranquil spot beside her lake back home. Forced her mind as calm as those still waters. She had one chance. One chance to live.

Nose-Picker tugged harder on the back of her head.

Tess gulped a breath.

Now or never.

Struggling to keep down the steak dinner she'd enjoyed, she ever so gently rose to stand, slowly enough not to spook him, coy enough not to upset him.

Eye to eye, she again smiled at him. Then headbutted him full in the face.

He staggered back, clutching his nose. Obviously dazed. Tripping over the pants knotted around his ankles, he almost fell. Almost. But he shuffled his feet and managed to stay upright.

Now, Tess had to finish him. Fast.

She spun around backwards.

Her leg shot up and out in a wide arc.

Her foot slammed into the side of his head.

He fell sideways and smashed into the floor.

Tess leapt on his back, her legs on either side of his head.

Still dazed and acting on instinct, he tried to push himself up.

The moment his head lifted off the floor, Tess hooked her right knee around his neck and wedged her ankle on top of her left thigh, trapping his head.

She leaned back.

Pushed up with her left leg.

Bent his neck way, way back.

197

He bucked. Clawed at her legs with his hands.

Horrible cackling, spluttering sounds came from the guy as he struggled to breathe and fought to cry out for help. But she'd caught him so tightly under the chin, his mouth was clamped shut.

Tess heaved back even harder.

He flailed. Spluttered. Then...

His neck crunched and he fell limp.

Tess rolled off. Without stopping for a breath, she scrambled across the floor to the crate and her backpack.

Getting in so close had been her only option because launching any other kind of attack could too easily have ended in failure: a kick to the head could have missed, or to the knee would have given him cause to cry out and thereby alert his friends. On top of that, his pants around his ankles had shackled his legs almost as much as the tape around her wrists had immobilized her hands. That had been a great equalizer.

With her hands tied behind her back, Tess had to rummage inside, identifying things by feel alone. Finally, she found her tiny knife. She opened the blade and sawed at the tape imprisoning her. Once she'd made a decent-sized cut, she pried her hands apart and the tape snapped.

She was free.

But still imprisoned God only knew where, by God only knew how many armed thugs.

She looked at the door. What was her next move?

Chapter 32

TESS CHECKED THE rounds in Nose-Picker's Glock: seventeen. She raced to the window and eased the striped cloth aside. The plastic sheeting was so filthy and scuffed it was impossible to see anything in the darkness outside. But seeing out wasn't the problem – getting out was.

A sheet of thick wire mesh covered the inside of the window. Tess pulled on it.

Fixed tight.

She planted her foot on the wall and heaved to get more weight behind it.

Didn't budge. She wasn't getting out that way.

At the back of the room, Tess levered up one of the wooden panels from the floor. Underneath was dirt. Solid dirt. So solid, she'd have a problem getting through it with a spade.

Tess looked up. The corrugated metal sheeting that formed the roof was either nailed or screwed into wooden joists. She could probably lever one up, but not without making a hell of a noise as the metal warped and scraped.

She couldn't go through the window. She couldn't go under the wall. She couldn't go through the roof. That left just one option.

She glared at the door.

Fearing someone might walk through the door at any second, Tess dashed to Nose-Picker and searched the right-hand pocket of his crumpled jeans, now twisted around his ankles. She stuffed a few rand into her jacket pocket. There wasn't much, but as she'd lost her ATM card, she needed every cent she could get. In his other pocket, she felt something small and hard. She pulled it out – an electronic key for a car. Now if she could find that, she'd have a chance.

Standing at the door, Tess drew a long slow breath, held it, then exhaled equally slowly. Slowing her breathing slowed her physiology and thereby steadied her mind. Adrenaline was great in the middle of a fight to boost her strength, but it did that at the expense of rational thought. Now, she needed a plan, and for that she needed a clear head.

Breathing slowly, she stared at the unpainted wooden door. If only she knew what was waiting on the other side.

One of her grandpa's favorite films had been *Butch Cassidy and the Sundance Kid*. If she'd sat on his knee and watched it once, she'd watched it a dozen times. Trapped here as she was, she couldn't help but picture those final few frames.

Tess lowered the flame on the lamp until it was all but out and then draped the coarse cloth bag over it to hide what little light it still shed – she didn't want to extinguish it in case she needed it later. Then, she took one last deep breath. Her heart hammered. How many guns waited for her on the other side, she had no idea. But whether it was three or one hundred and three, she had to open that door.

She pulled the door to open it just a crack.

But the door stuck.

She twisted the doorknob the other way and tried again.

Still stuck.

Was it locked or just jammed? She hadn't heard a lock click, so considering the dilapidated condition of the room, she guessed it was the latter.

She heaved a third time. The door opened, but creaked. Tess cringed and froze.

Holding her breath, she waited. Imagining the sound of stampeding footsteps heading her way any second.

Nothing.

Daring to breathe again, she peeked out through a small gap.

The room wasn't a room but a shack. Outside was *outside*. The clear night sky allowed the moonlight to illuminate shoddily made one-story brick buildings lining a wide dirt path. About fifty feet away, the building directly opposite had a porch. Beer bottles were scattered along a rectangular wooden table at which sat White Eyes and four other men, all talking loudly.

No car was in sight.

Tess eased the door almost closed, just leaving it open a fraction so it wouldn't stick again.

She had seventeen rounds against five men. Mathematically, that was an easy calculation, but realistically? Unfortunately, people tended to move when they were shot at, so no way could she shoot all five guys before some of them took cover and returned fire. Not to mention, she had no idea how many other guys might come running out of the nearby buildings, guns blazing.

On top of that, she didn't have a clue where her getaway vehicle was. Or even if it was drivable. For all she knew, it could be out of gas or even up on bricks.

No, there was a time for a full-on confrontation and a time for subtlety. If she played this right, she'd be away into the night without a single shot fired, and those thugs wouldn't even know it.

After extinguishing the light and snagging the bag that had been used to cover her head, Tess opened the door again and then lay down on the floor. She put the bag over her hand, then held the compact from her backpack in it. Easing her hand out at ground level, she hoped that if anyone saw it they'd only see an old rag and not study it long enough to realize it was moving. Tess turned the mirror left – four cars were parked about seventy feet away. Angling the mirror right revealed at least two cars, possibly three, the closest about one hundred feet away. Everything else was just a black blob in the darkness.

She pulled her hand back in.

One of those six vehicles might be her getaway car. But which? No way could she go running blindly into the night, just hoping to stumble upon the right vehicle. And no way could she risk clicking a button on the key from the shack to see if any of the cars responded – the car could be parked out of sight but so close that having the lights flash or the security system beep would arouse suspicion.

No, she had to know where to run to. Or at least to somehow stack the odds in her favor.

She leaned back against the door. Drew a couple of slow breaths to keep clear her mind.

Statistically, it made sense to go left because there were more cars there, which were also closer. She had to play the odds, and those were the best she was going to get.

But if she was wrong...

No. She couldn't think like that. This was not the time to second-guess herself.

There was only one way she was going to get out of here, and she had to do it now – there was no telling how long the biker would be getting to and from the ATM with her card. Once he was back, White Eyes would want that other chat. And after what she'd done to Nose-Picker, that could only end one way – bullets tearing in all directions.

No, she had to go and she had to go now. But which way?

She took another calming breath, then peeked outside again. She had to get this right. Had to.

There was one scrap of good news: an overturned armchair had been thrown out onto what passed for a sidewalk and was only about twelve feet from the door. If she could get to that, she'd be able to have a much better view of the area and, if she was really lucky, maybe even activate the car key without drawing too much attention to see if any of the vehicles responded.

So that was it. Her gut instinct said she was going left. More cars. Closer. And an object for cover. It was the only option that made sense.

Her heart hammering despite her breathing technique, she crawled out through the door into the night, staying as close to the ground as she could, gun in one hand, car key in the other.

The moment she was outside, she scurried over and dove behind the chair. She squashed herself against it.

Tess gulped, her mouth as dry as the baked earth beneath the shack. She took a moment to calm herself with her breathing again.

On the right of the shack, a narrow alleyway led away between the one-story buildings. Shadows drenched it in darkness, but in her situation, darkness was most welcome. If her luck continued, she might be able to circle around the back of the buildings and reach that first group of cars without being seen. If the key belonged to one of them, she could be away without the gang ever knowing. And if it didn't, she could just double back through the shadows to the other cars.

This really was going to be much easier than she'd thought. What had she been so worried about?

Without risking poking her head out to see what the men were doing, she broke cover for the alley. She dashed around the corner of the shack and pinned herself to the wall.

Her breathing came in fast gasps even though she'd exerted no energy. She swallowed hard again.

Maybe, just maybe, this was going to work.

Tess skulked down the alley, basking in the blackness. A chain-link fence bordered the land at the back of the shack, while the building on the other side had a fence made from odd cuts of wood. It was hard to see much of anything it was so dark. Tess stumbled over a rock sticking up out of the path. She grabbed the chain-link fence to save from falling. It rattled loudly. Or at least, loudly to her. Again, she held her breath and shrank as far back into the blackness as she could.

She heard nothing. Saw nothing.

Continuing along the passageway, she passed more buildings, all shrouded in darkness.

The scent of urine and feces hung in the air. Tess looked at the building beside her. Okay, the people were poor, but there must be water somewhere, so there was no excuse for their house to stink like a public toilet in a small-town Chinese bus station.

The alley curved around to follow the walls of a building before opening out onto another narrow dirt road. The smell was stronger here. Maybe it wasn't the house that stank but something else.

Tess warily peeked around the corner of the wall to make sure the coast was clear. Nothing stirred. Not even the wind.

Hell, this really *was* going to work.

The new road only had buildings on the near side, the far side being some wasteland and a row of ten upright wooden boxes around seven feet tall. The stench was almost overpowering now. Then it dawned on her – these houses didn't have running water, so residents would have to suffer communal toilets. Damn, she was slow at times.

She crept toward the row of outdoor toilets. There were no buildings immediately behind them, so there'd be no one to spot her. She might even be able to forget about the car and simply walk out of the township to a main road. The thugs would have no idea which way she'd gone and no idea where to look for her.

Tess glanced back to ensure she wasn't being followed, then approached the first toilet. And the door opened.

In the moonlight, she clearly saw the acne-riddled face of the man who'd been in the shack with Fat Guy and White Eyes.

He moved to pull a gun from his belt, but before he could draw it, Tess attacked.

She couldn't risk firing the gun and losing all the advantage she'd worked so hard to gain, so she slammed a kick into his knee. Even as his leg buckled and he was falling, she pistol-whipped him across the head.

He hit the ground and didn't move.

She blew out a heavy breath. That was too close.

Again, she glanced around to make sure no one was in the vicinity, then she knelt and grabbed for his gun – a six-shot Smith and Wesson revolver. Placing hers on the ground, she pushed the cylinder release and swung the cylinder out to check how many chambers were loaded. All six.

Yep, things were going great. She couldn't have asked for better.

Another toilet door opened.

Tess gasped.

Fat Guy hobbled out, zipping up his trousers and sniggering as he said something in that native language. Their eyes met.

He grabbed for a gun but fumbled it because of his finger splint.

Tess was quicker and made no such mistakes. She slammed the cylinder back into the revolver. Aimed. Squeezed the trigger.

Two slugs ripped into Fat Guy. One in the chest. One in the head. He reeled away and fell back inside the toilet.

Shouts came from back the way Tess had come before Fat Guy had even hit the ground.

Yep, things were going just great.

Tess bolted.

She couldn't go back the way she'd come, and now sneaking out of the place to safety was impossible. The car was her only hope.

Heading for the next alley she could see, she prayed she'd be able to circle back to where she'd seen the parked cars.

Voices shouted. Lights lit in some of the buildings. Footsteps pounded the ground.

As Tess reached the building on the corner of the alley, a gun thundered. She ducked as bullets tore into the metal wall with loud metallic cracks.

Tess dove around the corner and into the alley. But she stopped.

She crouched.

Waited.

Just a black mound lost in the blackness.

Two shapes shouting in that foreign language rounded the corner. Tess opened up with a gun in each hand. Two shots slammed into each man. Both in the chest. As if in some macabre ballet, they staggered back side by side and then both slowly turned to face each other and crumpled to the ground.

Tess was already tearing down the alley. She'd had to nail them. These guys knew the area, but she didn't, so she couldn't risk them knowing the direction she was taking, calling to the others, and them cutting her off.

207

With the proverbial cat out of the bag, Tess had nothing to lose by clicking the car key. She prayed she'd hear a beep nearby. She clicked the button. Far away to her right, a car security system beeped.

"Goddamnit." On leaving the shack, she'd picked the wrong way to go. It had been fifty-fifty. And her gut instinct had sent her the wrong way. Maybe Bomb was right and she was so messed up, she wasn't capable of working a job like this anymore.

"What the...?" This was not the time for self-recrimination. While she was enjoying beating herself up, some a-hole could just wander up and put a slug in her back. She bowed her head for a moment and took a steadying breath.

Focus. She had to focus.

At least now she knew roughly where the car was, so things just couldn't get any worse, only better. She darted down the alley once more.

Angry voices came from ahead.

She skidded to a stop.

More came from behind her.

With her back pinned to the concrete wall of a building, she peered up and down the alley, a gun pointing in each direction. She was trapped.

Chapter 33

HER HEART POUNDED like an express train as she glared up and down the alley. They'd be here any second. What the hell could she do with so little ammo?

Then it dawned on her – there was only one option open to her.

Tess stuffed both weapons in her belt and then heaved herself up the wall of the shack. A moment later, she scrambled across the roof of the one-story building. There was still a chance. If they didn't catch a glimpse of her up here, they might never think to look up, so she might, just might, be able to make it all the way to the car unseen.

The next building was about five feet away. Tess cleared the gap easily. With an almighty clatter, she landed on the metallic roof of the next building. Running from the moment she landed, every footstep was like she was hitting a giant gong with a sledge hammer.

She sprinted for the next gap ahead of about eight feet.

Tess tore for the edge. She leapt.

As she sailed through the darkness, guns blasted from somewhere below and behind her. A slug slammed her in the back.

A small-caliber handgun bullet wouldn't knock a person off their feet, no matter what Hollywood liked its audience to believe, and it certainly couldn't penetrate her Level IIIA vest. But the shock of being hit, and the jolt it gave her, made her arch her back in pain, knocking her off her line.

She slammed hard into the next roof, skidding across the concrete.

Rolling up to one knee, she swung around.

Took aim at the shadowy alley.

Blasted.

Both barrels.

Four slugs roared away into the night in four different directions.

Without waiting to see the result of her marksmanship, Tess dropped the empty revolver and was up and running again.

Behind her, someone cried out as a slug ripped into them. But someone else shot up at her again.

Missed.

To her right, flashlights jerked up another alley as their owners ran to intercept her. She leapt over the alley and tore across the next roof.

More shots zipped past her. But not from below – someone was up on the rooftops with her.

She spun.

Pulled the trigger.

Blasted three shots at a black shadow running over the roof four buildings back. The figure cried out, staggered, and fell off the roof into the blackness.

Tearing across the roof, Tess pressed the Unlock button on the car key. About thirty yards away, a car beeped and its lights flashed. Almost there.

Tess cleared another couple of roofs, then leapt down onto the main dirt track around ninety feet from the shack. Dashing to a silver sedan, she slammed a slug into the nearest tire of two other cars parked close by, then jumped into the vehicle.

She prayed it would start the first time and that, unlike in some corny movie, it wouldn't take three attempts and she'd only get away just as the bad guys clawed at the car.

The engine roared into action first time. Finally, a bit of luck.

But the car was pointing in the wrong direction, back toward the shack in which she'd been held captive, the direction from which the thugs were coming. The track too narrow to turn around without having to reverse at least twice, she had no choice – she slammed the stick into first gear and roared away.

As she stormed past the shack, three guys ran out of the alley alongside. By the time they'd realized she was in the car, she was past them.

They opened up on the car, firing like drunks at a fun fair, desperate to impress their girlfriend by winning a giant teddy bear.

The rear windshield shattered. Slugs pelted the bodywork.

Two other guys ran out of the next alley ahead on the left. They stood in the middle of the track and took aim.

Tess didn't wait. She fired through her open side window.

211

But the rough track jerked the car around so much her shots flew wild.

The thugs in the street didn't have that problem. They cut loose with everything they had.

Slugs hammered into the windshield, into the hood, into the lights, like it was raining lead.

Tess leaned sideways to hide behind the dash and heaved down on the wheel so the car jerked to the right. Turning, she blindly fired out of the window, just hoping she'd hit something.

As Tess hung a sharp right to tear down a sidetrack, she plowed straight through the corner of a metal shack, bringing the wall crashing down.

Bullets zipped at her from behind.

Tess hit the gas. Hard.

The car jerked and bounced, pummeling Tess as it careened down the rutted track between the buildings.

The car hit a particularly big pothole and veered to the left. It scraped down the side of a metal building. Sparks flew and metal screeched against metal. Tess eased the wheel back and brought the car under control.

The firing had stopped, so she glanced around.

The main track was so far behind her, she couldn't even see it now, let alone anyone up there running after her.

She'd done it – she'd escaped.

Tess blew out a huge breath and dragged her forearm over her brow. That had been way too close.

Now all she had to do was keep going in a straight line and at some point, she'd hit a real road and be able to get back to the city and safety.

There was still nothing following her, so she eased off the gas. The last thing she needed was to smash into something in the dark and ruin everything just when she was safe.

Then a strange grinding noise came from under the hood. Within seconds, the car lost power and decelerated.

Tess gasped. She stamped on the gas. But her speed slowed instead of quickened.

Smoke leaked from under the hood. A bullet must have hit something vital. After a few more yards, the car was barely crawling.

Tess punched the dash. "Come on, come on. Don't die on me now."

She pumped the gas. Changed to a lower gear as the engine struggled.

But the car got slower and slower.

Then it stopped.

She snatched her gun from the passenger seat. Though she'd counted as she'd shot, so she knew there was no real need, she checked the mag. One slug.

She leapt out of the car and looked back. Far in the distance, lights flickered.

Oh God, they were coming.

Her heart pounding, she ran, eyes desperately scanning for any sort of escape. The row of buildings on either side were homes. Homes belonging to ordinary people who had no choice but to live here and suffer the violence and squalor. No one would let her in knowing a vicious gang could storm in any moment, guns blazing. Who would put their own life at risk to rescue a stranger, especially when they didn't know what that stranger had done to anger a gang so?

No, her only chance was to run. Run and never stop till she hit asphalt and could flag down a bus or a taxi.

Twenty yards further, Tess came to an X-shaped intersection in the heart of the township. She pulled up in the middle of it, desperately glancing from one dirt road to the next. Two roads went in kind of the direction she thought might lead to the city, both of which curved so she couldn't see where they led. The remaining road veered off in the general direction of where she'd started, but again, she couldn't see the end of that either. The place was a maze. It would be hard enough finding her way around in daytime, but in darkness, it was impossible.

She stared at the two roads, switching rapidly from one to the other. Another fifty-fifty choice. Another that could save her or kill her. What did her gut say? And whatever it said, could she trust it?

If she'd made a better choice on leaving the shack, she'd already be out of this hellhole and the gang wouldn't even know.

What the hell was she going to do?

She stared at the one on the left. Would that take her home?

Then the one on the right. She buried her face in her hands. How could she choose?

She looked again. Still just two dark roads disappearing into blackness.

She spun around. Behind her, flashlights jerked around the alley down which she'd run. They were coming.

Standing at the intersection, she rubbed her brow. Two roads to choose from. Either might go to where she wanted to go. Or neither. Which to take?

The flashlights got closer and closer.

The shouts louder and louder.

And she still had two roads. And still only one bullet.

What was she going to do? What was she going to do?

Someone nonchalantly cleared their throat some distance behind her.

She spun around. Aimed her gun with both hands.

A man with a graying beard sat on a wooden rocking chair outside one of the buildings. He blew a cloud of smoke up into the night sky, then reached around and pushed open the door to his home. Light flooded out.

Tess stared at him. Was he trying to help her? Or was he trying to trap her in the hope of getting a reward?

Without saying a word, he rocked on his chair, hands clasped over a bulbous beer belly.

Tess looked at the two dirt roads. One could lead to her way out. Or both could lead to her death. She looked again at the man. At his open door. At light and safety.

The man gently rocked back and forth. The tip of the cigarette in his lips glowed bright red, then he blew another cloud of smoke.

Shouts came louder from the alley behind her. Beams from the flashlights shone more brightly.

The man stared at her with a calmness in his eyes. "I'd get your bony ass in here, if I was you."

Could she trust him?

In the alley, some of the furthest away flashlight beams silhouetted people running. So many black shapes storming toward her.

She checked the building. It had concrete walls. If she had to, she could hole up in there, blast the first goon that came through the door, and take his gun. With a full mag, she might be able to hold them off long enough for Bomb to get help from either the police or the US embassy. Assuming he could concoct a convincing enough lie for the authorities to be interested.

But that depended on her making a clean shot with her one round. And getting phone service in this god-awful place.

The shouts and lights were almost upon her.

Now, she had no choice. They were too close for her to run blindly into the night. They knew the area. They'd find her.

She dashed to the house. Flew through the door. Slammed it shut.

Chapter 34

TESS DIDN'T NOTICE anything about the interior of the house. She didn't see anything. Didn't smell anything. Didn't hear anything.

She stood. Barely daring to breathe. Gaze glued to the door handle. Gun raised.

Though she'd run barely more than a hundred yards, her heart pounded as if she'd just completed a triathlon.

She stared at the door.

Waited.

Beads of sweat ran down her face from her forehead.

Her gun felt slippery in her hands, but she dared not change her grip to wipe her palms. That very instant could be the moment someone came through the door, and if her aim was off by just a fraction, she might not down them, might not get their gun, might not ever see another sunrise.

Pounding footsteps came nearer. And raised voices. Ten or more of them.

Beams of light flickered on the thin red drapes of the window to the right of the door.

Tess held her breath.

She stared at the door. If someone walked through it, this could be her last few seconds on earth.

In their native tongue, angry voices shouted something outside, presumably to the man in the rocking chair. With the same calmness with which he'd spoken to her, he said something back to them.

More shouts came. Then finally, footsteps pounded away down one of the other tracks.

Tess didn't move.

Rooted to the spot like a statue, she stared at the door. Gun aimed squarely for a head shot.

Seconds crawled by.

Sweat ran into her eye. She squinted and blinked it away.

The door handle squeaked.

She gasped. Tightened her grip on the weapon. Looked straight down the sights.

The door opened. The man with the graying beard looked coolly at her, then waved the gun down. He closed the door and sat at a small table with a blue-and-white checker-patterned Formica top. At the other end of the table was a 1980s-style boombox with a twelve-inch television sitting on top of it, slightly lopsided. Beside this entertainment center was a kettle. He clicked it on and then reached for two of the four mugs alongside it.

Without looking up, he gestured to something behind Tess.

"Could you pass the milk when you've got a second?"

Tess gasped a huge breath.

Had she made it? Was she truly safe this time?

Her weary arms relaxed a little, dropping the gun a fraction.

He picked a tea bag from a battered cardboard box. "I hope you don't like it strong, because this is my last one."

Tess stared at the door. Quiet.

He said, "It was a nice thing you did in the square."

Tess frowned. And her gun lowered that little bit more.

Holding up a cracked white bowl, he said, "Sugar?"

She said nothing.

"I'll take that as a no." He dropped two spoons of sugar into one of the mugs. "These kids learn how to steal when they're still in diapers, so I don't think your gesture will make a scrap of difference, but you never know."

Tess's arms dropped till they were all but down.

The kettle made a bubbling sound as the water heated.

Watching steam come from the kettle, he said, "How are we doing with that milk?"

Finally, she looked at him. "You were in Greenmarket Square?"

"Someone has to sweep up all the litter you tourists drop." With his foot, he pushed out his other chair from being neatly positioned under the table. It scraped on the concrete floor.

She looked back at the door. And raised her gun again. She still wasn't a hundred percent sure all the gang had left the area.

"Tell me, are you always so forgiving?" he said.

Forgiving? Her? She couldn't help but snicker.

"So why this time?"

219

"An old friend once tried to convince me that a tiny act of kindness can change the world."

"Well" – he gestured to the chair – "hasn't it?"

It certainly appeared to have, though not in the way intended. But Tess shook her head. "I have to be sure they're gone."

"We won't be seeing them again tonight. They'll run around like headless chickens for a few hours, then get drunk and find some other poor grunt to pick on."

She looked at him. After all she'd been through, could it really all be so easy? Really all be over?

Without looking at her, he nodded to the chair.

Tess let her arms slowly fall. Finally, she pulled the chair further out to sit.

He held up his hand. "The milk?"

Behind Tess stood a tiny refrigerator. She opened it up. Inside was a cooked joint of meat with various bits hacked off it, some cheese wrapped in paper, a stick of celery, a few bottles of local beer, and a small bottle of milk about half-full. On top of the refrigerator stood a digital clock. It read 4:53 a.m. Her flight was 9:30.

She picked up the milk. It trembled in her hand with the nervous energy coursing through her body. She thought she'd finished with killing. Thought she'd left that death-filled life behind. How stupid she had been to believe walking away would be so easy.

Drawing a slow, steadying breath, she glanced at the man just as his gaze flicked from her to the kettle, as if he wanted her to believe he hadn't noticed her distressed state.

She passed him the milk. He nodded his thanks, then gestured for her to sit. She did so, putting the gun on the table beside her cup.

He shot her a sideways glance.

"Sorry." She picked up the gun and was going to drop it into her backpack, but he held out a blue plastic bucket with kitchen waste in the bottom.

He said, "I can make sure it's disposed of properly later."

Tess dropped it in. But noted where he put the bucket, just in case.

Behind him hung a long blue curtain, partly obscuring a second room. Tess could just see the end of a bed, the covers all messed up.

The kettle boiled and the man poured water into the cup with the tea bag in it. "I don't sleep much, these days. Age, you know. So if it's a choice between laying in here and staring at the ceiling, or sitting outside and staring at the stars…"

He pressed the teabag against the side of the mug with a bent spoon, then, for the first time since he came inside, he looked at her, as if expecting something.

She shrugged. "It's a long story. I—"

He held up a hand again. "I've seen the kind of person you are, and I know only too well the kind of people they are. Believe me, no way would I be sharing my last tea bag with someone who didn't deserve it."

He poured water into her mug and then quickly transferred the tea bag over with the spoon to avoid it dripping. "Now, you'll be wanting a way out of here."

"If I can get to a main road, where there's a taxi service or buses, I should be okay."

"Where is it you're staying?"

"A place on Long Street. But by the time I get back there, it'll be time for me to go to the airport for my flight home, so there's little point."

221

"So you just need to get to the airport."

"Yeah."

While pressing the tea bag in her mug, he nodded. He then added milk to both teas. Finally, he stirred his and took a drink.

Tess waited for him to offer information about transportation. But he didn't. He merely sat drinking his tea.

She stared at him. Waiting. But he said nothing.

What was wrong with this guy? He was supposed to be helping, not tormenting her.

When she could wait no more, she said, "So is there a bus route or anything nearby?"

"There is."

"So, I can get a bus to the airport?"

"You can." He took another sip of his tea. "Or I can drive you."

"You have a car?"

"A hovercraft."

"A hovercraft!"

"Made it myself from an old Volvo. It's great for getting across swampland."

"A hovercraft?" She wanted to sneak out, not draw crowds. "Seriously? You don't think it might draw the wrong kind of attention?"

"Tell me, are all Americans so gullible?" He winked at her. "Have I got a car? We might be poor here, but we aren't living in the Stone Age, you know."

Tess picked up her mug of tea. Steam swirled up from it. Yes, this place was poor, grimy, squalid, but it was safe. For now.

He held out his hand and the corners of his mouth turned up just enough for Tess to believe it was a smile. "Sipho."

Tess shook his hand. "Tess."

Sipho told her about the township, about the gangs, about proposing to his wife while they watched the sunrise from Table Mountain, and about how he'd lost her four years ago during a riot. He was now part of a neighborhood patrol that tried to improve the conditions and safety of the township. Unfortunately, thanks to the gangs, they were having very limited success. But success all the same.

Tess couldn't share details of how she was also trying to change the world for the better, not least for Sipho's own protection, but she could share the tale of that 'old friend' who'd inspired her act of kindness in the square. An act without which she'd be bleeding out in the gutter, instead of sitting there sipping warm tea. And all because she'd rescued an injured snake in a tiny Chinese town. Man, it was weird how the world worked.

Just after seven o'clock, Sipho fished out a green puffer jacket for her to wear. She put up the hood before leaving the house so her face was almost completely hidden. Sipho then guided her to his prized possession: his car. The vinyl seats were torn, the windshield had a crack running right across it, and the engine made a strange whirring sound whenever the vehicle turned right, but to Tess at that moment, it was better than a gold-plated Rolls Royce.

To avoid problems with airport security, Tess checked her backpack and then boarded her plane on time. She'd wanted to phone Bomb from the airport, but her phone had died. She'd found a charging point, but

223

then decided she had nothing new to tell him, and if he had more bad news to share it would only make her daylong journey all the more stressful. Phoning when she got back home seemed a better option.

She fastened her safety belt, settled back in her seat, and looked out the plane window at another beautifully sunny African day. It was a spectacular country. At least for a tourist with means. One day, she'd have to come back to explore it properly.

Her phone rang. It was not a number she recognized. Strange. She kept her number so private, only a handful of people had ever had it. Certainly no company had it to cold call. She'd check her voicemail later. Maybe change her number earlier than her schedule dictated.

Chapter 35

"TESS, I..." BOMB heaved a breath. It was most unlike him to be lost for words. "I don't know what to say, but I got nothing." He heaved another breath. "Hey, I can't tell you how sorry I am. But..."

If he didn't have anything, he couldn't conjure it out of thin air. Just like she couldn't.

Back home in Alpha apartment, Tess hammered her fist against the wall over her mantelpiece, staring at the unused plane ticket to China. It was over. Those bastards had gotten away with it. After all the sacrifices she'd made on behalf of others, what kind of a universe made her strike out on this job, the second-most-important job she'd ever taken on?

She looked at the date on the ticket. Looked at the boarding time. The gate number. It was all gone. Her new life was all gone. But worse, she'd never settle into *any* sort of life with this nightmare haunting her every waking breath.

No! She wasn't having this. There had to be something.

"Bomb, there must be something we're missing. We can't just let them get away with it. They've raped six goddamn women that we know of and God only knows how many that we don't. There must be something."

"Hell if I know what. In all the *Monster Bang* videos, plastic sheeting blacks out any identifying features of the van. Their masks never slip, even for a second, and the audio gives away absolutely squat. As for the email address you got in Cape Town – there's no IP data in the headers. I've tried phishing, but if they haven't bitten by now, they ain't going to."

"How about PayPal? Won't there be a street address registered?"

"Have you tried hacking PayPal? Without a back door, it's…" He sighed. "You've gone through the image files I sent you?"

"Before I left." It had taken her hours to scour all the portraits of med students that Bomb had found.

"And there's nothing?"

Finding nothing was so sickening, she didn't even answer.

"None of the victims you talked to have gotten back to you?"

Her voicemail was empty. She'd returned the call to that number she hadn't recognized but had got only a pay phone. It was likely kids, or some crank picking numbers at random.

Again, she didn't answer.

"Tess, I… I just don't know what to say. You know I never quit, but…"

Apart from his voice, no noises came from Bomb's end of the phone. It sounded so strange not to hear the clicking of his keyboard as he crunched data to crack the impossible. Had they truly reached the end?

No. She couldn't stop now. They couldn't just sit and pray another woman would be raped to give them a lead.

"Bomb, I... there must be... isn't there anything? Anything we... oh, Christ..."

"Tess" – Bomb's tone was serious, more serious than she could ever remember hearing before – "have you thought of just walking away from this one?"

"Bomb, there's something we're just not seeing, I know there is."

She pushed away from the mantel and paced around to behind the sofa. There was something. There had to be.

"Listen, Tess, the Veltman job nearly killed you, but did you feel the closure you thought you would when it was over?"

That was different. Completely different. She didn't answer.

"You devoted years to that job. Hell, it's defined your entire goddamn life. But when you got him, you said it yourself, you just didn't feel the way you thought you would. Now, what if this job goes down the same way? What if we spend the next ten years looking for these fuckers but never find them? That's another ten years of your life gone. Another ten years of struggle, when you could have had ten years of happiness."

"Happiness? How can I be happy, for Christ's sake?"

"You know what I mean. You could leave all this hurt and anguish behind. You could literally just walk away and be on a plane tomorrow. By this time on Saturday, you could be living the dream you've always wanted to."

She stopped pacing and hung her head, her mind a whirl of thoughts. Maybe he had a point.

"Tess, you can live that dream life. For God's sake, give me one good reason why you shouldn't grab it right now."

Rubbing her brow, Tess fought to find an answer. She wanted those bastards. She wanted to feel their blood on her hands. Wanted to feel their lives slowly draining away. Wanted the fury burning in her eyes to be the last thing they ever saw. But...

Her friend Indira would tell her to let it go.

And Chen Choa-An would tell her to let it go.

Hell, even that robotic bitch Antonnia Wosniak would tell her to let it go.

Tess sighed. Antonnia was right: how the event impacted Tess's future was entirely under Tess's control, and she could choose to not let it. But could she honestly make that choice?

An empty hollow twisted in her gut. Like someone had scooped out her insides with a giant melon baller. Just the thought of letting it go made her feel like she was being autopsied alive.

"Bomb, I'm sorry, but I can't talk now." She ended her conversation and slumped on the sofa.

Picking up the unused plane ticket to China, she sighed. She stared at the ticket. It had promised so much.

She shook her head. For the second time, she'd had her entire life ripped apart. Could she really turn a blind eye to all that hurt and just let it go?

"Fish, what do you think, buddy?"

He remained uncharacteristically quiet.

Tess huffed and returned to staring at her ticket.

Dragging over her backpack, she removed her tablet and fired it up. She gazed down at the ethereal landscape of the place she was supposed to be calling home now. A river snaked across a plain dotted with conical hills like a landscape from an alien world. Could she live there, work there, be happy there, knowing that those five bastards were still happy here?

After pulling up a comparison website, she checked for cheap flights to Hong Kong, that being the easiest place to get to from NYC to be able to travel onward to her prospective home in Guangxi Region.

Not because she wanted one. Just out of idle curiosity.

One flight caught her eye.

Curious, she clicked Flight Information. A new website appeared.

Knowing she could click away any moment she wanted to, she put her name into a little box.

Then her address. And passport number.

Before she even knew it, her personal details were complete.

Now what?

Her finger hovered over Buy Now.

Could she leave all this behind? Just walk away from everything she knew?

She pictured warm evenings sitting on her veranda with Fish, reading him Faulkner or Keats, pausing only to admire the river and those otherworldly limestone hills.

Could she leave behind pain and suffering and anguish?

Her finger tensed to click.

"Goddamn it!" She tossed the tablet to the far end of her sofa. There was no way she could do it. No way

229

she could run out on getting the justice she deserved, getting the blood she deserved.

But then she remembered Indira's tightrope. If Tess stayed in New York City and indulged in the killing spree she ached for, she might never be able to come back from that. And like her hunt for Veltman, the hunt for those five bastards could drag on for years. Years. Before she knew it, she could be 50 years old and still hunting them.

So, it was a simple choice: spend the best years of her life in pain and darkness, or get a flight and start a completely new life tomorrow. Literally.

She gazed at the tablet innocently lying at the far end of the sofa. At the 'Buy Now' button which begged her to click it.

Could she choose to leave it all behind and simply walk away?

She pulled her tablet back over. Raised her finger to click Buy.

A heavy knock on her apartment door stopped her dead.

Chapter 36

STILL SEATED ON her sofa, Tess craned around to stare at her door. Another knock came. She cringed. She never had callers. Never. And no one knew she was here anyway. Who the hell was that?

She glanced at Fish. He didn't seem anywhere near as perturbed as she was. Why not? Especially when it was all his fault. Every time she moved him, there was a risk she'd hurt him either through accidentally dropping him or shocking his system by immersing him in different water. That was the only reason she was at Alpha and not safe at Gamma still.

Not that she blamed him.

People thought fish were brainless blobs that floated around in water doing nothing and thinking nothing. But Tess knew differently. She knew they were living creatures with intelligence and personalities. Recent scientific evidence backed her up, suggesting that fish could not only recognize the different faces of other fish, but might actually be able to recognize their owner's face. Not a surprising discovery to anyone who cared about their fish.

Risking her life was one thing. Risking Fish? Hell, no. This was his home, so this was where he stayed whenever possible.

Another knock.

Tess winced. Now she knew who it was. And knew he wasn't going to go away anytime soon. If ever.

Detective Josh Hardy called through the door, "Tess, I know you're in there. I just need to make sure everything is okay."

Silent, she stared at Fish. Fish stared back. Still completely unfazed.

"Tess, can you open up, please? I need to know."

She held her breath. Tried to make herself as small as possible. Even though she knew he couldn't see or hear her.

"Do you honestly think I won't kick this door in if I have to?"

"Goddamnit." Tess trudged over and opened the door.

"See?" She twirled around in front of Josh. "I'm okay." So was that good enough for him? Would he fuck off now? If she couldn't be with him, why did he believe she wanted him here, rubbing her face in it? As if she didn't have enough to cope with.

"So are you going to let me in?" he asked.

"Twice in one week?"

He glared, obviously out of patience.

She sighed, stepped aside and ushered him in. Under her breath, she said, "Another fine mess you've gotten me into."

He glowered. "Really? Now?"

"What...?" The first time they'd met, Tess had referenced Laurel and Hardy as a joke, but it had

232

backfired completely, so she'd never brought it up again. "Oh, no, I was talking to Fish. Honest."

"You're blaming Fish?"

"It's his goddamn fault." It was, but saying it out loud didn't seem to have the same impact as it had in her head.

She slunk back to the sofa like a teenager who'd been caught smoking and slumped down onto it.

"So, how did you know I was here?"

"I offered fifty bucks to whichever of your neighbors called when they saw you."

"Oh." She'd have to find out which one had squealed. Then Bomb could crucify their credit history and get them thrown out of the building – she couldn't risk a nosy neighbor spying on her. God only knew who they might inform and about what.

He looked at her expectantly. "So?"

"Hmmm?"

"So how are you doing?"

Shrugging, she said, "Well, I'm not curled up in the bottom of my shower sobbing every day, if that's what you mean." It wasn't a lie – she'd done her sobbing on the bathroom floor, not in the shower.

"Have you considered the support group the hospital mentioned?"

Tess rubbed her face and drew a huge breath. "Look, I appreciate your concern and all, Josh, but let's face it, I'm not your problem, am I?"

"That doesn't mean I can't be concerned about you."

"Yeah, well, you might want to run that past the lovely Christine." She'd bet he hadn't told his present girlfriend he was helping out his previous one.

Smirking, he shook his head. "You know what, I'm going to let that one go because of what you've been through. Now, are you up-to-date with your meds?"

"My meds are fine. I'm fine. Everything's fine. Now, is this a social call, or are you going to tell me your colleagues have finally gotten off their asses and caught those bastards?"

"The detectives assigned to the case are good guys. I talked to them just yesterday, so I know they're doing all they can. Believe me, if they weren't, I'd be all over them."

"But no arrests anytime soon."

Realizing she'd left her tablet lying face up on the sofa with a ticket to China visible, she snagged it as she stood up and ambled toward the kitchen.

"Tea?" she said as innocently as possible.

"Look, forget the goddamn tea and talk to me, will you?"

"About what?"

He closed the space between them. Not so close that they were touching, but close enough that she could smell his Paco Rabane. She'd missed that.

"Tess, I can appreciate how angry you must be, but—"

"You can, can you?" Tears welled in her eyes. "Tell me, can you *appreciate* having five filthy dicks shoved inside you and you can't do a fucking thing about it?"

"Hey, I'm sorry." He stepped closer. Reached out. Lightly touched her arm. "I—"

She pulled away, wiping her eyes. "Don't." She shook her head vigorously. "Just don't."

His voice soothing, he said, "Sit down. Take a moment. And I'll make the tea."

"Don't you dare try to handle me like some goddamn helpless victim." She turned sideways, so she didn't have to look at him, and to put emotional distance between them.

He drew a heavy breath, but his voice remained calm. "Tess, I'm not trying to handle you. I'm seriously worried. That's why I'm here."

Without looking at him, Tess pulled further away. "Yeah, well, maybe I don't want you here. You ever think of that?"

He held his hands up in a conciliatory fashion. "That's okay. If you don't want company, I can get out of your hair."

Like a petulant child, Tess said, "Well, I don't want company."

Even as she said it, she knew she was lying. She ached to feel him hold her. To feel him comfort her. To feel his strong arms around her like a shield. She could kill him in just seconds with her bare hands, but she yearned to run to him and let him hold and protect her. God, she was pitiful. Tears welled again.

"Well, okay, then," he said. "If you don't want company, you don't want company."

He trudged toward the door. As he passed Fish's table, he placed his card on it. "There's my number, in case you've lost it. If you need anything – day or night – call me."

He waved a finger at Fish. "Look after her, buddy."

Tess bit her lip to fight back the tears. And the urge to run to him. That was the sweetest gesture she'd ever known.

235

Josh tramped to the door. She let him.

Pulling open the apartment door, he turned. "Tess, I—"

"Don't dawdle. You don't want Christine worrying where you are."

He hesitated a moment, as if he was about to say something, then turned and left. He didn't even have the decency to slam the door after him. Maybe he wasn't the strong man she'd always thought he was.

Tess stared at the door. Why, she wasn't sure. To see it open again? To ensure it didn't? To run through it? To run to lock it?

It remained shut.

And she remained rooted to the spot.

Her chin quivered. She felt as if someone had opened up her rib cage with one of Myron's retractors and then stamped on her heart.

She gasped a gigantic faltering breath.

A single tear escaped to roll down her cheek. Tess swiped it away. "What the hell's wrong with you, you weak-willed bitch?"

She kicked her bookcase. The top shelf flew off and her books scattered across the floor.

She shook her head. "Weak? I'll give you fucking weak."

Tess whipped up her tablet. Clicked Buy Now.

To hell with this goddamn place. She was going to China. Tomorrow.

Chapter 37

AS THE EARLY-MORNING sun streamed through her living room window, Tess slung her rucksack onto her back, shuffled it on her shoulders to get comfortable, then picked up her small backpack. Bomb had agreed to send everything else on for her, including her second rucksack, which she just couldn't be bothered to struggle with.

Picking Fish up from his table, she peered into the transparent plastic travel container in which he swam.

"Ready for our big adventure, Fish?"

She hoped the Homeland website had been correct in recommending this container, and that she wouldn't have problems with JFK airport's security. Unfortunately, she would bet it wasn't going to be straightforward. It never was with those by-the-rules jerks. But seriously, what could anyone smuggle inside a live fish?

After placing the container inside a padded bag for protection, she strode to her door. This was it. Goodbye, New York City. "And good goddamn riddance."

Tess whipped open the door, stormed out, and slammed it behind her.

As she marched down the dingy blue hall, her phone rang. Her hands full, she fumbled to get her phone out of her jacket pocket, only to find the number was unrecognized. Again. But it was impossible it would be another crank call.

Please don't let it be the airline saying there was a problem with her flight.

"Hello?"

"Miss Williams?"

"This is she."

"Antonnia Wosniak. We spoke recently."

Oh God, what did that anal-retentive control freak want now?

"Look, I'm sorry," said Tess, "but now isn't a good time." She hung up.

She marched for the stairs. Passing the door two down from the stairwell, she glared at it. She'd bet it was that old busybody that had phoned Josh. It was a good thing she was leaving, or else—

Her phone rang again. "Oh, goddamn it." Checking it, she saw it was the same number. She ignored it and stuffed it back into her pocket. To hell with the bitch.

She yanked open the stairwell door and started down the steps with her phone still ringing. It was strange to think this was the last time she'd ever see this god-awful flowery stair carpet that looked like a reject from a 1960s hippie commune.

Finally, her phone was silent. No doubt it had gone to voicemail.

But then it started ringing again.

"Oh, for fuck's sake," said Tess as she pulled the phone from her pocket. She answered it. "What?"

238

Antonnia spoke meekly, not with the commanding tone she'd had in the conference room. It sounded like she'd been crying.

Antonnia said, "I'm sorry to disturb you, Miss Williams, but you asked me to call if I remembered anything."

Tess gasped, the shock of Antonnia's words making her fumble Fish. He slipped from her grasp.

She grabbed, desperate to save her best friend. She caught him and cradled him in both arms, relief washing over her, but she'd dropped her phone in the process.

It bounced down the steps. She scurried after it. Snatched it back up.

"Miss Wosniak?"

"Yes?"

"Sorry, I thought I'd lost you. What is it you want to tell me?"

"I'm not sure. I... I don't know if it's real or not. It was probably talking to you, another victim, that triggered something. Maybe it unblocked a repressed memory. I... I'm just not sure."

A flicker of hope reignited in the pit of Tess's stomach.

"It might be nothing, yes, but you obviously think it's important enough to call. So...?"

After all the trauma, anguish, and disappointment of the last few days, Tess couldn't help but feel hope welling up from within her. But she didn't want it. She struggled to quash it. Struggled to remain detached. Struggled not to suffer even more heartache at even more failure. Even so, she couldn't help but mouth to herself, "Please let it be a name. Please let it be a name."

"I..." Antonnia hesitated.

Tess closed her eyes, silently mouthing, "Please, please, please."

"I saw an image as I was drifting off to sleep, and I've been awake all night trying to decide if it was real or just something I imagined because of all the drugs they pumped into me."

"So what is it?"

"I…" Antonnia drew a labored breath. "I…"

"Anything you tell me is strictly between us." Tess had a brainwave. "I want you as my lawyer. Will you accept me as your client?"

"Yes, but—"

"Great. Now, bill me for an hour of your time, then everything is covered by attorney-client privilege, isn't it?" Tess appreciated that the system usually worked to protect the client, but she had to offer the woman something to get her to spill.

"Sorry, this is a big step for me," said Antonnia.

"That's okay. Have you been to the police with this new information?" Tess's voice reverberated up and down the concrete stairwell.

"No."

Thank God. That meant Tess could investigate the lead first, could get to those bastards first.

"Are you going to?" Tess had to be sure.

"I've thought about that, but…"

"But?"

Antonnia sighed. "When we spoke, I got the impression that the kind of closure you're looking for doesn't come through a legal battle. Am I right?"

Tess leaned over the balcony rail and peered up and down the stairs. She couldn't see anyone. But even if someone overheard her talking, a one-sided conversation would mean little.

"Sometimes," Tess said, "justice doesn't come through following the letter of the law, but through following what your gut tells you is right."

"I was hoping you'd say that."

"You're okay with that?"

"Miss Williams, I've been in enough courtrooms to know what legal proceedings would involve, and I have no wish to be raped all over again by a defense attorney and made out to be either a liar or a whore."

Tess let her barriers crumble, and for the first time in days, she basked in the warmth of a real spark of hope. A tiny spark. But a living spark.

"So what is it you think you remember?"

"A…" Again she faltered. This was a gigantic step for someone whose life revolved around the law. Finally, she blurted it out. "A mole. I saw a mole."

"You saw one of them without his mask?"

"No. It was through the eyehole. He had a small dark mole – about the size of an aspirin – just outside the crease of his right eye, below the temple."

That tiny spark blossomed and flooded Tess's whole body with a warm glow. She didn't have a fingerprint, or a hit on a DNA database, or an eyewitness, but it was a lead. A real, hard lead.

"A Caucasian guy?" Tess asked.

"Yes. I'm sorry it's not more."

"No. No, that's great. Believe me, that's such a unique feature, it's a much bigger lead than you think." Tess's mind was already flying through all the possible ways they might trace someone with that identifying characteristic.

"You have to promise me one thing," said Antonnia.

Uh-oh. Here came the catch. Typical goddamn lawyer.

Antonnia continued, "Whoever you get to do the job, remind them that this could have happened to their wife, their girlfriend, or their daughter. After what those monsters did to us... after how they—" Antonnia broke down, and sobbing came over the phone.

"Believe me, Antonnia, those bastards are going to wish their mothers had aborted them."

Tess had them. She goddamn had them!

Chapter 38

HER BAGS SLUNG on her apartment floor and Fish placed back on his table, Tess spoke into her phone. "What do you think? I'm figuring we hack the DMV for Caucasian males, eighteen to thirty, and then facial recog to spot our guy."

Bomb clicked away on his keyboard. "Already on it. Just programming the parameters now."

Tess didn't remember seeing anyone with a mole next to their right eye. But then, she hardly remembered anything. Stunned, then drugged as she had been, that was no surprise. Or maybe the Mole Guy could have been driving, which would explain why she hadn't seen him. Whatever the reason, no self-respecting guy in his twenties didn't have a driver's license. Between the DMV database and Bomb's facial recognition software, she had them. She goddamn had them.

"How long do you need?" Tess asked.

"Tess, this ain't some cheesy TV cop show – it's going take some time."

"Sorry, it's just…"

"Hey, I know. Look, take a breather. You're going to need your head in the game when I find this guy."

It felt great to hear Bomb say 'when' they got this guy, not 'if.' Even though it had only been days, it felt like she'd waited a lifetime to hear that.

But Bomb was right. She'd been so excited that she finally had a solid lead that she hadn't thought through what was going to happen next – she was going up against five fit young guys who thought nothing of breaking the law to take whatever they wanted.

Tess ended the call, then eased Fish back into his little tank and set up his automated feeder so she wouldn't forget later.

Sitting upright on the sofa, she searched for a website on cargo vans. Bomb had said the gang had covered the interior of their van with black sheeting, but she hoped something might spark a memory, as it had for Antonnia, and give her another lead to go on. Maybe the sheeting had been torn and a wheel arch might suggest the make, even the model of the van. Anything could help them narrow the search, if only she could drag it up from the drug-addled corners of her memory.

A Ford site attracted her attention. Clicking it, she found page after page of van-related info and stats.

She clicked on the page for a van that looked about the right shape and size. The page opened and displayed close-up shots of the vehicle's main features, such as the sliding door on the side.

However, a 'take a tour' feature caught her eye. Tess clicked an image of the interior, and it opened in full screen. Dragging her finger over the screen, she maneuvered up and down, and around and around inside the van. It was a cool website feature, but it brought no memories crashing back to her.

She clicked on to the next van. Then the next. And the next.

On another website, she scrutinized Chevy vans.

Another search led her to a Dodge website.

Tess scoured image after image on website after website. But nothing worked. No memory came of the attackers. No recognition came of the vehicle.

She slung her tablet down and stared at her phone. There were no new messages from Bomb. She checked that it was set to ring. It was.

Heading for the door, she grabbed her leather jacket and her backpack.

A light drizzle fell to dampen the morning, but it didn't dampen Tess's spirits. The hurt was still there. The incessant need to wash was still there. The violation was still there. But there was something else now – the scent of vengeance.

She bustled through the streets to the park, where she made straight for her special place underneath her favorite willow tree. A rainbow arced over the trees at the far side of the lake. It was faint. So faint it was almost not there. But its subtle colors lit up her world. Now she needed inspiration to light up her mind, to conjure possibilities from the darkness that had consumed her for days.

Sitting on her small fold-up mat at the foot of the tree, Tess checked to be sure she hadn't accidentally set her phone to silent – she couldn't risk missing Bomb's call – and then closed her eyes.

Her mind drifted with the grace of the mallard ducks gliding across the water. She sensed the world slowly moving by before her, but she was no longer a part of it – like a cinema-goer watching a movie was both immersed in the movie world and yet distanced from it.

Slowly, her chaotic thoughts came together and flew through her mind like a flock of birds through the air – wheeling, arcing, swooping, so many and yet all one.

Two hours later, Tess emerged from her meditation. She had her plan now. In fact, she'd had it for nearly an hour. What she didn't have was a suspect. She checked her phone again. No, she hadn't missed any messages.

"Goddamnit."

There was no point in hassling Bomb – when he had something, he'd let her know.

The rainbow had long since disappeared. Now, a gray slab of cloud engulfed the city once more. At least the rain had stopped.

Tess closed her eyes again. After a struggle to clear her mind, to remove the nagging craving for a phone call, she returned to her meditation.

Forty minutes later, once more the urge to check for messages clawed its way so far into her thoughts, she could do nothing but succumb. But yet again, she hadn't missed a call. As she knew she hadn't. Good God, she was like a goddamn junkie.

As if the waiting wasn't bad enough, the drizzle returned with a vengeance. The sky turned almost black as heavy clouds squashed the world into submission.

The willow's trunk had sheltered her from the drizzle, but with proper rain, the leafless tree offered little protection.

Restless, Tess pushed up to her feet. She couldn't stay here any longer. She'd formulated a plan and cleared her mind, ready for the focus needed for a hunt, but this waiting was creating so much anxiety, it was undoing all the good her meditation had accomplished.

Tess pulled on her wool cap and headed out of the park and into the city, where, thanks to the rain, the traffic grumbled almost as much as the pedestrians.

That spark of hope that Antonnia's phone call had ignited still burned within Tess, but it was flickering like a candle flame in the wind. Tess needed to find those bastards. Needed to. She'd thought she was getting close, but now…?

"Goddamnit!"

Her head down, hands stuffed inside her jacket pockets, she lumbered down the street. Seeing a little café ahead, she checked her watch, trying to work out when she'd last eaten.

Everyone with a license could drive a car, yet only those with skills hewn from years of dedicated training could win the Indy 500. Likewise, though everyone was born with a body they alone controlled, only those with the discipline to train it could see it perform at its optimum level. Tess was a pro driver at the wheel of a Lamborghini. To ensure that when she hit the gas, the machine took off like a proverbial bat out of hell, she had to put fuel in the tank. If she didn't, when next she floored the pedal, she'd grind to a halt.

Her appetite had all but disappeared after the attack. Since then, she'd only eaten because she knew she had to, not to sate her hunger. However, if she intended to battle five men, she couldn't risk having low energy reserves cause her difficulties.

Tess ducked into the café.

247

Most of the tables were occupied, suggesting the food was either good quality or cheap. Or that people were prepared to pay to get in out of the rain.

A mirrored wall made the café appear twice its actual size, while wood paneling gave it a homey feel. The smell of freshly baked bread and luxurious desserts made even Tess's mouth water, despite her lack of appetite.

A tuna and egg on rye already being prepared for her, Tess pointed to a chocolate gateaux nestled amongst an assortment of desserts in a glass display case. "And just a tiny, tiny slice of that, please." She hated herself for being so weak, but after the last few days, like anybody could blame her for wanting to indulge herself a little.

The female employee behind the counter pointed to the chocolate cake. "This one?"

Tess nodded. "Please." She gestured with a thumb and finger. "Just the tiniest sliver."

A woman next to Tess said, "Oh, get a real wedge. With your figure, you can afford to treat yourself once in a while."

Tess looked at the smiling customer beside her – the woman was one pie away from her own mobility scooter. On the counter in front of her, this fat woman had three sandwiches, plus a large slice of lemon drizzle cake and one of ginger cake with frosting.

Tess said, "Excuse me?"

The woman serving Tess hovered her knife over the cake without cutting in.

The fat woman said, "I'm just saying, you should treat yourself. If I had your figure, I'd never worry about what I ate."

Tess gestured to her own body. "You want to look like this? What's stopping you?"

The woman laughed. "Oh, don't get me started. If you can name a diet I haven't tried, that's on me." She pointed to Tess's order. "I tell you, nothing works." She laughed again. "I've tried everything, believe you me. Everything."

The woman talked about failing as if it was something to be proud of. Tess could never get her head around people like that.

Tess said, "Have you tried willpower?"

The woman thought for a moment. "Hmmm...? Is that the one where you can eat carbs every third day?"

"No. It's the one where you stop cramming food down your throat 24/7."

The fat woman's jaw dropped.

Tess continued glaring at her.

"Well, I was only being friendly," the fat woman said. "There's no need for that."

Tess fully turned to face the woman, who was probably three times her weight. "Tried everything, huh? *Everything?* So whose fault is it you're this... this *blob*? The food manufacturers, for loading products with sugar and salt to make them more addictive than nutritious? The government, for not restricting what you can buy? Your family, friends, teachers, doctor, hell, maybe even your mailman, for not giving you the support you need? Is it their fault? Huh? Is it they who screwed up?"

Dumbstruck, the woman just stared. As did every diner in the café.

"No. It's you who screwed up. You. You've got a blob for a body because you've got a blob for a brain. So until you take responsibility for your life and start making intelligent decisions, this is what you're going to stay: a blob that dreams of being a person." Tess shook her head. "Jesus Christ, if people needed a goddamn license to operate a human body, you'd have lost yours years ago."

Sitting alone at a table, a skinny girl with thick glasses and spiky red hair applauded. She stopped when some of the fatter clientele glowered at her.

Tess stared at the blob, whose chin was now quivering and eyes filling with tears.

"Oh, for God's sake." Tess huffed. Typical. And there was the root of the problem – weakness.

Tess turned back to the counter. "I'll leave the cake, thanks." She calmly paid for her sandwich, snatched it off the plate, and stormed toward the exit. Like everything else, the rain could go to hell.

Traveling around India, Tess had found children working longer hours than most American adults just so they could buy food. Not video games. Not designer sneakers. Not candy. No, food. Goddamn food!

Then she'd come back home.

Talk about a wake-up call.

The USA didn't just dominate the rest of the world, it looked like it had eaten it. Gluttons. Everywhere. Why did everyone always want more? Why was *enough* never actually *enough*?

Tess ripped a chunk out of her sandwich as she yanked the door open to leave. But she stopped.

She drew a long steadying breath.

If she didn't constantly sacrifice pleasure to train physically and mentally, she wouldn't have this toned body. And if she didn't have this toned body, she'd never have been attacked. And if she'd never been attacked, she'd never have sunk into this stinking mood because Bomb hadn't called.

But was any of that this woman's fault?

Digging into her backpack, Tess trudged back to the counter.

"Here." Tess handed the woman a business card for one of her alter egos: Sam Waring. "If you really want a body like mine, give me one hour a day for a year."

Having totally destroyed the woman, the least Tess could do was offer to rebuild her.

As Tess slunk back out into the rain, her phone rang. Caller ID said it was Bomb.

Chapter 39

"**ADAM HENRY CARPENTER,**" said Bomb, "DOB six—"

Still standing outside the little café, Tess said, "I don't want any of that. Only the details I need to nail him."

These bastards weren't people; they were animals. No, that was an insult to the animal kingdom – they were goddamn scum. Living shit. No way was Tess going to treat them as human beings, so she didn't want any information that she would usually have asked for on a target. No family information, no relationship details, no hobbies, professions, achievements. Nothing. Hell, not even a name.

Nothing this guy had ever done or would ever do could transform him into a good person and compensate for the crimes he'd committed. Scum like that didn't just need to be exterminated; it needed to be wiped from existence. One way of achieving that was to deny him ever having lived, ever having meant anything, ever having done anything. She wanted to know nothing about him because he was nothing.

Tess studied the portrait Bomb had sent her – a white male with a pointed chin and dark hair. Just an ordinary guy. Nothing unusual at all. Even the mole was nothing special. He didn't look like a monster, but then they rarely did.

Tess looked in through the café window. The fat woman glanced away from staring at her. Tess stepped out of view of the diners. "How sure are you it's him?"

"Put it this way, his father owns a small vehicle rental business out of the Bronx."

"Jesus. And let me guess – some of those vehicles just happen to be cargo vans."

"So, if it's not him," said Bomb, "it's one hell of a freaky coincidence. And I tell you, they might be twisted little fucks, but you've got to hand it to them – they're shrewd. Using a range of vehicles instead of the same one all the time means any witness statements are bound to conflict."

It had to be him. He had a mole in the right place and easy access to the right kind of transport.

Tess clenched her fists as rage welled within her.

"Anything on the other four?" she asked.

Bomb clicked away on his keyboard. "I'm just getting into Mole Guy's Facebook and Instagram accounts as we speak. Most people have only a small circle of real friends, so it shouldn't be too difficult to isolate his."

"So where do I find him?" Tess asked, refusing to even use his name. A name made him a person. Like her. Except he was nothing like her.

"You're going after him by himself? Now?"

"Can you think of another way?"

That was her plan: isolate one, make sure it was the right gang, then, through coercion, force him to help her destroy each of them one after another, all on the same night. It wasn't the most elegant plan she'd ever devised, but it would sure as hell get the job done, and that was all she cared about.

Luring all five guys into a trap and taking them out all at once would be far easier *in theory*, but tackling a gang of five fit young men head-on would be too tough, even with her skills. So one by one.

The biggest problem would be nailing all five of them in just one night. But she couldn't afford to spread it out over days. Not so many. The logistics wouldn't work – she might be able to take out one or two without the others finding out, but five was way too many. She'd nail a few, but then the others would learn about it, get spooked, and disappear. No, she had to end them all. Tonight.

"Have you got a location?" asked Tess.

Bomb clicked on his keyboard again. "There's only one monthly payment from his checking account to a telecommunications company, so I figure he's only got the one cell phone. I've pinged the number and it looks like he's traveling. Maybe even in one of the vans, from the direction he's heading."

Tess turned and started jogging down the street, back toward the park. "He's heading to the Bronx?"

"That'd be my guess. The first cell tower ping put him in Brooklyn; the last was Chinatown. The guy lives in Queens, so he sure ain't heading home."

And he sure as hell hadn't snatched another woman or he wouldn't be driving into the heart of the city, but away from it.

Tess sped up. Back on Eighth Avenue, she turned left and ran through the shadows of the buildings while the park's trees hugged the opposite side of the street, now just shadowy blobs in the dusk's half-light.

A subway station lay ahead on the corner of Eighth and West Seventy-Second. If she could get there quickly enough and hop on a D train, there was a chance she could beat him to the Bronx. He had a head start, but most people in Manhattan didn't own a car for one reason – it was such a headache driving through the city compared to using the public transit system.

It was getting too late to rely on gridlock to hold him up, but she had a chance if only she could get there fast. Tess shot up the street and disappeared into the darkness. She needed to be lying in wait for him. Lying in wait the same way he had for her.

Chapter 40

A WHITE CARGO van rolled up to the metal gates of the parking lot on a darkened side street in the heart of the Bronx. The driver leaned out of his window and held an ID card to a scanning machine mounted on a post. An electric motor whirred, and the gates grated and rattled as they parted.

As the van drove in, Tess slunk in behind it, pulling on her armored gloves.

She'd gotten there in good time, time enough to don the rest of her armor in the shadows. Her titanium guards hugged her forearms and shins under her clothes, but she hadn't bothered trying to hide her bulletproof assault vest as she normally would. On the contrary, she'd just pulled it on over her shirt. She wanted him to see it. Wanted him to be terrified of someone who'd have such equipment. Wanted him to know death was at his door.

As the gates closed behind her, Tess spoke into her phone. "Now."

"Good hunting. Ciao, Tess," said Bomb.

She glanced up at one of the two security cameras, both of which Bomb would now have disabled with just a few clicks. The van had hidden her from the camera pointed at the gate, so now inside, she could take her time without worrying about video surveillance.

A couple of low-wattage lights illuminated the lot in a gloomy yellow, while a sturdy eight-foot metal fence with spikes on top protected it from intruders. Though the compound was big enough to hold sixty or more vehicles, it had only around a quarter of that parked inside.

Each vehicle was emblazoned with 'SelfDriiive.com' down the sides in big gold letters outlined in black, all inside a bright red box. How had she missed that? Surely she'd have noticed that on the side of the van as it turned the corner before she was snatched. Hell, remembering that could have relieved so much of her suffering because she'd have found this guy so much sooner. Unless he'd covered the branding with magnetized sheets the same color as the vehicle, of course.

The van drove over to a free parking space in the far-right corner. The engine died and its lights were extinguished.

She stalked toward the darkened van. This was it. This was the moment she'd been praying for, the moment she'd been aching for. Her heart pounded with a mixture of anticipation and anxiety.

As she walked, she inhaled slowly and deeply, using her four-second breathing technique to help her control the release of adrenaline and thus control her fight-or-flight response. The technique's simplicity belied its effectiveness.

A few seconds later, an average-sized guy sauntered out from behind the van. Dark hair. Pointy chin.

He saw her. "Hey! You can't be in here."

Tess stalked closer.

"You deaf, asshole?" He waved toward the gates. "Get the hell out or I'll call the cops."

Tess walked further into the yellowy glow from one of the two lights. As did he.

She wasn't close enough to see any identifying mole next to his right eye to be a hundred percent sure she'd found the right guy, but she didn't have to.

His mouth dropped open. His voice was hushed. "Holy fuck!"

He stumbled backward, then pointed at her.

His voice wavered. "What—what do you want?"

Silent, Tess prowled toward him.

He backed away. "No. No, you—" He spun around and raced back toward his van.

Tess smirked. "Jeez, what a real fucking hero."

Chapter 41

TESS STALKED ACROSS the parking lot after him. Her heart racing. Her back clammy with sweat.

He probably figured she had a gun and had come to kill him. Well, he'd gotten one out of two right, which wasn't bad.

Whoa... she had to cool it. The last thing she wanted was to kill him. Well, at least not yet. No, he'd be far more use alive, because he could give her the names of his friends to make the job of finding them infinitely easier. Yes, she'd take him alive and make him squeal. Squeal in so many ways.

Right now, he'd probably run to find a weapon. After what he'd done, there was no way he could call the police to come and protect him. And no one else would get here quickly enough to save him if she had a gun. So, the odds were that he'd gone to tool up.

Good. The more he fought, the more she could punish him.

Nearing the van, a little voice in her head screamed, '*Kill him. Kill the fucker. Kill him!*'

She drew another slow breath.

Calm.

She had to stay calm.

Take him alive.

Make her job easier.

As she rounded the back of the van to approach the driver's side, he leapt at her.

Screaming, he crashed a tire iron down at her head.

Without flinching, Tess threw an arm up. The iron clattered into her titanium guard, the seven-inch-long strip of metal dissipating the energy of the impact along the length of her arm so the blow didn't break her ulna.

Her block was so solid, it jarred the iron from his hand and it clattered to the ground.

She could have ended him there and then. But she didn't. Instead, she did something even worse from his point of view – she smirked. Yeah, he was a real hero. So heroic he needed a weapon to face a girl.

He gawked at her. Trembled. A patch of urine spread across the front of his trousers as terror flashed across his face. From her lack of fear and seeming imperviousness to injury, he must have thought she was a goddamn Terminator.

After a moment, he screamed again and flung a wild punch at her.

Barely moving, she blocked his strike again, only this time she let his fist hit her titanium forearm guard.

He yelped as bone crunched against metal.

Yes, let him think she was a Terminator. Let him feel true terror. Like the terror his victims had suffered.

And that little voice screamed, '*Kill the fucker. Kill him!*'

Clutching his hand, he backed away. "What the fuck are you?"

Her voice calm, eerily calm considering the crashing emotions inside her, Tess said, "Unstoppable."

His mouth dropped open again. He stared at her, then spun and ran. Ran for his life from a killing machine come to destroy him. Just like she'd known he would.

He skidded as he flew around the front of the van and crashed against the hood, but caught himself and disappeared from Tess's view.

Tess turned and walked around the back of the van again. She had all the time in the world. And was she going to use it to prolong the terror until she just couldn't hold back any longer.

He raced across the gloomily lit parking lot, heading for the gate and freedom. Glancing over his shoulder, he saw her stalking after him. He tore toward the gate with even greater urgency, head down, arms pumping.

Finally, he reached the scanner inside the compound. Barely waving his ID card over the scanner, he lunged for the gates to squeeze through the instant the gap was wide enough. But the gates didn't open.

"Fuck!" He scurried back and waved the card closer to the scanner, then looked at the gates. Shut tight.

He glanced at Tess. She was almost on him.

Whimpering, he pressed the card against the scanner's panel while craning his neck to watch for the gates opening. "Work, damn you. Work."

Defiant, they remained closed.

Bomb hadn't only disabled the security cameras but also the entry system, so Tess knew he was going nowhere and she could take her time.

Arms up, he cowered as Tess approached. "Please. Please. I–I've got money. A lot of money. My family owns this place."

Did he really imagine he could buy his way out of raping a woman? That he could buy forgiveness by turning her from a rape victim into a cheap whore?

Without saying a word, Tess stalked right up to him.

His face screwed up as if he was about to burst into tears.

She glared into his eyes.

He cowered behind his arms. Cowered like a school bully confronted by the big brother of one of his victims. Not like a man who deserved to live, who was prepared to fight for that right.

Tess stared at him. A small ball of cringing scum. Could she really end something so pitiful?

Peeping out from between his arms, he said, "Please. I–I didn't do it. They–they made me help them. I just drove the van."

"Stand up."

"Wh–what?"

"Stand up."

Peeking out, obviously believing it was some sort of trick, he slowly uncurled and stood erect.

"Hit me," Tess said.

He shook his head. "I–I don't want to hit you."

"Hit me."

Vigorously shaking his head, he said, "No. No, you'll hit me back."

"You wanted to fuck like a man, so now you can die like one."

Something must have clicked in his mind, and he realized the only way he was walking out of that compound was through her.

Unfortunately, that was where logic forsook him. Just like the average Joe, this guy's subconscious conditioning screamed at him to go for what he believed to be his opponent's weakest spot.

With a guttural yell, Mole Guy launched himself at her. He flailed his arms, fists aimed loosely at her head, obviously hoping something might connect, might knock her down, might give him those precious few seconds he needed to escape this nightmare.

Wildly swinging punches rained down on Tess.

Instead of counterattacking, she tucked her chin into her chest and, to protect her head, wrapped both arms horizontally across her face so her elbows jutted out toward him, left hand under her opposite armpit and the right next to her left ear.

Safe, she peeked through the gap between her forearms as he flailed away. He crashed in blow after blow, yet hit nothing but her elbows and titanium guards. If he hadn't been so hopped up on adrenaline, he'd have fallen in a pain-racked mound on the ground, his hands a mass of broken bones.

Moving back steadily, Tess drew him on. Letting him expend all his energy. Letting him cripple his hands. Letting him believe he might have a chance to nail her.

After only a few seconds, he panted for air, while his punches, once wild but forceful, were now sloppy and weak.

Tess had had enough.

Wrapped protectively around her head, her arms were in the perfect position for one of her favorite strikes – a hammerfist.

As he drew back his hand to launch another punch, the side of her fist lashed out and battered him in the ribs under his armpit.

Her other fist pounded into the side of his head.

He gasped and staggered sideways.

She slammed a roundhouse kick into his left thigh, the metal guard on her shin biting deep into his peroneal nerve.

He cried out and hobbled backward, the kick having given him a dead leg.

Spinning around, she slammed a sidekick into his body. He reeled back and crashed against the side of one of the vans.

Tess rushed in to finish him, right fist pulled back to pound his face to pulp.

He threw his hands up and wailed, "Please, I've a kid! I have a kid!"

Tess cried out and hammered her fist straight for his head. But she pulled it at the last moment. It crashed into the van alongside his ear.

Cowering with his eyes closed, he slumped to the ground. He cried, tears streaming down his face, his arms still raised as if they had a chance of protecting him. "I wanna see my kid again. Please, I just wanna see my kid."

Tess towered over him. Fury burned in her. She ached to see his blood. To see his life end. But...

If he truly was only the driver, could she sleep knowing she'd ended him? And if he truly was a parent,

264

could she face herself every day knowing she'd robbed a child of the joy of knowing their dad?

She screamed again. And again punched the van. Her armored fist dented the side panel as the pain of losing her own family amplified the conflict within her.

"Show me. Show me your goddamn kid."

His hands bloody, fingers twisted and bent at unnatural angles, he fumbled for his phone. She snatched it from his pocket. It had fingerprint security, so she grabbed his hand. He howled with pain, but she didn't care and pressed his index finger against the scanner.

The wallpaper that greeted Tess made her hit the van yet again, causing Mole Guy to flinch. The picture was of a man hugging a tiny girl. This man. Both were laughing as if sharing a special moment.

She grabbed him by the throat. "If you were only the driver, who attacked me?"

His hand trembling, he pointed to his phone. "Top four contacts."

She tightened her grip. "I know where you live."

He spluttered and his voice strained as he spoke. "Honest. Top four."

"Names."

"Teddy Cruickshank, Larry Kane, Niko Jossa, Johnny Graham."

She pinned his head against the van. Hard. His breathing rasped.

"Listen to me," said Tess. "Listen real good. You run and hide. You find the deepest, darkest goddamn hole and climb in. You stay there one week." She repeated that instruction to make sure it stuck. "*One week*. If you come out sooner, I'll kill you in front of your daughter. Contact anyone – anyone – I'll kill you in front of your daughter.

Hell, breathe too goddamn loud and I'll kill you in front of your daughter. Understand?"

"Yeah. Yeah."

"For your kid's sake, you better." As she stood up, the frustration overwhelmed her and she couldn't resist punching him in the side of the head one last time. He collapsed sideways.

Heading for the gate, she checked his phone. His most contacted numbers would be either his family or his close friends, so even if the names he'd given her didn't pan out, any calls that aligned with the dates of the attacks would likely be to those involved.

As she checked out his phone, a folder caught her eye. It was very plain. Only had five letters to describe it. VIDEO. It was so ordinary, she almost skipped straight over it. But then...

She looked at it again.

What could that be? His daughter's birthday party? A gig he'd loved? A spectacular touchdown he'd seen? Something innocent. Something completely inconsequential. Something that wouldn't interest her one bit.

So why was a sickness clawing from her gut?

Her stomach knotting and heart racing, she hovered her finger over the folder's icon.

It would be innocent. She was sure of it.

But her heart skipped a beat when she opened it and faced a list of videos that weren't titled, but merely differentiated by a date. The most recent was the date of her attack.

That was either a freaky coincidence or...

She drew a trembling breath and clicked Play.

After only a few seconds of viewing, she lurched forward and hurled her guts all over the asphalt.

Since that night, she'd lived the rape every moment of every day in her mind. No way had she wanted to see the video that Bomb had uncovered. Not least because part of her still hoped it had never really happened. That it was some horrendous nightmare that sooner or later she'd forget. The last thing she wanted was to see it in dazzlingly vivid color. To see indisputable proof of what they'd done to her.

Sweating and panting for breath, Tess wiped her mouth. Only the driver? Only the fucking driver?

Tess raced back. Mole Guy had clambered to his feet and was leaning against the side of the van. Trembling, he cradled his broken hands.

He saw Tess. Saw the rage in her eyes.

His face contorted. "Oh no. Please, no." He burst into tears.

Tess grabbed him around the neck in a Thai clinch and pulled him forward and down. She hammered knee strikes into his body. Crashed them in over and over and over.

As he collapsed, sliding down the side of the van, she thundered elbow strikes and hammerfists down onto his head.

Tess pummeled him as if he were a punching bag, as if he were nothing but an unfeeling object. She slammed in blow after blow, until he was slumped on the ground with his back against the van and she was down on one knee to be on the right level to continue punishing him.

Holding him around the back of the neck with one hand, she pounded her free elbow into his face again and again and again.

She shrieked, "You fuck! You fuck! You fuck!"

Letting go, she leapt to her feet.

Stamped on his crotch.

Screamed.

Stamped and stamped and stamped. Pounded it into mush.

Finally, she slumped against the van, exhausted, gasping for breath, arms and legs trembling. Tess had endured far harder, far longer fights, so the physical exertion was negligible. The emotional release, however, was utterly draining. Draining, but so incredibly satisfying – she felt better than she had in days. More like her old self.

After a few moments, her pulse slowed and her breathing eased, so she pushed away from the vehicle. She stared down at her prey.

A bloody mass of burst flesh and jagged bones stared back at her.

So much for taking him alive. Though she'd always secretly known she wouldn't.

Now what?

Chapter 42

TO BE SAFE, Tess checked the back of the van Mole Guy had driven into the parking lot. To her relief, there was no woman in the back. With the elation of ending the first gang member waning, she ached to get at the others, so she phoned Bomb to share the fresh information she'd gleaned.

Leaning against the van, she had her phone in one hand and Mole Guy's in the other.

"Next one," said Bomb, "Jonathan Graham, probably listed as Johnny?"

Tess scanned the contacts on Mole Guy's phone. "Yeah, I got that."

"And finally: Edward Cruickshank, maybe look for—"

"Teddy. Got it."

"And get this: that guy did two years' pre-med."

That explained his technique for administering injections, and probably how he obtained restricted drugs – he still had contacts.

She stared at the picture of him that Bomb had copied from Facebook and sent to her. A shiver slithered from deep within her and made her cringe. Blond hair. Square jaw. That was him – the blond Dracula.

Bomb had continued investigating while she'd ambushed Mole Guy, and so far, the fresh information he'd dug up meshed with the info she'd just obtained.

Bomb said, "Okay, so as far as I can tell, those are the four guys he's had the most interaction with and who his phone account says he contacts most often, including on the night they snatched you."

"That's what I got here."

"I only had time to run a Level 3 on them. Sorry," Bomb said. "What info do you need?"

"I don't. They aren't people; they're objects. I don't need to know the tree a piece of toilet paper came from before I flush it down the crapper."

"You don't want anything?"

"Not unless you're going to tell me one of them has combat training. Or a gun permit."

"Not that I've found. Okay, so now that we've got their phone numbers, I can track them, but where do we go from here now that we ain't got the fall guy?"

She'd killed the first rapist. The guy who was going to help her reach the others. That had tanked her plan. Thank God she had a backup.

Chapter 43

BEING A FREELANCE journalist in her brighter moments, Tess used her writer's eye to study a sample of the text messages that the members of the gang had exchanged, looking at colloquialisms, syntax, punctuation, and spelling mistakes. While scanning the messages, Tess spotted something else. An abbreviated name of a possible location cropped up in many of the texts: St Eds.

Tess googled 'Saint Edwards NYC.'

Saint Edward's Elementary School sat in the heart of Queens, the borough in which all the members of the gang lived. From the context, the location was obviously the meeting point.

"Bomb, I think I've got something."

"Me too. Get this – I got the GPS data for all their vans from SelfDriiive.com's system. Turns out every single night there was an attack, one of the vans stopped for five to ten minutes in the exact same location, as if picking people up."

"Don't tell me: Saint Edward's Elementary, Queens."

"How the hell...? Never mind. So what's the plan?"

"I'll fill you in on the move. I'm squeezed for time here."

"Okay. Ciao, Tess. Good hunting."

Using Mole Guy's phone, Tess sent each of the gang a text telling them to meet at the usual spot at a time they'd met before: St Eds at midnight.

'gr8 surprise in van. OMG DDG!!! ur gonna luv it. 12 usual 20. BFG!'

Tess spent the next three hours tearing back to Beta, her closest apartment, to fetch the equipment she hadn't been able to take with her earlier. Then, at the location she'd settled on to execute her plan, she undertook the necessary preparations.

Her backup plan was sound. On the whole. However, it did have one potentially fatal flaw. One that she'd known existed and had always intended to avoid but now had to face head-on. After nailing Mole Guy, she'd have to take on all four of the remaining gang at the same time. Tackling multiple opponents was always dangerous. So many things could go wrong. But she'd made her proverbial bed, so...

Just after midnight, she drove the van along a gloomy street with a row of apartment buildings on her left and a darkened school on her right. Three young men sat on the small stone wall outside Saint Edward's Elementary School, while a fourth stood in front of them, gesticulating as if recounting an anecdote.

Instead of stopping next to the gang, Tess drove a few car lengths past, then pulled in and parked. She gave a quick blast of the horn, then leapt into the back of the van and slid the side door open onto the sidewalk.

272

Immediately, she jumped back into the front and, as quietly as possible, got out of the driver's door.

She stood silently in the road, back against the side of the van.

Her heart hammered. The Glock 19 semiautomatic she'd brought from Beta felt slick in her right hand. She swapped hands and wiped her right palm on her jeans. It didn't help.

The four men neared, laughing and joking about some alcohol-related incident.

This was it. This was what had consumed her every moment for days, what she'd been praying for since that horrendous night they'd snatched her.

The voices got louder.

Someone called out. "Yo, Adam, where's this big fucking surprise?"

When they heard no answer, someone else said, "You jerking off in the back, you dirty little fucker?"

They all laughed.

Tess peeked around the back of the van. No one was in sight – they were all standing on the opposite side of the van.

Someone said, "Where the hell is he?"

Tess slunk around onto the sidewalk, holding the gun discreetly by her thigh.

Two guys were peeking in through the open sliding door, the two other still on the sidewalk.

Her voice deathly cold, Tess said, "Get in."

Four men turned to her. Big grins turned into questioning looks.

Raising her Glock, she flicked it toward the open door.

Each of the guys flinched. A couple froze, eyes wide, mouths agape, while the other two cowered behind their raised arms and tentatively shuffled back.

"Whoa, take it easy." A tall, broad-shouldered, sporty type stepped back, bumping into one of his friends, who pushed him forward again.

The blond guy's jaw dropped even lower. "Oh fuck. It–it's her."

Seeing Dracula, Tess felt her stomach knot. How she dearly wanted to end it right here, right now. But she resisted.

A pudgy one beside Dracula said, "What? Who?" Then he scrutinized Tess. "Oh shit."

Dracula said, "We don't want any trouble."

Tess aimed the gun at his head. "Too bad. Trouble's here."

She panned her gun across each of them. They each cowered as the muzzle stared them in the eye.

"Get in," said Tess. "Backs against the far wall."

Sporty said, "Fuck you. Like you're ever going to use that."

"Do you really want to take that risk?" Tess racked a round. The slide barely made a sound as it loaded a 9mm shell into the chamber, but it was loud enough to transform the four guys from boisterous big men into frightened little boys. Just as she'd expected it would.

Dracula shoved Sporty. "Get in, you dick."

Muttering and cursing, they clambered in one by one.

At a safe distance, so they couldn't jump her, Tess stood in the doorway and admired her catch all lined up sitting against the van wall.

274

Sporty glared at her. "You won't get away with this, you dumb bitch."

Pudgy elbowed him. "Shut up, Larry, for fuck's sake."

"On your knees," said Tess. "Or I'll do you here."

More cursing. But they each complied.

Tess threw a bunch of white zip ties to the pudgy guy. They hit his chest and fell to the van floor. "Everyone. Left wrist to right ankle. Right wrist to left ankle."

Pudgy picked them up, then turned to the scrawny guy next to him, who started to cry as he held his hands out. Pudgy bound him.

Tess had learned the hard way that just because someone had their hands tied, maybe even their feet as well, it didn't mean they couldn't move or they couldn't fight. But hands tied to feet – it was pretty much game over, mobility-wise.

Sporty, the broad-shouldered one, glowered at her when Pudgy shuffled along to him. He did not hold his hands down by his feet.

"Dude!" Pudgy said.

Glaring at Tess, Sporty spat on the van floor.

Tess reached just inside the near side of the van and pulled a tarpaulin off a mound lying there. Dead eyes stared up from the bloody, battered face of Mole Guy.

Scrawny whined. It could have been words, but it came out as just a squeal.

Sporty's eyes popped wider as his glower transformed into a look of shock.

They each scrambled back, pressing tight against the far wall, as far from their mangled friend as they could get.

275

A warm glow of satisfaction flowed through Tess. She wanted them to feel pure terror, to feel all hope was lost, to feel they were completely helpless at the mercy of a psycho. Just like their victims.

Glaring at Sporty, Tess aimed the gun square in his face. "Hands. Or you join this asshole right now."

Sporty glared at her.

She locked his gaze.

But he put his hands out and let Pudgy bind them to his ankles.

As Dracula was secured, he said, "You won't fucking get away with this."

She stared coldly. "I already have."

Dracula bound, Pudgy looked at her for instruction.

Having watched him, she knew which his dominant side was. "Right hand to left ankle."

Sullenly, he bound himself as instructed.

With everyone else secured, she got into the van and bound his left hand to his right leg. Then, she reached onto the passenger seat and grabbed a handful of balled socks.

She looked at Dracula. "Mouth."

He glared at her, a mixture of hatred and fear burning in his eyes.

Without flinching, she cracked him in the side of the head with her pistol, knocking him sideways into Sporty.

Scrawny whined again.

Tess hadn't hit him hard enough to do real damage, but blood dribbled into those lush blond locks of his, turning them a nasty dark color in the little light that crept in from the street.

"Mouth," she said again.

He opened his mouth. Tess shoved the socks in.

She then stuffed a ball into the mouth of each of his friends.

Finally, Tess stared down at her captives. They couldn't have been more predictable, having done exactly what the average Joe does in a hostage-taking situation. They'd surrendered their freedom and done whatever they'd been told because they believed that at some point, they'd escape, or be rescued, or their captor would relent and free them.

Tess smirked. "You dumb fucks."

Their best shot hadn't been to comply and to pray, but to have immediately jumped her and to have fought like hell to remain in control of their own fate. Sure, one or two of them would have been injured, maybe even killed, but the others would have had a fair chance of escape.

But they weren't trained in combat. They were just ignorant, sadistic scum. Scum that didn't know they were already dead.

Chapter 44

THE VAN'S TIRES screeched in the long-term parking garage as Tess took a corner to go up another ramp. An overhead sign said 'Level 4.' The concrete walls seemed to close in more with each level, as if trying to catch the little van and crush the life out of it.

The orangey glow from the garage lights barely illuminated the all-pervading gloom, leaving the water-stained concrete draped in hungry shadows, while the darkened vehicles lined up like row after row of corpses in a hangar after a disaster.

On such short notice, this was the most appropriate location she could find, considering the equipment at her disposal. Especially as it was only a few miles from Saint Edward's. She'd have preferred to drive further away, but the further she drove, the more likely she was to encounter some sort of trouble, despite Bomb having hacked SelfDriiive.com's computer system and amended the records to show the van had been rented for the next two weeks. It wouldn't be reported stolen, but if one of the brake lights failed, or if someone drove into her, it could not just wreck her plans, but pit her against armed law enforcement officers when a routine traffic stop revealed four hostages and a dead body in the back. Talk about ruining a good day.

So, the closer the better.

Circling around the penultimate level to the final up ramp, Tess glanced at the ramp down from the top level. Slewed sideways, a car blocked that exit, cordoned off by police crime scene tape. Any staff member would simply assume they'd merely been left out of the loop of what was happening, so no one would attempt to move it. Like the location, it was the best makeshift solution Tess could come up with given the time constraints.

Finally driving out onto the top level, she was greeted by a light rain and a starless sky. The van splashed through the puddles that dotted the level.

Neighboring high-rise buildings gazed down like disapproving parents. Though peppered by lights in some windows, they were offices, not residential premises, so she doubted there would be any Peeping Toms to alert the authorities once proceedings were underway. And even if there were, she couldn't control everything – this was the best option, so it was here, now, or never.

Cars dotted the level, but it was highly unlikely that someone would leave their vehicle in a long-term garage and then choose to pick it up in the middle of the night. But just to be sure, Bomb had checked the garage's database. It said she would be undisturbed.

Tess drove out and stopped at the far end, near the walled balcony overlooking the alley below.

Opening the backdoors, she said, "Out."

Her four hostages gawked at her.

She pulled the Glock out of the back of her belt. "Maybe I didn't make myself clear." Stepping away to give them room, she beckoned with a flick of the gun.

Scrawny capitulated first. Whimpering, he shuffled out on his butt, his bound wrists and ankles making his movements jerky. He toppled from the van and let out a muffled cry as he thudded into the oil-stained concrete.

The others followed.

When they were all sprawled on the hard concrete, Tess backed away. Training the gun on them as long as she could, she got back in the van and fired up the engine. She drove away.

They must have thought it was all over and that being bound and abandoned to the elements all night was to be their punishment.

Foolish boys.

Tess hit the gas, and as the entrance ramp neared, she yanked on the steering wheel. The van slewed sideways and battered into concrete walls, jamming itself in to block the entrance.

Tess prowled back, screwing a suppressor onto her Glock.

The four guys shuffled backward to squash up against the balcony wall. Not surprising. A gun said someone was dangerous. A gun with a silencer said that someone was a killer.

As she approached, Tess pulled out a hunting knife. The blade glinted in the garage's eerie orange light.

Amid muffled whines, the guys all pulled even further away, trying to flatten themselves against the concrete.

Tess singled out one of them and stalked toward him.

Scrawny squealed like a pig sensing it was about to be carted into the slaughterhouse. He shook his head, his gagged yelps getting more frantic the closer she got.

She stood over Scrawny. He screwed his eyes shut and twisted away.

She smoothed the blade across his cheek and then delicately circled his right eye with the tip.

Scrawny froze.

A pool of urine spread across the concrete from Scrawny's crotch.

Removing the knife, Tess reached down and slit the zip tie binding his right hand.

His eyes popped wide open.

Her gun in one hand, she tossed the knife over in her other to catch the blade, then offered the black composite handle to him. "Free the others."

"Huhhh?"

Tess shoved the knife closer.

His hand trembling, he reached out.

Almost touching the knife, his gaze shot to her as if he expected this to be a sick joke and that she'd let him get within a fraction of an inch and then stick it in him.

He reached further and winced, as if already feeling the pain she'd inflict at any moment.

His fingertips brushed the handle, then his fingers curled around it.

Tess let go of the knife, her gun trained on him.

With an almost joyful gasp, he gulped a huge breath. Maybe he thought she'd relented and was going to set them free.

Foolish, foolish boy.

Scrawny freed his other hand and foot, then cut loose his three friends.

They all huddled together and eyed her, terror mixed with curiosity and the tiniest glimmer of hope.

"Toss the knife," Tess said, nodding over her shoulder.

Scrawny threw the knife. It clattered away into the darkness.

With a flick of her fingers, she beckoned them to stand. They slowly all clambered to their feet.

Tess passed her gaze over each of them, staring deep into their eyes, and letting them stare deep into hers. If they hoped to find compassion lurking there, they'd be horrified at what they found instead. Horrified like a swimmer staring into the emotionless dead eyes of a great white shark.

She gestured with her free hand. "Up."

They shot anxious looks to each other. They were already standing, so they didn't get what she wanted.

"Up." She nodded to the balcony wall, which reared up six stories above the street.

With quizzical looks, they glanced at the wall, then each other, then back to her.

Tess squeezed the trigger of her Glock. A shot blasted between Dracula's legs and into the foot-wide concrete wall.

Dracula jumped in shock. His friends all cowered back from him.

She panned the gun across them. "The next goes in someone's ballsack."

With a mixture of stifled whimpers and cursing, one by one, they clambered up onto the wall. Physically, the wall was easily wide enough for a man to comfortably stand on; however, once its height above the ground and the threat of the gun were factored into the situation, the wall became a precarious sliver of doom.

Facing Tess, with the drop behind them, the men teetered and swayed. They grabbed onto each other for support.

Still holding the gun on them, Tess said, "What defines us, what separates us as a species and elevates us above animals, isn't logic or tools. Not even language. No, it's the moral code by which each of us lives through the choices we make. Now, I'm no angel, but some people..." She shook her head. "Jeez, some people just don't give a damn about how their choices hurt others. And even if they wanted to, there's rarely a chance for such people to make amends for what they've done wrong. But you guys... you guys are real lucky, because I'm going to give you that chance."

Again, she stared coldly into each of their eyes, then she nodded toward the dark city stretching out behind them. "Jump."

Dracula ripped the gag from his mouth. "Are you shitting me, you psycho bitch?"

She trained the gun on him, aiming at the center of his right eye. "Jump."

"Fuck you." He splayed his arms wide in a typical male gesture of aggression. "You want to shoot me? Shoot me, you crazy fuck." He spat at her.

Tess ached to end him. Ached to see him bleed.

She lightly squeezed her trigger. Squeezed so gently for so long that the gun almost fired. But then she relaxed. She hadn't come here for that.

"It's all about choices," Tess said. She tossed the gun away. It skidded into the shadows.

Dracula jumped back onto the parking garage floor. The others followed.

Tess smirked. "I was hoping you'd choose that."

Chapter 45

"I'M GONNA THROW you off this goddamn roof, you stinking whore." Big burly Sporty swaggered toward Tess.

Dracula called, "Go on, Larry, do the bitch."

Tess stepped back to make some space. They obviously thought she was backing away from fear.

Dracula chanted, "Larry, Larry, Larry." The others joined him, clapping in time.

Sporty closed in. His fists up, chin tucked in, he looked like he'd done a little boxing.

He threw a jab, then a hook.

Tess slipped both with ease.

Yes, a 'little' boxing – the punches lacked finesse, being rather slow and technically clumsy. Plus, while there was anger in his eyes, he punched with the commitment of someone sparring with a friend, not fighting for their life. Or maybe he didn't appreciate that was what he was doing.

His friends chanted to egg him on.

He threw a three-punch combination. Tess slipped the first punch again, then blocked the next two.

Grimacing, he snarled, obviously getting frustrated that he wasn't hitting her. It must have been doubly infuriating considering he had an audience.

A third time, he came at her.

But Tess was already weary of this game.

As he lunged to attack, she slammed a kick into his gut.

He wheezed loudly and staggered back.

Tess surged forward. She leapt at him, flying through the air to hammer her knee into his body. He threw his hands up to protect himself, so Tess crashed her elbow down onto his head.

The instant she landed on her feet, she fired in a body punch, then lashed a side elbow across the face, then spun backward and hammered in a backfist to his jaw.

Sporty stumbled back.

Instead of moving in, she let him make some space between them. Just enough for her to move.

She spun around backward and pounded a side kick into his stomach with such force he reeled away with his arms flailing.

He crashed into the balcony wall.

Couldn't catch his balance.

Toppled over.

Wailing, he plummeted to the dark alley six stories below. His scream ended abruptly.

Tess turned to his cheerleading squad. His gaping-mouthed, wide-eyed cheerleading squad.

Unable to prevent her top lip curling into a sneer, she said, "Who's next?"

It didn't take a genius to figure out what these heroes were going to do now.

Their champion fallen, the remaining three guys did the only thing they could do – they ran.

Tess might have thrown her Glock away, but a skilled killer didn't leave home with only one weapon.

She pulled out a Berretta Bobcat – a gun so small, she'd had it secreted in her pocket.

A single shot blasted into the night sky.

The three guys lurched to a standstill. Cowering behind their arms, they shuffled around to face her once more.

Pudgy said, "Please. Please, don't hurt us. We're sorry. We–we can pay you."

Striding toward them, Tess glowered. "Are you suggesting I'm a hooker?"

"No! No, please, I'm not. No. It's–it's compensation."

Tess marched on. "You sure? Because it really sounds like you're calling me a hooker."

He cowered, his voice whiny. "I'm sorry. I didn't mean any offense."

"See, you pay a hooker for sex, so as you boys have banged me and are now offering me money, I can't help but feel you're calling me a hooker."

Tess strode right past them to stand between them and any possible escape other than over the concrete balcony.

Pudgy's voice was even whinier. "No, really. I was just—"

"Hey, I'm messing with you. Don't you know how to take a joke?"

Pudgy twitched a nervous smile. "So... you're going to let us go?"

Tess snorted a laugh. "Good God, no. I'm going to break every last one of you and smile while I'm doing it."

Training the gun on them, she said, "So, here's the deal: you've been in me, now, to get out of here, you're going to have to go through me."

She glowered at them. "Who's first?"

They shuffled back, exchanging anxious looks.

"Oh, this little thing?" Tess looked at her gun. "Okay, I can see where you might think this makes it a little one-sided."

She tossed that gun away as well. It skidded under one of the few parked cars.

"Better?"

They still hung back, obviously terrified after seeing how she'd destroyed the biggest member of their gang.

"No? So how about now?" Tess put one hand behind her back.

There were no takers.

"Still not fair?" She put her other hand behind her back too. "How about now?"

The gang exchanged anxious glances, but still no one stepped up to face her.

"Come on," said Tess. "Surely one of you has balls enough now, you pussies?"

Pudgy must have snapped under the pressure. He screamed and ran at her, drawing his right fist back to pummel her.

She waited until he was almost on her, then skipped sideways and fired a roundhouse kick into his midriff.

Pudgy doubled up, clutching his gut, then fell on all fours. He vomited.

287

Spinning around backwards to gain power through momentum, Tess lashed out a kick. Her heel cracked into the side of Pudgy's head, whipping it sideways.

His neck crunched and he keeled over.

Sprawled on his back.

Empty eyes stared up at the blackest of skies.

Tess looked to the last two attackers. "Okay, who's—"

Dracula shouted, "Now!"

He ran one way and Scrawny ran in the opposite direction, each tearing toward one of the stairwells at either side of the building. Both ramps were blocked by vehicles, so the stairs were the only escape routes.

That was very shrewd – she couldn't chase both of them, so while she dealt with one, the other would have a good chance of getting away. And maybe getting help for his friend.

After a moment's hesitation, Tess darted to her left, after Scrawny.

As with a lot of skinny guys, Scrawny was very quick on his feet. He dashed between a couple of parked cars and shot for the exit.

As Scrawny neared the stairwell door, he shouted. "Shit!"

Reaching the exit, he grabbed the chain sealing it shut which Tess had padlocked in place earlier. He rived at it, but it held fast. Putting his foot up on the gray concrete wall, he grabbed the steel handle with both hands and heaved back.

"Open, damn you." He strained, but the door didn't budge.

He must have heard Tess's footsteps because he spun around.

Too late.

Tess leapt into the air. Her body angled sideways, she flew through the air and then kicked her leg out straight. Her foot slammed into Scrawny's chest, flinging him backward.

His head smashed into the hefty door. As he slumped to the ground, he left a splatter of blood down the door where his head had cracked open.

But Tess had to be sure she'd finished the job.

She crouched and hammered her fist into his face.

"Fuck me, will you? Fuck me? Fuck me now, you puke!"

Tess crashed in punch after punch after punch, her armored fists mashing his face as if she was pounding a sack of tomatoes.

Finally, realizing she was pulverizing dead flesh, she cursed and leapt up.

She'd let her emotions get the better of her. Now she'd no idea where Dracula was. For all she knew, he'd managed to climb over the sedan with which she'd blocked the down ramp and was now racing away into the night. If he went to ground, it could be months before she found him again.

"Goddamnit." She couldn't lose her self-control like that.

Well, what the hell did she expect after the scum had raped her?

She drew a long slow breath as she strode through the parked cars and around to the down ramp.

Focus. She had to stay focused. Arguing with herself was the worst thing she could do at a time like this. Hell, she'd been hunting scum for long enough to know better.

She peered over the hood of the sedan and down into the eerie orange shadows of the lower level.

Nothing moved.

Nothing made a sound.

She strained to hear running footsteps. To see a flicker of a shadow.

Nothing.

She studied the ramp. Maybe there were wet footprints to prove he'd escaped down there.

Again, nothing.

He was still up here. She was sure. Kind of.

Everything had been going so smoothly as well. Why the devil hadn't she thought of that particular escape tactic? Why? Because she was only human. And hadn't she just said to stop beating herself up?

"Focus, goddamnit. Focus."

Something clicked in her mind. She patted her pockets. Didn't feel what she wanted to feel.

"Oh, hell." Had she removed the van keys from the ignition? She strained to hear an engine trying to start.

Nothing.

But that didn't mean it wouldn't any second.

One of this gang had been clever enough to plan how to snatch women and get away with it. It could have been Dracula. If it was, he was clever enough to figure that merely running away was not the best option against someone like her.

She raced around toward the van.

The van stood slewed inside the entrance ramp to this level, and looked exactly as she'd left it. But Tess stopped running.

He might be hiding inside, ready to pounce.

Or he might have found a weapon in there. Something she'd missed.

Oh, God.

What if he hadn't run to the stairwell at all? What if, instead, he'd run to retrieve one of the two guns she'd casually tossed away so she could not just end them, but truly terrify them?

"Oh, shit."

She scanned the area, looking for the slightest of movements or a shadow that appeared out of place.

Instead of heading straight to the van, she moved sideways to use the angles to check it out. She breathed slowly, trying to calm her mind as visions of a killer leaping from the blackness flooded her body with adrenaline.

From fifteen feet away, she peered through the driver's window.

Gloom shrouded the van's interior. It looked empty, though she couldn't be certain. That begged another question – if he wasn't in the front, was he hiding in the back?

Again, she spun around and checked the parking area. The last thing she wanted was to be jumped from behind.

And again, she saw nothing.

Moving sideways still, she circled around so that she could see the back of the van without getting near enough for someone to leap out. The doors were still open, but the interior gaped so black it looked like it would swallow her whole if she went too close.

Tess swallowed hard.

Nervous energy coursed through her body. To try to dissipate some of it, she clenched and unclenched her fists repeatedly.

Creeping forward, she strained to see into the depths of the van.

Impossible. There could be anything in there.

Nearer.

Still she strained to see. Still impossible.

She glanced about her. She couldn't risk being caught off guard and jumped while she was preoccupied with something else.

The shadows were silent and still.

Creeping ever closer, she squinted, desperate to see what was in the back of the van. He was here. Somewhere. She was sure of it. And any second, he'd leap out at her, brandishing God only knew what kind of weapon.

Clenching her fists tight, ready to smash anything that moved, she stalked closer. So close she could almost touch the open door if she reached out.

Hardly daring to breathe, Tess shuffled nearer and nearer. With her heart thumping like a jackhammer, she shot her gaze around the darkness all around her, desperate to lock onto something lurking, something moving that she could tear apart.

She swallowed hard as she reached the van.

She held her breath.

Peered in. Half expecting a muzzle flash to be the last thing she ever saw.

"What the…?"

Nothing. He'd escaped.

She hammered her fist into the door, denting the panel.

How could she have been so goddamn stupid? Why hadn't she just nailed Scrawny instead of wasting time on punishing him?

This could mean months of searching to track Dracula down.

Again, she pounded the door. "Damn you!"

Furious with herself for losing it and screwing up, she slouched a few steps from the van, then stopped. It would be pushing it to stay here too long after blasting off shots, not to mention hurling someone off a six-story building to splatter in the alley. Someone would have heard or seen something. She had to get away. Now.

She peered away into the shadows. Where the hell had she slung her guns?

Something scraped behind her.

She spun.

Too late.

Dracula leapt down off the van roof and crashed into her.

Tess crunched into the concrete.

Before she could roll away or get up, Dracula hammered a kick into her gut.

Tess wheezed, then instinctively curled into a ball on her left side. She wrapped her left arm up over her face and the top of her head, while her other she flattened against her right ear so she could hold the back of her neck. Together, her arms shielded her head to stop him crushing her skull under his boot. She pulled her knees up to protect her torso.

Kicking and kicking, Dracula laid into her, pounding her body and head.

Her shin and forearm guards protected her from the ferocity, but even so, it was only a matter of time before one shot broke through and busted a rib to puncture a lung, or fractured her skull to knock her out cold. Either way, it would end the same – Dracula would be able to take his sweet time finishing her while she was defenseless. She needed an opening. Needed a clear moment when she'd be able to counterattack before one of his shots blasted through.

But Dracula was relentless. Kicking and kicking and kicking.

Changing tactic, he stomped down on her head.

Tess's arms took the sting out of the blow, but her head still cracked into the concrete. If one of those broke through her defenses, it would cave in her skull – game over.

Dracula lifted his foot higher so he could stamp down with more force.

Tess grabbed that small break in his onslaught. She caught his foot. Twisted it with both hands, while lashing a kick up to slam into his side.

Dracula staggered back.

Tess leapt to her feet as he balled his fists to face her.

She glowered at the man who'd snatched her, drugged her, raped her. The man who'd ruined her life a second time.

And he glowered straight back.

This time, he didn't run away. He must have figured that because he'd downed her once, she wasn't indestructible. Yes, he obviously figured he could take her.

Fists up, she shuffled forward.

Dracula scowled at her. "I'm going to fucking break—"

Tess flicked a kick at his crotch. Slowly. So slow he had plenty of time to see it coming. His hands shot down to protect himself.

Dracula's hands protecting the wrong target, Tess smashed a hammerfist down into his left clavicle.

He squealed and clutched his smashed collarbone, grimacing with pain. He wouldn't be using his left arm again.

She fired a hook at his head. A slow hook.

When he threw his good arm up to block it, she caught his wrist and twisted it to lock his arm. She punched clean through his elbow. A sickening crunching sound cracked the darkness of the parking garage.

He yelped and hobbled back.

"You fuck," he shouted, hunched over like a broken puppet with his arms dangling at odd angles. "I'll kill you, you—"

Tess slammed a sidekick at his leg.

His knee broke and he toppled to the ground.

While he wailed in pain, she stamped on his other shin, shattering both his tibia and his fibula.

He writhed on the cold concrete, screeching as torment racked his nervous system from all over his body.

Tess stared down at him. Each of his limbs broken and useless, he was almost as helpless as she had been when he'd gotten her in the van. Almost.

Straddling his chest, Tess sank down to sit on him. She clutched his throat with both hands. Squeezed.

To end him, she could simply have stamped on his head, but he didn't deserve that. She hadn't suffered so much and come so far only to give him such an easy out.

Tess tightened her grip.

Choking someone to death is easy. And amazingly fast. It only takes seconds to cut off the supply of blood to their brain and that's it. Dead.

Strangling someone? That was a whole other ball game. That was messy. It took minutes, not seconds. And the person was conscious for most of that time – struggling to breathe, fighting to live, sensing their life was slowly being ripped from them. And the noises...

Dracula made horrible gurgling sounds – he spluttered and gagged and squealed and wretched.

Yes, strangling someone was a nightmarish and lengthy process. Which was why Tess never used the technique – it was way too ugly and inefficient. And it always left those gargled noises in her head for days afterward.

No, she never strangled her targets to death. Never.

Dracula's face darkened in color and his eyes bulged. Gobs of saliva spat from his mouth.

He flailed his broken limbs, but he had no strength or maneuverability to stop her from killing him.

Again, Tess shifted her hands to constrict them around his throat even more.

Dracula's flailing stopped. His gasped, spluttered breaths drew shorter, less frequent.

It would only be seconds now.

So Tess relaxed her grip.

Dracula gulped a gigantic breath as life once more surged through his body. His world would once more be filled with hope, with a chance to live, with a belief that he was going to survive this nightmare.

But Tess immediately tightened her grip again.

His eyes widened in horror and again, he choked and gagged.

Sometimes, justice shouldn't be swift, but agonizingly long.

Tess leaned down and peered into his eyes, so close she could smell curry on his sputtering breath. If he'd known, would he have chosen that for his last meal?

She squeezed harder.

He'd destroyed her life. Violated countless women. Reveled in his power over them. Left them broken. Battered. Shells. Some would never recover.

If there was an afterlife, Tess was going to make damn sure he entered it screaming in such agony that the feeling haunted him for all eternity.

Black pools of terror stared up at her from where his pupils had been. Wide and dark. Deep enough to drown in.

Tess stared into his eyes as he sputtered one of his last breaths. They still sparkled with life, but also with a sadness, as if he realized this would be his last moment on this earth.

In barely a whisper, Tess said, "You did this. Through the choices you made, you did this."

He gurgled one last agonized breath. And then his eyes didn't sparkle quite so much.

Everything was still and silent.

Tess stared into his empty, dulled eyes.

Could the windows to the soul tell her what made some people so evil?

Deeper and deeper she peered.

And deeper still. Searching through that blackness.

But no answer came.

It never did.

Chapter 46

NINETY-FOUR MINUTES LATER, Tess turned the water off and stepped out of her shower in Alpha apartment. She toweled herself dry, then picked up her deodorant, but stopped and put it back on the shelf. How wonderful it felt to feel truly clean. She closed her eyes and savored the feeling for a moment.

Standing in front of the mirror, she dragged a wide-toothed comb through her long chestnut locks to leave wet, matted spikes of hair hanging down over her shoulders and breasts, so long they covered her dark pink nipples.

She loved long hair. Always had.

But...

Long hair was easy to grab, so it was a hazard in combat situations.

With a pair of scissors, she hacked away until her hair barely reached her shoulders.

She dropped the long wisps into the trash next to the washbasin. They lay on her ripped-up plane ticket to China.

How stupid she had been to imagine her life could ever be any different. All she'd ever known was pain, hardship, and anguish, so it was foolish to think it could be any other way. Talk about deluded.

No, this was where she belonged.

This was the life she deserved.

So, if God or Fate or the Universe or whatever decreed this was to be her lot, she was fine with that. Just as long as no one expected her to roll over and play nice.

She stared into the mirror. "Who's next?"

The End
Tess Williams will return.
In the meantime, discover the white-knuckle adventure that brought her to this point. Grab a MASSIVELY DISCOUNTED Bumper Edition which includes the first FOUR books in the series.

MASSIVELY DISCOUNTED 4-Book Edition

http://stevenleebooks.com/4owr

Free Library of Books

Thank you for reading *Kill Switch*. To show my appreciation of my readers, I wrote a second series of books exclusively for you – each Angel of Darkness book has its own Black File, so there's a free library for you to collect and enjoy (books you cannot get anywhere else).

Start Your FREE Library with *Black File 10*.
http://stevenleebooks.com/hwr1

This also entitles you to get my VIP readers newsletter every month, with some combination of:

- news about my books
- special deals/freebies from me or my writer friends
- opportunities to help choose book titles and covers
- anecdotes about the writing life, or just life itself
- behind-the-scenes peeks at what's in the works.

Angel of Darkness Series

Book 01 – Kill Switch

This Amazon #1 Best Seller explodes with pulse-pounding action and heart-stopping thrills, as Tess Williams rampages across Eastern Europe in pursuit of a gang of sadistic kidnappers.

Book 02 – Angel of Darkness

Set in Manhattan, Tess hunts a merciless killer on a mission from God in a story bursting with high-octane action and nail-biting suspense.

Book 03 – Blood Justice

Blood Justice erupts with the intrigue, betrayal and red-hot action surrounding a senseless murder. Thrust into the deadly world of crime lords and guns-for-hire, only Tess can unveil the killer in this gripping action-fest.

Book 04 – Midnight Burn

An unstoppable killing-machine, Tess demands justice for crimes, whatever the cost. But even 'unstoppable' machines have weaknesses. Discover Tess's as she hunts a young woman's fiendish killer.

Book 05 – Mourning Scars

Crammed with edge-of-your-seat action, suspense, and vengeance, this adventure slams Tess into the heart of a gang shooting and reveals the nightmare that drove her to become a justice-hungry killer.

Book 06 – Predator Mine

Bursting with nerve-shredding intrigue, this page-turner plunges Tess into the darkest of crimes. And dark crimes deserve dark justice. Discover just how dark a hero can be when Tess hunts a child killer.

Book 07 – Nightmare's Rage

If someone killed somebody you loved, how far would you go to get justice? How dark would be too dark? How violent too violent? Vengeance-driven Tess is about to find out in an electrifying action extravaganza.

Book 08 – Shanghai Fury

Tess Williams is a killer. Cold. Brutal. Unstoppable. In a white-knuckle tale of murder, mayhem, and betrayal, discover how her story begins, how an innocent victim becomes a merciless killing-machine.

Book 09 – Black Dawn

Everything ends. Including a life of pain, hardship, and violence. Tess has sacrificed endlessly to protect the innocent by hunting those that prey upon them. Now, it's time to build a new life for herself. But a news report changes everything.

Book 10 – Die Forever

A brutal gang is terrorizing NYC. Tess's hunt takes her to one of the deadliest places on the planet, for one of her deadliest battles. How will she get out alive?